Melody of Life

Beth E. Westcott

Scrivenings
PRESS
Quench your thirst for story.
www.ScriveningsPress.com

To my writers' group, Foothills Inkspires.
Your friendship and encouragement mean so much to me

CHAPTER ONE

ark Chambers knocked on the open door of Dave Wilkes's office and entered. "Good morning, Dave. You wanted to see me?"

Mark settled into the chair facing Dave, who looked up from his chair on the other side of his desk. Dave nodded. "Yes. Good morning, Mark."

For all the time they'd worked together, Mark had been on good terms with his boss. Now, the tight lines around Dave's mouth and the crease between his eyes worried Mark. His gut tightened. What troubled Dave?

Two weeks ago, Dave informed Mark he'd recommended Mark to supervise the development of projects in a new southern district office in Tennessee that Building and Engineering Concepts, the BEC, planned to open. A major increase in pay and benefits went along with the greater responsibilities.

He'd accept the new position if offered. Although it would be hard to leave Millvale, his hometown, moving to Tennessee might be just what he needed to get a fresh start at this point in his life.

Dave folded his hands on his desk. "How are things in Millvale?" Dave always showed an interest in his employees' lives.

"About the same as usual."

"Did you have any trouble on your trip in today?"

Mark tensed. Dave's troubled expression hadn't changed, and now he appeared to be stalling for time. Why didn't he say what he had to say?

"Traffic was heavy, and I had to stop twice for road construction, but the trip was otherwise uneventful. The forecasted storm held off." He took a deep breath to relax.

"Glad to hear it." Dave tapped his desk and cleared his throat. "I called you in here, because there's been a change of plans. Last week, the Board of Directors took a merger vote. Maxwell Corporation took over Building and Engineering Concepts. We'll be closing our headquarters here and moving out of state."

What? He leaned forward. "I—I didn't know a merger was being considered."

"Yes, for a while now. I thought we'd decided to expand on our own, but the Board made a turnabout and went along with the merger."

Mark tried to wrap his mind around the implications. "What does this mean?"

"I'm sorry. I'll have to take back the offer for you to manage the new office." Dave sighed and leaned back in his chair. "Maxwell Corporation will lay off most of our people." He dropped his eyes to his desk and shuffled some papers. "You'll get a good severance package and help finding a new placement."

"But I've been with the company for eight years. You've been satisfied with my work and that of my team. We've helped build this company."

"I know, and I'm sorry to do this to you." Dave finally looked up. "I have no complaints about your work, but the Maxwell Corporation owns a controlling interest in the new company and wants to make decisions about its employees. You may apply for a position with them. I'll write you an excellent recommendation."

Mark took a couple of deep breaths to refill his lungs. Instead of a promotion, he'd get a severance package. How did this happen?

On top of everything else, a job loss. Why, God?

"Your team will finish work on your present project with your meeting next week. You've done a great job with the senior citizens' complex. You're right on schedule."

Mark nodded. His team had already begun preliminary work on their next project, which would either be scrapped or passed on to Maxwell. How would the members of his team afford to live? Autumn had a baby due in six months. Ian's wife needed chemo for breast cancer. The others on his team had children.

"Please don't talk about this with your co-workers until I've had the opportunity to speak with everyone here today."

"I won't." Mark stood, his legs like jelly, his chest tight. He wanted to say he understood and didn't take it personally. But it was personal. Life-changing. "I'm shocked. However, I want you to know I've enjoyed working for BEC and with you." Mark held out his hand.

Dave also stood and clasped Mark's hand. "Thank you. I wish this could have had a different ending. It's out of my control and I'm sorry."

"Me too." With trembling hands, Mark lifted his briefcase and walked out of Dave's office. He still had a project to complete. A glance at his watch indicated he had forty-five minutes before meeting with his team. He rode the elevator to the café on the first floor of the BEC building. A cup of coffee might calm and prepare him for what lay ahead.

Unlike most of his co-workers, he no longer had a family to support. Rachael's autoimmune disease and vulnerability to respiratory illness left him a widower five years ago. Fourteen months ago, his daughter, Blythe, had joined her mother in heaven. If he could have them back, he'd willingly give up everything, including his job. But he was alone, and now he was jobless.

His brother, Jack, had been excited when Mark told him about the new job offer with BEC, and it would be hard telling him he'd be unemployed in another week. Outdoors, lightning flashed, and rain splashed against the windows. The weatherman that morning predicted the storm, but nothing had prepared Mark for the news that caused the turmoil now swirling within him.

How would he make it through the next couple of days?

CHAPTER TWO

*D*ragging her suitcases, Alana Somers opened the door with her key and pulled her luggage inside. She shut the door, closed her eyes, took a deep breath, and released it slowly.

Home!

Her sister, Ellie, and brother-in-law, Ben, wanted to pick her up at the airport late last night, but she insisted on getting a room at the airport motel and hiring a ride-share to bring her home this morning. With their new baby, Ian, and their jobs, they needed sleep.

The apartment, with a bouquet of sweet, mild-scented flowers in the middle of the table, smelled clean and fragrant. Ellie's work for sure.

She found a note wedged under the bouquet.

Dear Alana,

Welcome home! Kate and I decided you needed home-cooked food, so she made the soup, and I made the stew. Your favorite cookies are in the cookie jar.

You'll have to let us know more about what your stomach can tolerate.

Ben, Ian, and I want you to have dinner with us tonight. I'll be home just after five. See you then.

Please call me to let me know when you arrive.

Love,

Ellie

Alana's stomach growled, reminding her she ate an early breakfast at the airport motel and needed to eat again. Not that she was particularly hungry. Even though she'd had the malaria shot, she contracted the disease anyway. It had taken away her appetite and drained her strength. She yawned.

Like Old Mother Hubbard, her cupboards were bare. Clearly Ellie had been shopping for her and filled the refrigerator. The drawers contained some fresh fruits and vegetables, and eggs and milk sat on the top shelf. On the second shelf, a container labeled "beef stew" sat beside another container labeled "chicken soup."

Alana's stomach growled again. She poured the chicken soup into a pan and set it on the stove to heat. While she waited, she called Ellie to let her sister know she'd arrived home.

ALANA AWOKE and blinked her eyes several times at the painted walls and curtained windows. She squeezed the soft pillow under her head, inhaling its fresh sweetness.

She was in her apartment in the basement of her parents' home in Millvale, not the International Aid Society refugee camp. Bright sunlight shone on the green grass outside her window. She checked her watch. Three o'clock. She'd intended to rest for a few minutes, but she'd slept for two hours. Although in no hurry to get up, she wanted to unpack before going to

Ellie's. She snuggled against her pillow. She still had a couple of hours.

In the refugee camps, noise and activity seldom ceased, and she had little time to relax and think. Her heart broke for the refugees, although she loved what she did. While ill, she'd had little activity and much time to think about the future. When her contract with the IAS came up for renewal in less than a year, would she sign on for another five years? Or was there something else for her? She turned to lie on her back.

How would Mark Chambers react when he learned she was home? The last time they corresponded via email, she was still in Africa. They'd been friends for a long time, but when they talked at Mark's brother's wedding last fall, a spark of hope for more than friendship ignited within her.

Wide awake now, she grabbed her bag of toiletries and headed for the bathroom. After washing her face and brushing her teeth, she transferred her bathroom items to the medicine cabinet and drawers. Returning to the bedroom, she emptied her suitcases of clothes and pushed her luggage to the back of the closet.

Someone knocked on her front door. Who could that be? Hurrying from her bedroom into the living room, she fluffed her hair and smoothed wrinkles from her white T-shirt imprinted with the IAS logo. She peered through the peephole in her front door and threw it open. "Ellie!"

Ellie walked in with a sleeping infant in a carrier and set down the carrier.

Alana stepped into her sister's embrace. "I missed you so much." Alana had seen Ellie six months ago when she came home briefly for Jack and Kate Chambers's wedding. But as she lay ill with malaria on the other side of the world, she longed to be with her sister and family.

Ellie held her in a tight hug. "I'm so glad you're home. Kate's working today, and she insisted she'd take care of the shop and lock up later. She almost pushed Ian and me out the door because I kept talking about you." Ellie released her. "I also have a floral delivery to make."

Alana looked down at the sleeping baby, and the desire to enfold him in her arms became irresistible. "May I hold him?"

"Of course." Ellie unbuckled Ian and lifted him into Alana's embrace.

Alana savored his baby softness and sweetness. She'd held many babies, and she even helped birth a few. But Ian, her six-week-old nephew, was special.

"When I was lying on the cot in the infirmary, I thought I'd never see your baby on this side of heaven. And now I'm holding him." She drew in a deep breath, and tears pooled in her eyes.

"Thank God." Ellie pulled her into a side hug and rested her head against Alana's.

Alana followed her sister to the sofa and sat beside her. Ian snuggled against her shoulder.

"Ian couldn't wait to meet his Aunt Lanie." Ellie rubbed her arm.

"I could hardly wait to meet him." Alana laid the sleeping baby on her lap with her arms on either side of him. "Oh, Ellie, he's beautiful! You and Ben must be so proud." Would she ever have one of her own? She laughed when he pursed his lips, then frowned and smiled in his sleep.

"Ben loves his little boy. He spends all the time he can with him. He's a great daddy."

Ian stretched, and his eyes fluttered open.

"Hi, Ian. I'm your Aunt Lanie. I'm so glad to meet you." Brown eyes focused on her face. "Thank you for sending the pictures of Grammy holding him."

"Mama and Daddy brought Grammy to see him the day after we came home from the hospital."

Ian turned his head toward Ellie when she spoke. She smiled and touched his cheek. "Hi, baby."

"Mama felt bad she couldn't be here for his birth and stay and help me at home, but they brought some casseroles for the freezer, and Grammy baked cookies for us on one of her good days. Ben's parents helped a lot, and our church family supplied meals for us for a week."

"How is Grammy?" Her dear grandmother's dementia lay heavy on Alana's heart.

Ian looked at Alana again. She chuckled at his puzzled expression, a tiny frown on his brow, as if he was trying to figure out her identity.

Ellie shrugged and shook her head. "She has good days and bad. The bad ones are becoming more frequent. They've had to remove the knobs from the stove at night, and Mama and Daddy must be especially careful she doesn't get out and wander away. She still enjoys going to church and cooking, although Mama supervises closely."

Alana's heart clutched. This was so unlike the grandmother she knew. "What about her physical health?"

"She sleeps more and is losing weight. Mama takes her out for a walk nearly every day and fixes food Grammy likes. She doesn't eat every meal. It's like she forgets to eat, even though Mama coaxes her."

Grammy had always had a hearty appetite that maintained her active body. Maybe Alana could encourage her to eat. Maybe her time home wouldn't be wasted.

"It was a good day when they brought her to see Ian. She talked with us and laughed. She loved holding her great-grandson. We had a good time."

"Mama and Daddy must be getting tired. Being a caregiver isn't easy." A lesson she'd learned in refugee camps. If she became a nurse, a onetime dream she had set aside when she joined the IAS, she could help people like her grandmother even more.

"I think it's like having a baby—be ready for the unexpected and many nights of interrupted sleep." Ellie yawned.

"I suppose. It's like that at work too." Ian smiled at Alana and cooed. "Look, Ellie, he smiled at me. I'm smitten." She lifted the baby and kissed his cheek, her arms trembling. Then she held him to her shoulder and rubbed his back. "I'll have to give him to you, though. Fatigue is catching up with me." She placed Ian in his mother's outstretched arms and leaned back on the sofa.

"Are you all right?"

"I'm getting better. The aches and fever are mostly gone, but I still get tired quickly. I've lost fifteen pounds, and I have little appetite." She could sympathize with Grammy, but starvation wasn't a healthy option, especially if she wanted to return to work.

"I'm glad the IAS sent you home so we can take care of you." Ellie cuddled her son. "I got to thinking that you didn't have a car and would have to walk to our house. Then I remembered Daddy had Grammy's car serviced, so if your license is up to date, you have a car to drive while you're home. He left it in the garage for you."

"I thought about borrowing or renting a car, then Mama mentioned Grammy's car on the phone."

She wouldn't play the helpless invalid and make people wait on her, although there would probably be times she'd need help. Having a car would allow her to drive to doctor's appointments and go other places without having to depend on others. With careful spending during her time out of work, she'd have enough money to live on, and her IAS health care plan would take care of her medical expenses. In six months, she'd be back at work.

Ian fell asleep. Ellie placed him in his carrier and fastened the harness. "I have a quick flower delivery to make. I promised the arrangement by supper time. Do you want to come with me? It won't take long."

"I still have a few things I'd like to get done here." She looked down at her sleeping nephew, then waved her hand. "I guess the rest can wait. I'll have plenty of time to do it tomorrow. Sure, I'll ride along."

She grabbed her purse and a sweater from her bedroom and rejoined her sister in the living room. "I'll have to go grocery shopping soon."

She held open the door for Ellie to go out with the baby carrier.

"Will you be all right shopping by yourself? Do you want me to go with you?"

Ellie would always be her big sister and want to take care of her.

"I think I'll be fine by myself, but let's see how I feel tomorrow."

CHAPTER THREE

About halfway back to Millvale, dark clouds released their moisture. Mark turned the wipers on high and peered through streams of water as rain pounded the windshield. The wind pushed his car sideways, and he gripped the steering wheel tighter, slowing to keep from hydroplaning on the slick highway. Tension radiated through his neck, shoulders, back, and arms and down to his feet.

Vehicles ahead of him disappeared in the veil of rain. Emergency signals blinked through the haze from several cars that had pulled to the shoulder of the road. He prayed and continued driving.

The rain and wind stopped. Blue sky appeared as the dark clouds rolled away. Mark released the tension from his body and flexed, stretching his fingers.

"Thank you, God."

The sun peeked through the opening in the clouds and spread its rays across the fields and hills, like God's smile on the day. And with the sun came hope.

The company offered a generous severance package, including several months of health insurance. With that and his savings, financially, he'd be all right, barring an emergency. He wouldn't have as much to give to the church or to support the homeless shelter in Break-a-Bean. He'd try to continue sending support to the children's home in Peru that had been dear to Rachael's heart.

Taking the exit toward Millvale, he turned onto a less-traveled, shorter route into town. A few miles from Millvale, the front right wheel of a red SUV disappeared into a water-filled ditch, sending the rest of the vehicle leaning sharply after it.

Mark gasped, and his right foot jerked to the brake pedal.

Skid marks streaked the road where the driver had applied brakes and still ended in the ditch slumped forward over the steering wheel.

He drove past, pulled over, and turned on his emergency flashers.

As he approached the SUV on foot, he pulled his phone out of his pocket. Taking a deep, calming breath, he peered in the window. A woman's head was turned away from him, blonde hair splayed against a deflated airbag. Was she breathing? He jerked on the door, and the vehicle rocked in response, but the door wouldn't open. Locked or maybe jammed. He tapped on the window. The woman didn't respond.

She needed help he couldn't give her. He called 911.

He craned his neck until he could see her profile. The wedding band and diamond on her left hand teased his memory. There was something familiar about the woman. Did he know her?

Movement from the back seat drew his attention. A frightened little boy stared at him through the back window from a child's car seat. His face crumpled, and he began to cry.

Mark smiled. "It's okay, buddy. We'll get you out."

The back door refused to open. The vehicle rocked again. Mark feared the moist soil beneath the wheels might break away, then the SUV would slide farther into the ditch.

The boy stopped crying, but his little body still shook with sobs.

The water in the ditch wasn't deep enough to seep into the vehicle. The child seemed in no immediate danger, but concern for the woman gripped Mark. Although he didn't see blood or detect an injury, she hadn't moved or responded to his knocking or the boy's crying.

Let her be all right, God!

"Damaris Cook." She'd been a member of Mark's grief group. Her husband had died suddenly from an undetected heart problem, if he remembered correctly, leaving behind a wife and infant son.

Mark had met the boy once at a grief group social event.

What was his name?

He snapped his fingers. "Harrison, and she calls him Harry." When he tapped on the back window, Harry stared at him, his thumb in his mouth.

"Hi, Harry. I'm Mark. Do you remember me?" Could the boy hear him?

Harry shook his head.

"Someone is coming to help you and your mommy get out of your car. Do you hurt?"

He shook his head.

"I'll stay right here and talk to you, okay?"

He shook his head.

Mark chuckled. Either the boy couldn't understand him or couldn't hear him.

"Who is that you're holding?" He raised his voice and pointed to the purple and green stuffed toy Harry cuddled in his arms.

Harry held it up, dangling it by one leg.

"Is that your dinosaur?"

The boy nodded and smiled.

"He's a handsome fellow."

~

After delivering the flowers, Ellie took the back road into Millvale.

"I think there's an accident up ahead." Ellie slowed her van.

In the back seat where she conversed with Ian in his car seat, Alana's head snapped up. "I hope no one's hurt. It looks like that red SUV is stuck in the ditch. Do they need help?"

The sun had been shining when they left Millvale, but the wet road and water flowing in the ditch indicated it had rained here.

As they passed by, Alana turned to gaze out the window. A man peered into the back window of the SUV. *Is that Mark Chambers?* The driver appeared to be slumped over behind the steering wheel, but Alana couldn't see into the back. *Please let them be all right, Lord.*

"That looks like Mark Chambers's car parked ahead. I'll pull over to see if they need help." Ellie parked along the road in front of Mark's vehicle.

"Let me go, Ellie." Alana opened the door. With her experience in crisis situations, she might be able to help. "You stay in the car with Ian." Cold moisture seeped into her shoes when she stepped on the grass.

"Be careful," Ellie called after her.

"I will." She shut the door and made her way to the shoulder of the road.

Alana's heart rate accelerated when familiar dark hair and blue eyes met hers as she approached. Surely the flutters in her stomach could be solely a response to the emergency.

"Alana, what are you doing here?" Mark's eyes widened, and he took a step toward her.

This wasn't how Alana imagined her first meeting with Mark after returning to Millvale.

"Is anyone hurt? Do you know them?" There would be time later to answer his question. "Is there anything I can do?"

"The woman is Damaris Cook. And this is her son, Harry." He bent and regarded the boy through the window. "How are you doing, Harry?"

Alana leaned in to see Harry. As her shoulder brushed Mark's, she caught the scent of his aftershave, and a tingle zipped down her arm. Trying to ignore the sudden warmth, she finger-waved to the small, blond boy cuddling a green and purple dinosaur.

"Hi, Harry."

He stared back at her, his little face streaked with tears. She longed to gather him in her arms. "Is he all right?"

"He doesn't appear to be hurt, only scared. I've been trying to distract him until the emergency responders get here."

"So, you've called 911." *Of course, he has.*

"Yes." He gazed at her for a moment, his forehead creased between his brows.

She should probably explain why she stood here on the road outside Millvale rather than in an IAS camp overseas.

"Mama!" Harry stretched his hand toward the front seat and sobbed. "Mama!"

Mark tapped on the window. "Harry, I'm right here." Mark made faces at him, and giggles replaced sobs. She admired the way Mark interacted with Harry and distracted him. But then, he'd been a good father to Blythe.

A cool breeze blew, and Alana folded her arms across her body and shivered. The familiar weakness invaded her body. She couldn't offer much help here and should probably go before she needed medical assistance. But she didn't want to leave yet. Mark knew the woman and the boy. How close were they?

"What about her?" Alana peered at the woman in the front seat. "You said her name is Damaris Cook. How long has she been unconscious?"

"She hasn't awakened since I arrived, although she's breathing. I believe I found them soon after the accident happened. I can't tell about injuries. The doors are locked, and I can't get in."

Two sirens sounded from the direction of Millvale. A third came from the opposite direction.

Mark tapped on the window again. "Okay, Harry, the police and ambulance are almost here. Have you ever met a policeman or someone who works in an ambulance?"

Harry looked at him and blinked.

"I don't think he understands you, Mark." Even so, Mark's chatter kept the little boy occupied so he didn't think about his mother.

"It's a little hard talking through the window." Mark pointed to the flashing lights as a sheriff's car pulled up behind them, and a fire truck and an ambulance stopped across the road.

Harry's eyes widened, and he squeezed his dinosaur in his arms.

A sheriff's deputy approached. Alana moved to the shoulder of the road a few feet away and stood behind Mark's car.

Her phone pinged. She pulled it out of her pocket. Ellie texted.

> What's going on?

> A woman and a boy are locked inside the SUV. I want to make sure they're all right. Give me just a few more minutes.

Mark stepped back from the SUV. The deputy peered in the windows and tried to open the doors. The vehicle rocked. Alana held her breath, willing it not to tip.

The deputy turned to Mark. "Are you the person who called 911?"

"Yes, I am."

While Mark talked to the deputy, two firemen jumped from

the fire truck. They examined the position of the vehicle and moved a couple of large rocks to prop the wheel in the ditch. When the SUV no longer rocked, they broke the window and unlocked the door. Alana released the breath she didn't know she was holding.

The EMT and ambulance driver helped Damaris, now conscious and able to stand after smelling salts had been administered, from the car to the gurney they had ready. Damaris talked with the EMT while he examined her.

One of the firemen unlocked and opened Harry's door. The other fireman leaned in and came out with the little boy in his arms.

"Thank you, Lord," Alana whispered.

Harry stared at the man holding him but didn't cry. He twisted to see his mother.

Alana's heart did a little gallop when Mark walked over and stood beside her.

His eyes remained fixed on the accident scene. "They're safe."

He sounded relieved, yet the lines around his eyes revealed stress or fatigue. Her hand reached for him, then dropped to her side. "I'm glad they didn't get hurt. Ellie and I were passing by and saw you here. We stopped to help, but you have it all under control."

Mark nodded and glanced over his shoulder at Ellie's van. "Thank you for stopping." His attention then locked on the scene unfolding before them.

Clutching his dinosaur, Harry reached for the woman. "Mama!" The EMT allowed him to be placed in her arms and checked him for injuries. The mother cuddled him as she talked to the deputy.

The ambulance driver approached. "Ms. Cook wants to speak with you, Mark."

"Thanks, Vinney."

Once Mark spoke Vinney's name, she remembered him. He and his family lived in Millvale.

Before Mark headed over to Ms. Cook, the deputy strode up to them. "If I have any more questions, I'll contact you, Mr. Chambers."

"All right." With a nod to Alana, Mark walked with Vinney toward Damaris.

"Did you witness the accident?" the deputy asked Alana.

"No, sir." Her insides quivered, whether from nervousness or fatigue she didn't know. Or maybe it was disappointment that Mark had left.

She explained her presence, and the deputy wrote down her name, address, and telephone number and returned to his vehicle. Ellie was probably worried about her, and Ian might be getting antsy. She'd better go. She glanced in Mark's direction, and her stomach took a dive.

Mark held Damaris's hand between his two.

Alana frowned. Mark must know Damaris well. Was she just a friend? Were they a couple? In his email correspondence, Mark hadn't even hinted he was dating anyone. Not that it was her business. She had no claim on Mark's affections. Just hoped she might one day.

DAMARIS HELD OUT A TREMBLING HAND, and Mark gently clasped it between his. He didn't know Damaris well, their acquaintance was based on their loss of loved ones. But he was glad he'd been here to help her and her son.

"How are you, Damaris?" Her hand was cold.

She grimaced, drawing attention to a bruise coloring her left cheek. "Oh, a few bumps and bruises and a lot of embarrassment. Thank you for your help, Mark."

Letting go of her hand, he dropped his to his sides. "Of course. Did you skid during the downpour?"

"Just as it stopped. I saw movement in the trees, a deer, and I put on my brakes, a little too hard, I'm afraid. We were on our way to visit some friends. Going through Millvale is the shortest route."

He smiled at Harry. "How about you, little buddy? Are you happy now that you have your mama?"

Harry held out his dinosaur. "Purple."

"Is Purple your name?" Mark shook the dinosaur's right front foot. "It's nice to meet you."

Harry's giggle reached Mark's heart. "Do you have someone you can call, Damaris, someone who can help you and look after Harry?" He'd volunteer if she needed his help.

She nodded. "Our friends will watch Harry until my parents get here. They'll meet us at the hospital. So, we're all set." She must have made calls while he talked to the deputy.

He could follow the ambulance to the hospital, but Damaris had people to look after her. Hospitals weren't his favorite place, with Blythe's death still too fresh.

He wanted to do one more thing before leaving, if she'd let him. "Damaris, may I pray with you and Harry?" He didn't know her views on God, faith, and prayer.

Damaris glanced at Harry, who was talking quietly to Purple. Her eyes met Mark's. "I'd like that."

He nodded and bowed his head. "Father in heaven, thank you for protecting Damaris and Harry and keeping them from serious injury. We're thankful for these first responders who came and for family and friends who are on their way to help. We ask for Damaris's quick and complete healing, and we ask that Harry won't have bad memories of this time. And we pray that Damaris's parents will arrive safely. In Jesus's name, Amen."

"Amen!" Harry said.

Mark and Damaris laughed.

"Thank you, Mark," she said.

"You're welcome." He grasped Harry's hand and shook it. "'Bye, buddy."

As he headed for his car, Mark pulled his key from his pocket. Harry reminded him how much he missed Blythe—how much he wanted a family of his own.

He paused before opening his car door. Oh, no. He'd left Alana standing by the road when he went to talk to Damaris, but now she was gone. Why was she home? She didn't tell him she was coming. Her last email came from the IAS camp in Africa.

He got in his car and started it. Checking for traffic, he turned on his blinker and pulled out onto the road. His friendship with Alana had meant a lot in the months since they'd talked at Jack's wedding. They stayed connected through emails about twice a month. She'd prayed for him in his grief for Blythe, and he'd prayed for her work with the refugees.

He hoped she didn't leave the country before he could see her again.

CHAPTER FOUR

ark climbed the stairs to his apartment with legs made of lead. After two long and difficult days, he looked forward to a hot shower and bed. He removed a TV dinner from his freezer compartment and heated it in the microwave while he emptied his duffle bag and put his dirty clothes in the laundry hamper. The microwave beeped, and he headed for the kitchen, when someone knocked at his door.

Mark groaned. He just needed time alone to unwind.

Another knock sounded.

He'd make this interruption quick.

Mark opened the door and faced Jack, his brother. Even though Mark was five years older, they were sometimes mistaken for twins: same blue eyes, same dark brown hair, same build.

"Hi, I saw you were home. How did it go? I've been praying all day."

"Come in." Mark stepped aside and gestured toward the kitchen table. "Have a seat."

"Well, what did you decide? Did you take the new job?" Jack

pulled out a chair and sat, leaning back and stretching out his legs.

"I got home about ten minutes ago." The aroma of food made Mark's stomach growl. He glanced at the microwave but left his supper there. Pulling out a chair across from his brother, he sat. "Thanks for praying. But no, I didn't take the job." He tapped the table with his fingertips. "The offer was withdrawn, and I was laid off." A wave of hopelessness washed over him.

"What?" Jack leaned forward.

Precisely! Mark hadn't had time to work through the shock and grief yet and forced out the words that felt like a death sentence. "Building and Engineering Concepts is merging with Maxwell Corporation, and they don't want to keep most of us on the payroll. They're sending us off with a severance package and a recommendation for our résumé."

"I'm sorry, Mark." Jack clasped his hands together on the table. "I thought I'd be celebrating with you, so I came crashing in here. I didn't know."

Mark gazed around the kitchen without seeing and took a deep breath before responding. "It's okay. You couldn't have known." He shrugged. "I guess I'm a little angry. I need time to think things through, get some perspective."

"What will you do?"

"I have enough money set aside to live a year if I use it carefully. The company will cover health insurance until the end of the year or until I find a new job, whichever comes first. I think with my age and work experience, and a good recommendation, I should be able to find another job." His words expressed an optimism he didn't feel. "Or maybe God is directing me in an entirely new direction. I don't know. Right now, I'm beat. I need food, a shower, and bed."

"Do you want to come over for supper? I can give Kate a call." Jack pulled out his cell phone.

"No, although I appreciate the thought. I need to be alone for a while to pray and work through this. And I'm just too tired to be good company tonight."

"Tomorrow night?" Jack stood and pushed in his chair.

Mark nodded and got up.

Jack turned to the door. "I'm sorry. Kate and I will be praying, and if you need to talk or anything else, I'm here."

"Thank you for stopping by. It was good to have someone to talk to. And thank you for praying."

"Glad to do it. We've shared many hard times, haven't we?"

Mark nodded. His brother had been with him through all his losses.

Jack stepped out and closed the door.

IN MARK'S dreams last night, he watched Rachael and Blythe run laughing through the meadow filled with emerald grass and purple, yellow, and red wildflowers. They stopped to listen to the wind blowing through the blue spruce. He'd awakened with a sob, his pillow wet with tears. Dreams like that didn't happen as often now. How could he stay strong when his heart was so shattered?

Some mornings were harder than others. This was one of the hardest. Even the sunshine peeking in through the window blind didn't appeal to him. There was a reason for what happened. Still, his pain was real.

And losing his job made everything seem so much worse.

Pushing back his covers, Mark lowered his feet to the floor. He performed his usual morning routine, but focusing on his Bible reading and praying were especially hard this morning.

The clock on the wall reminded him it was time to go to his office, but he took a few more minutes to gaze out his front window overlooking Main Street. He recognized several of the children passing by on their way to school: Blythe's former classmates, second graders, chattering and skipping and running ahead of the adults accompanying them.

He sipped his morning coffee from a yellow mug Blythe gave him one Father's Day. His fingers traced the words printed on the side of the mug: "World's Best Daddy." That was a lie, though, because he couldn't protect her from the illness that took her life fourteen months ago.

Grief carved a hollowness in him.

He turned from the window. There must be a purpose in all his pain, even if he didn't understand it now. Romans 8:28 says that *all things work together for good to those who love God, to those who are called according to His purpose.*

He inhaled deeply and let his breath out slowly. He still had work responsibilities to fulfill at his rented office space. He'd have to notify his landlord he'd be closing the office.

He washed out his mug and cereal bowl and set them in the drainer, then brushed his teeth. Lifting his briefcase from the kitchen table, he headed for the door. Although tempted to hibernate in his apartment after work, he'd promised to eat with Jack and Kate tonight. He needed to be with family, and they expected him to eat with them at least once a week, except when he was out of town.

He didn't regret his decision to let Jack and Kate live in his cottage in exchange for the apartment above Jack's computer business. His family cottage without his family would never be home again. Now the place looked different inside. Kate had good taste in decorating, and some of Kate's paintings hung on the walls, along with wedding and framed photos of Kate's parents and her brother's family. They still kept him there in spirit, with a photo of Jack and him on top of a bookcase.

Shutting his apartment door, he climbed down the stairs to

the parking lot. A cigarette butt lay at the foot of the stairs. He frowned as he kicked at it. Neither he, nor Jack, nor Jack's employees smoked, and they were the only ones who used the back entrance to Jack's business, JC Computers.

He stepped up to the back door of Jack's store and tried the handle. Locked, with no signs of tampering. If someone tried to break in, the security system would go off.

Who else would come back here, and for what purpose? He'd have to be a little more vigilant.

MARK PULLED into the driveway at the cottage, turned off his car, and sat for a minute, consciously forcing the tightness in his chest to relax. When he got out, he gazed over the roof of his car at the familiar meadow, the one from the dream, alive with the colors of wildflowers. A soft breeze blew across his face and set the spruce trees singing.

"The blue spruce are performing their meadow song, Blythe," he murmured.

He closed his eyes, and the echo of his daughter's laughter filled his mind.

When tires crunched on the driveway beside him, he opened his eyes, reluctant to release the bittersweet memories.

"Glad you could make it, Mark." Jack climbed out of his van.

Kate pushed open the screen door, hopped down the steps, and threw her arms around her husband. Jack grasped her waist and twirled her around.

Blythe had once said that Jack should marry Kate. She'd been right. Kate was good for Jack. They belonged together.

He longed to hold and be held, but his wife had been gone for five years. The void couldn't ever totally be refilled again, but many people remarried and had wonderful second marriages.

Still, grief struck at the most unexpected times. And his most recent loss of his job seemed to magnify his other losses, at least for the moment.

Kate turned to him with a welcoming hug and sparkling green eyes. "Hi, Mark. You're just in time for supper."

"Hello, Kate. Thank you for inviting me over."

Did she know she had a spot of blue paint on her chin?

Jack whispered to Kate, and he rubbed her chin with his thumb. Kate wiped her chin with her palm. Her eyes flickered to Mark. He grinned at her. Her cheeks turned pink, and she led the way indoors.

"You guys sit. Everything's on the table but the spaghetti."

As he followed Jack to the dining room table, Mark's stomach growled, and his mouth watered at the wonderful aroma of tomato and garlic in Kate's spaghetti sauce. After Jack gave thanks, Mark enjoyed his meal of spaghetti and meatballs, tossed salad, and homemade bread with marble cake for dessert.

Across from him on the wall hung Kate's painting of Blythe that now held his gaze. She had captured his daughter's sparkle and sweetness. How his little girl would have loved spending time with her *aunt* Kate. He loved the painting, but his heart cried out for her presence.

"A delicious meal, as usual. Thank you." He laid his napkin beside his plate and leaned back in his chair. "I'm glad I came tonight."

Kate smiled. "Thanks." She rested her arms on the table. "Are you all right, Mark? You look tired."

"I am tired." Memories of Rachael and Blythe had haunted him all day. And, of course, job worries.

"Jack told me about your job. I'm sorry."

"I still have work to do, but I didn't accomplish as much as I planned to on my project today." Mark took a sip of coffee.

"Some days it's hard for me to make progress on a painting when I have a lot on my mind."

"That's probably why."

Kate nodded. "Why don't you and Jack sit in the living room and visit? You haven't seen much of each other lately." She stood and collected the plates.

"Are you sure, honey?" Jack grasped her hand. "We'd be glad to help you."

"No, clean-up will be easy. It will only take me a few minutes, and I'll run the dishwasher. Thanks for the offer. Go, enjoy yourselves." She shooed them away with a flick of her hand.

Mark looked away when Jack kissed his wife. For a man who'd been afraid to get married, Jack sure enjoyed married life.

He remembered Rachael's gentle touch and caring and longed for it now.

"I'm going to show Mark our garden, Kate. We'll be out back."

He followed Jack outdoors.

Jack had prepared a plot for a raised bed vegetable garden. "Kate would like to buy a couple of blueberry bushes to plant out here." Jack walked to one side of the backyard to indicate the place. "And she has her eye on a dwarf apple tree for over there." He pointed to an area beside the small building that housed Kate's painting studio.

"It's fine with me. This is your home while you live here, and I know you and Kate love it as much as Rachael and I did."

"Thanks. I'll let her know."

Mark tucked his hands in his pockets and walked around the backyard. His heart pinched at the new grass sprouting where Blythe's swing set had stood. He'd given the set to a couple at church with small children. Blythe would like that, and leaving the set to rust away would be a greater reminder of his loss.

Daffodils nodded their bright heads, and the green leaves and buds of tulips pushed their way through the soil in the perennial bed beside the studio he'd built for Rachael because she loved to paint. Kate, a professional artist, now used the building. He stared across the yard, remembering but not seeing, until Jack spoke beside him.

"You had a rough day?"

He focused on his brother. Jack had loved Rachael and Blythe and had walked with him through his losses and grief. "The dreams don't come as often now, but the one last night hit me hard. I dreamed about Rachael and Blythe in the meadow, and this morning, I saw some of Blythe's classmates skipping by on their way to school. I've been grieving for them and for my job all day." He shook his head and tears threatened to spill out. "I couldn't concentrate on my work, and I have to finish the project before my meeting next week."

Jack laid a hand on his shoulder. "I'm here for you."

Mark put his arm around Jack's shoulders and pulled him against his side. "I know, Jack, and I'm thankful I have you and Kate. Maybe one day the pain won't be so great." He hoped the happy memories of his family would one day take precedence over the pain of loss.

When they returned to the house, Kate joined them in the living room. She sat beside Jack on the sofa. He stretched his arm out behind her, and she leaned her head against it. Mark rocked gently in the rocking chair across from them, soothed by the motion.

Kate spoke. "Ellie told me that Alana came home yesterday."

Mark stopped rocking. Like his family, Alana and Ellie grew up in Millvale. Mark had married Rachael by the time Alana graduated from high school. "Yes, I saw her. I'm surprised she's home so soon. She thought she'd be gone for at least a year."

Last fall, at Jack and Kate's wedding, Alana had told Mark about her work with the International Aid Society. He admired Alana's courage and compassion as she helped the victims of trauma in Third World countries. Since then, she'd sent him email updates about her work. He responded with tidbits about life in Millvale and occasionally wrote about his grief.

Alana's responses were always sympathetic and understanding, and he'd enjoyed their correspondence.

"She contracted malaria." Kate curled her legs up beside her. "She's on medical leave so she can rest and get the proper diet."

"Will she be okay? Don't malaria symptoms keep coming back?" Jack put his arm around his wife, and she snuggled against him.

"Lanie told Ellie her symptoms are lessening, and she's expected to make a full recovery with medication, diet, and rest."

"She mentioned that malaria was a concern in the camp, but I didn't know she was ill and had to leave her job." Mark resumed rocking. "At least she's getting better."

"Ellie's worried about Alana, and she's glad she's home where she can keep an eye on her. It will take some of the stress from their parents as they care for Grandma Somers in Kellersville. Besides, Ellie wants Ian to know his aunt, and she believes Ian will help Alana heal faster."

"He's a cutie." Jack grinned. "His smile makes me smile."

"Babies are like that. I remember when Blythe was a baby." Mark couldn't continue against the lump in his throat.

Jack nodded. "I remember."

Mark blinked several times against the prick of tears.

With wet lashes, Kate gazed across the living room at Blythe's portrait hanging on the dining room wall.

Wiping moisture from his eyes, Mark stood and stretched. "It's time for me to go. Thank you for the meal."

Jack got up. "I'll walk you out."

Since Blythe's death, Jack had become his watchdog, checking up on him regularly. "It's been a hard day. Lots of memories."

"Can I get you anything before you go? Coffee? Another

piece of cake?" Kate stood. "How about a piece of cake to take home with you?"

Mark nodded. "A piece of cake to go would be good. Your desserts are always delicious."

Kate led the way into the kitchen.

Jack laid his hand on Mark's shoulder. "That's because I'm the guinea pig. I get to sample her trials." Kate turned and raised her eyebrows at her husband. "Oh, they're mostly good. You can see I'm not losing weight." He patted his stomach.

Mark chuckled.

"Here you go." A generous slice of cake covered with plastic wrap lay on the plate Kate handed him.

"Thanks, Kate." Mark kissed his sister-in-law's cheek. He turned to his brother. "Jack, I don't know if it's a cause for concern, but I found a cigarette butt at the foot of the stairs to my apartment. Everything else looked to be all right, but I don't know anyone who should be back there that smokes."

"I didn't notice anything out of order in the store today."

"I'll try to watch more closely. You have a good security system, but an electronics store might be a target. Some area businesses have had attempted break-ins, and a couple of homes in Millvale have been burglarized recently."

"Thanks for the warning."

"You're welcome. Good night." Mark went out to his car.

An owl hooted from the giant blue spruce, which now kept a quiet vigil over the meadow. The scent of flowers filled the air as memories filtered through his mind. He took a deep breath and let it out slowly.

Today had been one of the hardest he'd had in a long time. He never expected to face a day like this again. Added to the lingering grief over Blythe's death and memories of Rachael, losing his job had left him hanging from a precipice, the loneliness and grief nearly cutting him loose from his moorings. Today, he felt abandoned.

He couldn't fathom God's purpose in all this hurt and loneliness. He didn't pretend to fully understand God's ways. God had left him a brother to anchor him. Jack looked after him now as he had looked after Jack when they were young. Spending the evening with his brother and sister-in-law had been good. They shared his grief and accepted his need to grieve. He had a church family, and he had friends. And the promises in God's Word.

Tomorrow had to be better.

CHAPTER FIVE

$\mathcal{M}$ark sat at his desk, determined to let nothing distract him from his work today, and so far, it had worked. He'd made good progress since arriving at his office early this morning.

Looking up from his computer, he recognized Alana Somers walking by on the opposite side of the street. Kate had been talking about Alana last night, and after their awkward meeting at the accident scene, he'd hoped to see her again. He saved his work and hurried out the door.

"Alana!" He jogged across the street.

As she turned with a smile, a rush of excitement passed through him. Her brown hair had been cut short, and it curled. Dark lashes framed her hazel eyes. Her face, however, was thin and pale. Of course, she'd been sick.

"Mark, it's good to see you! How have you been?"

Seeing her triggered a zing of attraction he hadn't experienced since Rachael. He wanted to hug her but hesitated. She stepped up to him and gave him a one-armed side hug, which he returned, fighting her scent and softness that touched the longing he'd been battling since the dream. He stepped away first. Their eyes held briefly, leaving him shaken.

He stuffed his hands in his pockets. "I'm well physically and improving emotionally. How about you? How are you feeling? Kate said you came home because you contracted malaria."

"I'm much better now, but it will be awhile until I will be able to return to work." She dropped her gaze and played with the buttons on her coat. Then she smiled at him again and pushed a curl away from her face.

"I'm glad to hear that." Mark had more work to do on his project, but he also wanted more time to talk to Alana. "Are you out for a walk, or do you have a destination in mind?"

"It's such a lovely day for a walk, and I need the exercise. I'm on my way to Ellie's shop."

"Do you have plans for lunch?" He hadn't asked a woman out since Rachael, but he longed for companionship to ease his loneliness. He and Alana could talk and get caught up over lunch.

She shook her head. "No special plans. Why?"

"I have to get back to work now." He gestured toward his office. "How about having lunch with me at Mill Pond Diner?" He'd call this lunch with a friend, but his heart told him it might be more.

"I'd like that. Okay." Her smile formed dimples on both sides of her mouth.

Letting out the breath he didn't know he'd been holding, he checked his watch. "Will you be at the florist shop for a while? I can meet you there. Or you could meet me back here around noon."

"Why don't you meet me at Ellie's place? The diner is closer to the shop than here. I don't want to stretch my strength to its limits."

"Tell you what: I'll get my car, so you don't have to walk. Then I can drive you home afterward." She had been ill.

When she touched his arm, a spark zinged through him. "That's thoughtful of you, Mark. Thank you."

"I'll see you later."

"Yes. I'm looking forward to having lunch with you." She turned and walked away but looked back once and waved.

He watched her retreating figure. Although he considered the spring day to be warm, she just returned from a hot climate recuperating from a serious illness, which was probably the reason she had her fleece jacket buttoned to the top.

He became friends with the widowed women at the grief group he attended after Blythe's death, but he hadn't been inclined to date them. He'd discovered in Alana a friend with whom he could share some of his hardest moments of grief and who had been open about her struggles while working with refugees.

Could the future hold more than friendship for them? Too soon to tell. In his present state, he wasn't ready to make such a decision. And whether she'd be interested in being more than friends, he didn't know, but today he looked forward to having lunch with her.

MARK CHAMBERS INVITED her to lunch! Alana's stomach still fluttered from the solid feel of his hug and his warm gaze. However, she wouldn't read too much into the lunch invitation. He'd loved his wife very much and might not be ready for more than a friendship.

Alana had enjoyed her email correspondence with him for the past six months. He seemed genuinely interested in her work, and he shared his walk with grief. There was no harm in joining him for lunch at the diner.

She had few opportunities to date while working at the IAS

camp, although the workers's schedules usually allowed a day off every week, unless an emergency intervened.

Something about Mark, his blue eyes, his smile, the warmth of his greeting, made her want what Ellie had—a home and family of her own.

Alana enjoyed the heat of the sun on her face as she placed her hands in her pockets and pulled her fleece jacket closer. It would take a few days for her body to adjust to the cooler temperatures. How she'd always loved spring in Millvale with the fresh, warm air, and new plant life exploding into a symphony of color.

At Mill Valley Florist, a bell jingled when she opened the door. Inside, she searched the shop. No Ellie. And that meant no Ian to cuddle. She'd counted on seeing and holding him.

However, Kate Chambers rushed up to greet her. "Lanie, it's good to see you."

"Hi, Kate." Alana returned her former college roommate's hug. "Thank you for not asking how I am. I know people are concerned for me, but I'm finding it hard to respond to the same question all the time."

Kate nodded. "After my fiancé, Tim, died, people did that to me. And when my mom was sick. I wasn't sure if they really wanted to know, or if they didn't know what else to say." She grinned. "How are you?"

Alana wrinkled her nose at her friend. "I'm alive, I'm getting better, and I'm home."

"That's good. Ellie said you might stop by this morning. I'm working on some floral arrangements. I'll get a chair from Ellie's office so you can be comfortable while we chat."

Alana waited by the worktable as Kate entered the office. Several vases stood at one end of the table, along with floral tape and wire, foam blocks, scissors, and wire cutters. Kate dragged the padded chair through the office door and left it on the opposite side of her workspace. Alana sat down and leaned back with a sigh.

"Are you all right?" Kate inserted a fern into an unfinished flower arrangement on the table.

"I'm fine." She drew in a deep breath and blew it out. "I walked here from my house. It feels good to sit." She didn't want to dwell on her health. "I thought Ellie would be here this morning."

Kate smiled. "You're disappointed that Ian isn't here, right?"

Alana shrugged. "Well, yes. But I want to see my sister too."

"Ellie and Ian will be in soon. I've been working more hours since Ian's birth. She'll keep Ian here with her for as long as she can before getting a sitter for him."

"I hope she'll let me help with Ian while I'm home."

"She only works a few hours a day right now, but she's hoping to start full time again in a couple of weeks."

"Well, I told her I plan to spoil him, and I can't do that if I don't spend time with him." She'd make up the time she'd lost since his birth when she was on the other side of the world.

Kate chuckled. "I think she'll let you do that once she's convinced you're well enough."

Alana credited Kate's skill in arranging leaves, ferns, and flowers in the vase to Kate's artistic gift along with Ellie's training. However, she suspected the glow on Kate's face wasn't entirely from arranging flowers.

"How's Jack?"

Kate looked up. "Jack's fine. He enjoys having his own business, and it's doing well."

"You look happy." *Ellie and Kate make marriage and family look blissful. Will I find happiness like theirs?*

"I am." She clasped her hands. "Jack is wonderful. I have my studio, and I love living in the cottage. God has blessed me so much."

"I'm glad for you, and that Jack found you."

"God had something special in mind for us both when He brought me to Millvale. When Ellie invited me to work for her, I came to escape my pain and memories. Then I met Blythe." Kate bit her lip. "And Blythe led me to Jack." She picked up a daisy, snipped its stem with scissors, and inserted it in the vase. "God had something better planned."

"Definitely." According to Kate, Blythe had insisted from the beginning that her uncle Jack should marry Kate.

Ellie said she doubted there was a dry eye in the packed church by the time Blythe's memorial service ended. Alana hadn't been there, and Kate hadn't either, because she was in Mountain View caring for her mother who had cancer.

"How is your mother, by the way?"

"My mother's doing well." Kate smiled, shifting a daisy in the bouquet. "She goes in for a check-up every six months, and so far, the cancer remains in remission. That's another answer to prayer."

The bell jingled, and they both turned toward the door.

"Good morning." Ellie pushed through with the baby carrier in one hand and a diaper bag on her other shoulder.

"Hi, Ellie. Alana's been here waiting to see Ian."

Alana glared at her friend as she stood to give her sister a hug. "You, too, Ellie. I wanted to see you as well."

"It's okay, Lanie. I understand. Ian and I talked about seeing you today, and we're both glad you're here. Did you walk over? I didn't see Grammy's car outside."

"It's such a beautiful day for a walk. I hated to take the car out."

Ellie handed Ian to her, and she sat again in the chair. As she held her nephew snuggled against her shoulder, contentment spread through her. And a deeper desire to have a family of her own.

"You look tired. I can run you home when you're ready. I have my car." Kate examined the finished arrangement.

If she leaned back and closed her eyes, she could probably fall asleep. She blamed jet lag combined with the aftermath of malaria. She may have made the wrong decision to walk this morning, except she wouldn't have encountered Mark.

Alana shook her head. "No, thank you. I have … Mark invited me to have lunch with him at the diner. He'll take me home afterward." Alana wasn't ready for her romantic sister or anyone else to think there was something happening between her and Mark.

Ellie gazed at her. "Huh," she said and went into her office.

Alana stared after her. Did Ellie think she couldn't have a romantic relationship with Mark?

Kate set the arrangement in the cooler. "When did you see Mark?" She checked the next order and chose a vase.

"He stepped out of his office when I walked by this morning. He has work to do now, but we're meeting around noon for lunch."

"Good," Ellie said as she came out of her office with several papers clutched in her hands. Her face didn't reveal her thoughts about Alana's lunch date with Mark.

"I'm glad he asked you." Kate's voice drew Alana's attention back to her friend. "He came over for supper last night. He misses Blythe so much, and he's lonely. His team's project is nearly completed, and he's stressed about …" She pinched her lips together.

What was Kate not saying?

Although Alana hadn't experienced the personal loss of a spouse or a child, her heart had been broken many times by what she had witnessed in IAS camps after a natural disaster or war that left people without a home or family. She understood more than most.

Mark had lost much, but he had a home and a job, and Jack and Kate. If nothing else, she could help ease his loneliness by being his friend, with no strings. She could do that.

Ellie leaned over and rubbed her son's back as he lay cuddled against Alana's shoulder. "Since I have an in-house babysitter for the next hour, I'll get some work done. Just let me know if you get too tired."

She waved the papers in her hand. "I see Sarah and Matt have finally set their wedding date and want to meet with me to discuss flowers. Corinne and Janice want some arrangements and corsages for their parents' fiftieth wedding anniversary party. I have to make some phone calls and set up appointments. I'll help with those arrangements afterward, so you can go to lunch, Kate."

"Thanks, Ellie. Jack expected he'd have a busy day, so I packed a lunch. We'll eat together in his office at the store."

"Ben's at work, so I'll have my lunch here with Ian." Ellie returned to her office, and Alana heard her say, "Hello, Sarah? This is Ellie Jakobs at Mill Valley Florist. I had a message that …"

Two women entered the shop. Kate greeted them, and Alana quickly lost track of Ellie's phone conversation as the customers cooed over Ian. Kate finished the second arrangement, then went to help the customers.

"I guess it's just you and me, Ian." Alana got up and walked around the shop with Ian resting in the crook of her arm. She flipped through Ellie's catalog of flower arrangements and stopped to examine a couple of dish gardens. Fatigue forced her to sit again.

Should she cancel lunch with Mark? She didn't want to. Hopefully, food would ease her tiredness.

CHAPTER SIX

Brown vinyl seat covers and faux wood table and countertops in the diner had replaced the red ones Alana remembered. A few well-placed painted landscapes hung on beige walls. Wooden planters filled with decorative foliage divided the diner into three sections. The plants were probably artificial, but Alana couldn't tell from the doorway where she lingered.

"I like the new décor, but I kind of miss the old red and chrome." She glanced over her shoulder at Mark standing behind her.

The mingled scents of coffee, grilled hamburgers, and other food caused her stomach to growl. Embarrassed, she mentally commanded it to stop.

"I know what you mean. It's a big change from what we grew up with." Mark directed her to a small, corner table beside a window facing the street. "I hope you don't mind sitting here."

"Not at all. Although it would be fun to watch the ducks on the Mill Pond. I've thought about taking Ian to see the ducks when I'm feeling better. Blythe loved the ducks, didn't she?"

A shadow flitted across his face, and his shoulders sagged.

"Yes, feeding the ducks became a ritual for her. I haven't been back there since …" He shrugged.

Now she'd done it. Reminded him of his loss. Why did she do that? "I'm sorry." She touched his arm. He flinched, then nodded. An uncomfortable silence followed.

He helped Alana remove her jacket and hung it on the back of her chair. Assured she was seated comfortably, he took his seat across from her.

"Hi, Mark." The waitress laid menus on the table in front of them. She glanced at Alana, and her eyes widened. "Alana? I thought you were in Africa or South America with the IAS."

"Hello, Hannah." Alana had been Hannah's babysitter long ago, and in their small town, Alana's work with the IAS was no secret. "Well, I should be, but I'm home for a while unexpectedly." Alana didn't feel like explaining more. Hannah would find out soon enough.

Queasy and light-headed, she opened her menu, hoping to find something that sounded and tasted good. Agreeing to have lunch with Mark today may have been a mistake. Between her unruly tongue and her misbehaving digestive tract, she wouldn't be the best lunch companion.

Pulling a pad and pen out of her apron pocket, Hannah asked, "Would you like me to bring your drinks while you decide what to order?" After jotting their drink orders down, Hannah said, "I'll return in a few minutes to take your food orders."

Mark nodded as the waitress moved away. He picked up his menu and said to Alana, "Please order whatever you want, whatever you can eat that sounds good to you."

His down-turned mouth and refusal to look at her stabbed her conscience.

"Thank you, Mark. I think I'll have the chicken noodle soup and a half sandwich. I don't want to eat too heavily yet." She hoped she didn't have to make a quick visit to the restroom.

"That's fine." He opened his menu.

Alana peered at him through her lashes. She and Mark's brother Jack had been classmates in school. Along with almost every other girl in junior high, she'd had a crush on Mark Chambers, a senior and the baseball team captain.

With the help of a great-uncle, Mark had shouldered the responsibility of caring for Jack after their parents died in a plane crash. He'd remained strong in his Christian faith, even when his dear wife died, followed by the death of his sweet daughter. He still carried grief, like today, but he hadn't turned away from God like so many others did.

The IAS could use a strong, compassionate man like Mark.

Hannah returned with their drinks and set napkin-wrapped eating utensils in front of them. Mark glanced up, and Alana quickly lowered her eyes to her menu.

MARK LOOKED FORWARD to having lunch with Alana. Her comment about Blythe and the ducks hurt and sent a fresh pang of grief through him, but that hadn't been her intention.

He'd been friends with both Somers girls for most of his life, bubbly Ellie and quieter Alana. However, until Jack's wedding, he'd never taken the time to sit down and talk with Alana. She was sweet, smart, and compassionate, and her spiritual insights encouraged him. Through their email correspondence, she'd helped him navigate life after Blythe, perhaps because she dealt with suffering in her line of work.

A light blush crept along Alana's cheeks. He'd been staring at her. He looked away quickly, his face warm, and glanced around to see if anyone had been watching. He peered out the window and took a deep breath.

Turning back to Alana, he folded his hands on the table in front of him. "Thank you for agreeing to have lunch with me today."

Alana unwrapped her stainless tableware from the napkin. "Thank you for asking me."

Mark swallowed. "Our email correspondence has meant a lot to me. I hope I didn't overburden you. Attending grief group meetings helped a lot, but emailing you was like having a personal discussion with a friend."

"I'm glad I could help. And I appreciated that you kept me up to date on news from Millvale." Alana sipped her water. "I heard from my sister and Kate, but you gave me a different perspective."

"I guess the benefit was mutual."

Hannah brought their lunches, and Mark asked the blessing on the food.

Alana stirred her soup. "Kate said you're working hard on a project for your job."

He hesitated. "Yes. The project is nearly complete." The reality of being laid off still had a nightmare-like quality, as though he'd wake up and discover he hadn't lost his job. Plus, he'd told only Jack, who had told Kate. "My team has to work out some problems and plan a promotional presentation for our client." There was no need to tell Alana more because she was already struggling with her illness.

"How is everything?" Hannah stopped beside their table.

Alana nodded. "It's good."

"Everything's fine, Hannah, thank you." He smiled at the waitress.

"Let me know if you need anything else."

"We will," Mark said.

Several acquaintances walked by and greeted them. Their eyes flitted between Mark and Alana as though trying to figure out the meaning of the couple's lunch together.

Mark took a bite of his Reuben sandwich. He wanted their conversation to be an easy and enjoyable one between two friends, not polite and forced. Tired lines grew prominent around Alana's mouth and eyes, and her complexion paled.

He leaned forward. "Are you all right? You haven't touched your sandwich."

"Just tired." She stirred and finished her soup. "I'm sorry, Mark. I can't eat another bite."

"You can take the sandwich home with you." They had shared so much in their email exchanges. Why was face to face with her in the diner so uncomfortable?

On the drive back to her apartment, she sat with her head back and her eyes closed. Her silence and pallor worried him. "Do you miss your work?"

"I miss being there to help the people." Her eyes remained closed. Her dark lashes lay against pale cheeks. "There are never enough aid workers, and every day I'm gone means more work for the others." Her voice held frustration. "I'm glad to be home for now, where it's quiet, and I can rest when I need to. But I can't get back there soon enough."

"I imagine you're looking forward to returning."

She sighed. "Most of the time." She turned her head toward him. "You said your team is nearly finished with a project. It must be satisfying when you finish."

"It is." But this time it meant the end of his job, which seemed like more loss than he could handle. And with Alana planning to leave, maybe he should reconsider what he wanted before he scheduled another loss in his very near future.

He pulled into the Somers's driveway, and she opened her eyes.

An awkward silence lay between them as they walked to her door. He matched his pace to hers, ready to assist her if she needed it.

"As a world traveler, I'm sure you're thankful for a place to come home to."

"Yes, I am. Especially now." She opened the door and turned toward him. "Thank you again for lunch."

He didn't want to leave her there alone. "Do you want me to call Ellie?"

"No, I'll be fine. I can call Ellie if I need to. I'm going to rest for a while, then I'm going grocery shopping. I'm just tired. Jet lag and malaria. I think I did too much this morning."

"Well, if you're sure." He stepped back. "See you later."

"Okay." She waved and shut the door behind her.

With his hands in his pockets, he returned to his car.

Mark's grief group leader had encouraged the attendees to not be afraid to date and get married again after taking time to work through their grief.

His head was ready, but his heart … called him traitor.

Maybe it was fear. He couldn't expect any woman to marry him if he was unemployed.

And he didn't want to risk ever losing another wife to illness.

Besides, Alana would be leaving Millvale when she regained her health, anyway.

It was time for him to focus on the things he could control, to get back to the office and finish his work.

THE DING of her phone brought Alana back to consciousness, the dream about refugee children in camp clinging to her. After Mark dropped her off from lunch, she'd over thought every word of their conversation, procrastinated her grocery shopping, then snuggled under her quilt and fallen asleep.

The clock on her phone said it was two p.m. She'd slept for an hour. And Ellie had texted.

How was lunch?

Good.

Ellie doesn't need to know it was disappointing. My foolish tongue and that rotten malaria!

Pushing back the quilt, she swung her legs over the side of the sofa and tucked her feet into her shoes. She had to make out her shopping list. But she didn't get up. Instead, she plopped back against the sofa.

Do you want me to take you shopping?

She shook her head, too tired to make out a list.

No, I still have food. I'll wait until tomorrow.

She would stay in, watch a good movie, if she could find one on TV, and rest. *And not brood about the disappointing time with Mark.*

Let me know if you need anything.

Okay.

Could she have said or done anything to create a different lunch outcome? She'd expected too much. It was just as well she'd be leaving Millvale in six months.

CHAPTER SEVEN

*B*irdsong greeted Alana through her open window. In the camp, human voices usually woke her, sometimes laughing, sometimes scolding—voices like that of Nicholas Ames, a physician's assistant who worked on her IAS team and triaged refugee health needs while she registered the refugees as they arrived. She and Nicholas had worked through many emergencies together. Nicholas liked to spend time with the children, especially the boys without fathers, and she had formed a special bond with two children who often followed her around camp.

She checked her bedside clock. "Nine o'clock." She sat up. She'd slept eleven hours.

Refreshed by the much-needed sleep, she propped her pillow against the headboard. She still had to fill the hours she usually worked with something more than sleeping and eating, like caring for Ian while Ellie worked—she smiled at the thought of his sweet face and cuddly body. When her stamina returned, she could help care for Grammy from time to time, to give Mamma a respite. Pastor Clary at Valley Community Church might suggest ways she could help at church.

She yawned, stretched, and pulled her Bible and notebook

from the bedside stand. In the refugee camps, she squeezed her devotional time into spare moments, never knowing when an emergency might arise that demanded her attention. She'd make the most of her quiet days at home.

Her phone dinged. A text from Ellie.

> Hey, do you want me to drive you to the grocery store? You said you planned to go today.

> No, you have plenty to do. I'm feeling much better today.

> Okay. I'll be available if you change your mind.

After reading her Bible, Alana began her grocery list while she ate breakfast, checking the IAS doctor's care recommendations, including food suggestions, that lay on the table beside her dishes. She also recorded what she ate in a food journal.

ALANA PULLED a shopping cart from the outdoor supply and pushed it through the automatic doors as they swished open. The trip to the store had been uneventful, but she hadn't driven a car for a while. Her ankles ached a bit, probably from using the brake and accelerator pedals.

"Alana Somers, how are you, dear?"

Startled, Alana turned her head toward the familiar voice. "Good morning, Mrs. Matthews. It's nice to see you."

The gray-haired woman stood a couple of inches shorter than Alana's five-foot-five frame. Alana had known Mrs. Matthews all her life, and they both belonged to Valley Community Church. She was a bit of a busybody, but her concern for people was real.

With a smile, she gave the older woman a side hug.

"I heard you were sick with malaria and had to come home. Are you feeling any better?" Mrs. Matthew's pale blue eyes twinkled behind her dark-rimmed glasses.

"I am, but I still have to be careful not to do too much."

"Are you here alone?" Mrs. Matthews peered behind her.

Alana nodded. "Yes, I have my grandmother's car, and I'm well enough to drive."

Mrs. Matthews patted her arm. "I'd love to stay and chat, but I must get home. My husband's waiting for me. Be assured that Mr. Matthews and I are praying for you, and if you need anything, please don't hesitate to call on us. Will I see you in church this Sunday?"

"I expect to be there, Mrs. Matthews."

The older woman bustled out of the store, pushing her cart.

Alana picked out some bananas, oranges, and red grapes, then she looked over the display of fresh vegetables. She'd always enjoyed helping her father in his garden. Maybe she'd grow her own vegetables this year. She'd benefit from the exercise and fresh air and the extra nutrition from home-grown vegetables.

Her legs ached, so she leaned on her cart for support. Adding milk, yogurt, and cheese from the dairy section to her cart, and oatmeal and a whole wheat cereal from the breakfast aisle, it became harder to push the cart as her arms tired. Then she yawned.

After completing her shopping and paying for her groceries, she pushed her cart out into the sunshine, ready to go home for a nap.

Alana enjoyed the sense of freedom and independence the use of the car gave her. However, she wasn't ready to conquer the world—yet.

～

THE NEXT MORNING, Alana caught up on updates and messages from the IAS.

One of her tentmates messaged, "I miss you. It's not the same without you." The other wrote, "I've had to take over some of your work. Working with Nicholas is a hoot."

A message from Nicholas made her chuckle, which often happened with him. "How soon will my partner in crime return?"

She loved her work with the refugees in the camps, even though it was exhausting. What she and her co-workers did mattered, and working together to aid the victims of trauma gave them a special bond of caring for one another. She prayed for them each day.

But did she want to be an aid worker for the rest of her life? Could she do that and be a wife and mother, because she definitely wanted to do that? She worked with two married couples. Was there another way for her life to have a greater impact, like becoming a nurse? The IAS could always use more medical professionals. What did God want her to do?

AFTER LUNCH THE NEXT DAY, the bell over Mill Valley Florist's door jingled when Alana entered. Ian cooed in the background as Ellie created an arrangement at the worktable.

"Hi, Ellie."

"Good, you came. Kate went home at lunchtime, so it's just Ian and me here now."

"What can I do to help?" She peered at Ian over the edge of his portable crib behind the work counter. His big brown eyes caught hers and he smiled, kicking his legs and waving his arms.

Ellie paused her arranging and smirked. "Go ahead and pick him up. He'll enjoy the attention. It's almost time for his nap."

"Hey, sweet boy." Alana lifted the baby into her arms.

Savoring his softness and warmth as she walked around the shop, Alana talked to him, and he smiled and cooed. After a few minutes, he snuggled against her shoulder and fell asleep. She laid him in his crib, tucked a blanket around him, and gazed at his tiny form. Would God ever give her children of her own?

Ellie finished the floral arrangement.

"What can I do to help you, Ellie? Ian's asleep, and I don't want to sit in a chair and fall asleep myself."

Ellie placed the arrangement in the cooler. "I don't want you to tire yourself out. You've been helpful just looking after Ian."

"I'm getting plenty of rest, Big Sister. I'll stop when I get tired."

"Okay. I need an inventory check of these things. Here's a list I printed off for Kate for when she works next time, but you can do it instead." She held out a paper. "You know where I store things."

Alana examined the list and nodded. "I can do this."

"You're planning to come to our house for supper tonight, aren't you?" Ellie chose a vase and started another arrangement.

"Yes, I am. And one day soon, I'll fix a meal and have you, Ben, Kate, and Jack over."

"Deal." Ellie wrapped her arms around Alana. "I'm so glad you're home. I know your work is important, but I've missed you."

Alana embraced her sister. "I've missed you too."

Things like illness, death, and even birth revealed life's value and the preciousness of family and friends. If she signed on for another five years with the IAS, she'd miss Ian's first words, his first steps, and his sweet hugs. She'd miss birthdays and other family celebrations, and time with her beloved grandmother. *God, would it be selfish to choose these things over helping suffering people?*

On the way back to her apartment that evening, she passed

JC Computers. Mark's car sat in the parking lot. Had his day gone well? Had he finished his work project yet?

FROM HER BASEMENT apartment within her parents' home, Alana climbed the stairs to close the windows she'd opened earlier to let the spring air refresh her parents' house. A cool breeze made her shiver, and she wrapped her sweater across the front of her body.

Her mother's cloth-covered, baby grand piano in the living room caught her eye. Alana had taken lessons for twelve years. She'd also taken voice lessons and loved to sing.

Pushing back the cloth, she opened the lid covering the keys and ran her fingers up and down the keyboard. A little out of tune, but not bad. She sat on the bench and played.

One after another, the hymns poured out from her fingertips. "It Is Well with My Soul," "Great Is Thy Faithfulness," "How Great Thou Art," and several more washed over her like the waves of the ocean lapping up on shore, soothing her tired body and mind.

Her body might be weak and her future uncertain, but her faithful God was the keeper of her soul. She just had to wait for Him to direct her on the path she should follow.

CHAPTER EIGHT

Mark lay in bed with his eyes closed. He opened one eye, and as far as he could tell, the sun wasn't up yet—too early to be awake on a Saturday morning. He plucked his clock from the bedside stand. "Five o'clock." Replacing the clock, he rolled over on his stomach and pulled the pillow over his head. It didn't help.

He had no plans for the day, no place to go, nothing to do. He moaned and kicked back the bedcovers, too restless to stay in bed.

Yes, he'd go for a long run.

Dressed in his running shorts and T-shirt, he grabbed a bottle of water and stared for a moment at his cell phone lying on the kitchen table. No. He wanted to be alone.

When he stepped outside, the glow of sunrise hovered on the eastern horizon. Bird twitters broke the stillness. He breathed in the cool air and released his breath slowly.

There it was again, rustling in the bushes and the tap-tap-tap of a runner's footsteps.

"Is someone there?" He listened, but all was quiet. His imagination was working overtime.

He took off for his run. Light shined from the windows of a few of the homes he passed. Quiet reigned, broken only by the song of birds and the barking of a dog. Almost of their own accord, his steps took him out of town in the direction of his family's cottage.

In high school and before Rachael's death, a daily run had been common for him. For a while, he'd worked out in the gym in Break-a-Bean, but lately, even that had fallen by the wayside. His whole life lay stretched before him, like an empty and lonely landscape.

Lights came on at the cottage where Jack and Kate would be getting ready for the day.

Crossing through the grass in the meadow, he stopped under one of the blue spruce trees and brushed his hand against the rough bark. Sap stuck to his fingers, and a memory surfaced of Blythe, who had touched the bark and earned sap-covered fingers. She hated sticky fingers, and she ran to him in tears, demanding he get it off. He pulled his hand away and stared at it, rubbing his fingers with his thumb. How was he supposed to go on like this? He slid to the ground, his hands cradled his face, and sobs broke from his chest.

Mark wiped his face with his sleeve and looked up. "God, are You there?"

The sun rose above the horizon, and the dewy grass sparkled in its rays as wildflowers opened their faces to the sun. He took in the beauty of creation. A breeze whispered through the tree branches. Rachael and Blythe had said the trees sang.

I am with you always. God's whispers stirred hope within him.

He filled his lungs with air and released it slowly. "Thank You, Father."

Today he'd start looking for another job. He'd update his résumé and do an online search with the list of potential employers Dave had sent him. The sooner he finished his run, the sooner he could begin his search for a new job. Stepping onto the road, he began a slow jog, enjoying the warmth of the sun on the way back into town.

Would finding new employment mean moving away from the place he loved? A life-long resident, Mark knew most of the people in and around Millvale. He remained active in the community through the Chamber of Commerce and church, and he often helped a family or individual in need. Many people had reached out in a caring way during the worst times in his life, when Rachael and Blythe passed away. Millvale was his home.

A red minivan parked in a neighbor's driveway reminded him of Damaris and Harry Cook.

"I wonder how they are?"

Their grief counselor had encouraged the whole group to find and be open to a second love. Did Damaris wish to marry again? The little boy with the purple and green dinosaur needed a father. He'd like to get to know them better, but Damaris didn't live in Millvale, and he didn't have her email or phone number.

Maybe his grief group counselor could help him get in touch with her.

As he continued his run, he decided to make an appointment with Pastor Clary at Valley Community Church. He'd often gone to the pastor for wise counsel and prayer which he needed now. He'd helped Mark and Jack through the loss of their parents, counselled Jack through his angry, rebellious period, and supported them when Rachael and Blythe died. He'd call the pastor later this morning and set up a meeting.

Why had God allowed him to lose so much? He didn't know.

But he trusted that God knew what He was doing. *"You will keep him in perfect peace,"* he repeated softly as he jogged, *"whose mind is stayed on You, because he trusts in You."* *

---

* Isaiah 26:3

~

ALANA REACHED for the door handle to the church office and jumped back when the door opened from inside.

Her hand flew to her chest. "Mark, it's you!" She took a deep breath to slow her heart rate and breathing. The cobalt blue of his polo shirt intensified his eye color.

"I'm sorry if I startled you." He held the door open, and she stepped inside. He let the door close behind them both. "How are you today?" His shoulders hunched, and he shoved his hands in his pockets.

She turned to respond, the short sleeves of his shirt revealing toned arm muscles, and she tried to cover her blush with a smile. "Every day I feel less tired, stronger. I'm getting restless. I need something to do. Something not strenuous." He didn't return her smile. "Is everything all right?"

He sighed. "I'm looking for a job."

"A job?" She frowned. "I thought you worked for Building and Engineering Concepts." He'd worked for them for a long time. Had they been displeased with his newest project? Or worse, was he unable to finish it in time?

"I do, for a few more days. The company's been bought out, and I'll be let go, along with most of my coworkers."

"How awful for you! I'm so sorry. What will you do next?"

"I don't know. Pray a lot, I guess. Polish my résumé and look for another job."

He sounded so uncertain and discouraged. She wanted to hug him and assure him he'd get another job, but sometimes life didn't work out that easily, considering what happened with his wife and daughter.

If he applied to the IAS, maybe they'd work on the same team. Working side-by-side with Mark Chambers appealed to her.

No. Now wasn't the right time to talk to him about it. She wanted to plan what she'd say, have information about the IAS ready.

"Is Pastor Clary in his study?" She gestured down the hall with her hand.

"Yes, he's there. I had an appointment with him." Mark rested his hand on the door bar.

"Oh, I didn't think to make an appointment." She bit her lip. "I need to speak with him. If he doesn't have time now, I'll make an appointment for another time."

Mark's warm smile reached his eyes. "I'm sure he'll be glad to see you." His eyes met hers and seemed to say she was special and he was glad to see her. Butterflies invaded her stomach.

Warmth spread over her face. She drew her eyes away and looked toward the study. After their uncomfortable lunch date earlier in the week, she feared she might read more into his smile than he intended. Mark had a warm way with people. Better she end the conversation now before things turned awkward again. "I'll pray for you."

"Thanks. I have to go. See you later." With a quick wave, he pushed open the door and left.

She frowned at his abrupt departure. Her hope for a romantic relationship with Mark tugged at her heart, but he probably would never think of her as more than a friend. She'd have to be satisfied with that. She sagged and headed for the pastor's study.

From the doorway of the secretary's office, she peered in at Pastor Clary sitting at his desk. The church secretary didn't work on Saturday, so Alana knocked on his open door and waited. Pastor Clary looked up.

"Alana!" He stood. "I heard you had come home. Please, come in." He walked around his desk and clasped her extended hand. "Mark Chambers just left."

"I know. I met him at the door."

With his hand he indicated a chair for her and sat behind his desk. "How are you? Ellie said you've been ill."

She leaned back in her chair and folded her hands on her lap. "Yes. I had the malaria immunization as recommended, but I still contracted it. It was awful. They had to send me home so I could get better."

He picked up his cell phone. "I'm so sorry. Let me call my wife. She'd like to see you."

"I'd like to see her as well."

Mrs. Clary had been her middle school Sunday school teacher and a mentor throughout high school. The pastor's wife often sat in on her husband's conversations with women or was present nearby when his secretary wasn't available.

While he made his phone call, Alana looked around. The walls had been painted a pale blue. Books lined the bookshelves in neat rows. Books, papers, and a laptop computer cluttered his desk.

He laid his phone down. "She'll be right over."

Alana nodded. "Mark said he got laid off from his job."

The pastor folded his hands and leaned on his desk. "Yes, it's a hard and unexpected situation for him."

"I don't understand why life has to be so difficult for him. He's one of the nicest men I know." She licked her lips, and her face warmed.

Pastor Clary gazed at her for a moment, as though reading her thoughts. "We don't always understand what God has in mind."

"I know. I've wondered why God allowed me to contract malaria. The IAS needs workers, and we were quite busy when I left. If I'd had a choice, I'd have stayed in the field to convalesce. I could have done a lot behind the scenes." *And not had this confusion about Mark.*

"They probably knew too much would have been demanded of you had you stayed there."

Alana looked down at her hands in her lap. He spoke the truth. The temptation to help would have been too great, and rest would have been nearly impossible. And she didn't regret being home. In fact, she was enjoying her time with Ellie and Ian more than she ever could have imagined. She nodded. "I know."

Mrs. Clary, a slender, smiling, gray-haired woman, entered. "Alana, welcome home, although I'm sorry illness brought you to us this time."

"Hello, Mrs. Clary." Alana rose from her chair. Mrs. Clary's reputation for warm, comforting hugs still held.

The pastor set another chair beside Alana's and dragged his chair into position to form a small circle. "How long do you expect to be home?"

"The doctor said six months or less, depending on my health. I'll have a check-up and blood tests each month."

"Will you go to your own doctor for this?"

"No, there's a clinic that specializes in tropical diseases about two hundred miles from here. My first appointment is in three weeks."

"If you need someone to drive you, I'm sure we can find volunteers." The pastor smiled at his wife.

She nodded. "I can think of several women who'd probably do it."

"Thank you, I'll keep that in mind. I have my grandmother's car, so I can drive myself. I think Ellie or Kate might go with me if I ask."

Pastor Clary crossed one leg over the other. "I expect you won't just sit around while you're here, although you'll need time to rest. Do you have plans for your time at home?"

"That's what I've come to discuss. I'll have to spend time with my parents and Grammy." She grinned. "And I told my sister I'd spoil Ian."

Pastor and Mrs. Clary both laughed.

"That won't be hard to do," Mrs. Clary said. "He's a sweetie."

"I can't do anything strenuous, at least right now, but I want to do more, to make this time at home matter."

Pastor Clary clasped his hands around his knee. "We can always use more substitute Sunday school teachers."

Teaching a Sunday school class would take more brain power than muscle. "I'd like that. In the field, a few of us have a Bible story time for the children. The IAS is respectful of religious beliefs, so we have to be careful not to offend."

"Would you be willing to talk to our women's fellowship about your work and experiences?" Mrs. Clary looked at her husband, and he nodded.

Alana gulped mentally. Public speaking had never been her forte, even though she had sung with her sister in church. Teaching a kids's Sunday school class was a lot different than getting up in front of a group of adults and talking, but she didn't want to disappoint Mrs. Clary.

"Let me think about it." Just the thought made her stomach wobble.

Pastor Clary clapped his hands. "Why don't we wait until after your appointment at the clinic before we decide? We want to be sure you get well. In the meantime, my wife and I will keep our eyes and ears open for things you might do, and we'll pray for you."

"Thank you. Will you pray with me now?"

Alana left the church a few minutes later and headed home.

As a young girl, she dreamed of traveling the world, of visiting exotic places she heard and read about in books. In the four years she'd been with the IAS, she'd been to South America, Africa, and Europe. She still didn't want to be confined to a small town for the rest of her life, but she had doubts about signing another contract with the IAS.

Only a few of the people she worked with had remained with

the relief organization for more than five years, and they were mostly middle-aged. The physical, mental, and emotional stress of being in the midst of so much suffering took its toll. Many workers went on to other careers and marriage.

But if Mark wasn't the one, if God had other plans, then how was she to know what to do next? Until she heard from God, she couldn't decide about her future.

CHAPTER NINE

efore their parents's death in a plane crash, a Chambers family vacation at a Rhode Island beach had been a high point of each summer. Mark had honeymooned there with Rachael, one summer they'd gone with Blythe, and he and Blythe came once after Rachael died. Perhaps there he could recover some of the joy he so desperately needed.

Mark made his reservation for the beach cottage from Monday afternoon through Thursday morning at off-season rates. He'd be willing to pay higher summer rates just to be there.

"I need time, and I have to get away," Mark told his brother. "I'll be back in time for Kate's dinner on Friday night."

He'd already closed his office in town. No sense in paying rent for something he wouldn't use. That had been hard and sad, like a finale for the past eight years of his life.

Monday morning, he packed his suitcase, filled his car with gas, and headed for the Rhode Island shore six hours away. Already, he felt better.

The sun hung two-thirds of its way to the western horizon late Monday afternoon when Mark pulled into the parking space in front of the small, white cottage with blue trim and a porch. Getting out of his car, he stretched and inhaled the salty sea air. Exhaling, a wave of tension rolled off his shoulders. The cool ocean breeze ruffled his hair. This early in the season, few tourists would be here. That was fine; he'd come to be alone.

The familiar sound and scent of the ocean drew him, and he couldn't wait. Jogging the half mile down the road, he then followed the well-worn path to the beach. The sand stretched before him to where it met the frothy waves, and sea gulls called to each other as they circled above the water and dove into the waves. The swoosh of breakers welcomed him.

Climbing to the top of a sand dune, he sat and gazed out to where the sea met the sky. As a child, he'd wondered how far away that was. The last time he was here with Rachael and Blythe, he'd watched Rachael showing Blythe how to build a sandcastle.

An overwhelming wave of grief suddenly overtook him. Hunching his shoulders and leaning his arms on his knees, he released the tears he could contain no more. He let go of the emotion and pain that had lodged within him, and he sobbed. God created humans with emotion, and tears were an expression of grief. He wasn't ashamed.

After a few minutes, his tears spent, he wiped his face with the bottom of his shirt for lack of a handkerchief or tissue. He pulled in a deep breath, held it for a few seconds, then released it. He probably looked a mess, but he felt better.

Tomorrow morning, he'd fly Blythe's kite. That was one reason he had to come here. Blythe talked about flying a kite at the beach, and he made reservations for their summer vacation, but they never came.

He wiped his eyes on his shirt sleeves. After returning to the cottage and changing his shirt, he pocketed several tissues and went in search of something to eat at the nearby deli.

EARLY THE NEXT MORNING, Mark bit down on his lower lip as he tied the string on the kite he'd made in Blythe's memory, her sweet face lingering in his mind.

"A pink kite, Daddy, with sparkles."

She painted a picture of herself flying a kite on the beach and sent it to Kate. When she died, he wasn't prepared to lose her. Even though she was prone to respiratory illness like her mother, her lively mind and body belied her underlying vulnerability.

He missed her.

As he walked to the beach, Mark inhaled the cool morning air. He paused and closed his eyes, listening to the whoosh of the waves. The sound never failed to soothe him and unleash good memories. Too early in the year to go swimming, the nearly empty beach gave him plenty of space to fly his kite and, hopefully, release him from his melancholy.

Kicking off his flip-flops, he tucked them into the back pocket of his jeans. The sand, not yet warmed by the sun, gave way beneath his bare feet as he walked out to the edge of the waves, and he shivered as the cold froth touched his toes before receding.

A sailboat appeared along the horizon, and seagulls dove into the surf. Mark waved to a fisherman who cast his line into the water from rocks along the shore. The fisherman would probably have a fish breakfast or lunch.

The sun popped up on the horizon. He ran, releasing the kite little by little as it rose on the wind into the sky, tugging against the string's restraint. He stopped unrolling the string but continued to adjust the tension.

The kite danced in the wind and sparkled in the sun's rays, reminding him of Blythe's joy and laughter. He imagined that, if he let go of the string, the kite would soar up to heaven, to

Blythe and Rachael. They were there, with Jesus, and he'd see them again one day.

Mark's stomach growled. "Just a while longer," he whispered. The kite floated. "I wish I could join you, merry kite. Up there, maybe I could break free from this terrible weight in my heart."

A white-haired couple came down the wooden walkway and strolled arm-in-arm along the beach. Their voices and laughter carried to Mark. She leaned her head against the man's shoulder. He kissed her forehead.

Mark's parents had talked about growing old together, and he and Rachael had dreamed of doing so.

"Will I be alone forever, Lord?" He stood, small and lonely, beside the vastness of the ocean that stretched beyond him.

A voice whispered to his heart. *I love you and am with you, My child.*

Yes, God was his Father, and he belonged to God's family. God loved him, and he was never alone.

I will never leave you or forsake you. *

He drew in the kite, winding the string around the reel. He'd come out again tomorrow morning and Thursday before going home.

AFTER MARK ARRIVED home on Thursday, he received a text message from Damaris Cook.

> Harry invites u to his 3rd b'day party Friday at
> 4 with a few family members and friends. He'll
> be sad if u don't come.

Somehow, Damaris had learned his personal phone number,

---

* Hebrews 13:5

maybe from their grief counselor. Immediately, he changed his mind about going to Jack and Kate's for dinner on Friday.

If Harry wanted him at his birthday party, he'd go. He would see for himself that Damaris and her son were all right after the accident and perhaps discover if there could be more between Damaris and him than the trauma of loss.

Guilt nudged him when he phoned Kate and told her he'd miss her Friday dinner after he said he'd be there. "I don't want to disappoint little Harry."

"I understand, Mark. Go, and have fun. I've also invited the Jakobs and Alana. We'll all miss you."

He'd seen but not spoken to Alana for more than a week. Of course, he'd been away for part of that time. Did he avoid her because she stirred something in him he was afraid to explore?

He'd go to Harry's party because Harry expected him.

Leaving Millvale in pouring rain, he followed his GPS to the address Damaris texted him. Here, the sun had already chased away the clouds.

As he headed up the sidewalk, he heard voices from the backyard. A small boy rounded the corner of the house and raced toward him. "Mark! Mark!"

"Hi, Harry." Mark crouched, set the gift he carried on the ground beside him, and held out his arms to catch the boy.

Harry threw himself against Mark and clung to his neck. Harry's enthusiastic greeting surprised him and warmed his heart.

With a welcoming smile, Damaris walked toward them. Her white slacks and pink sleeveless blouse accentuated a lovely figure. "Hi, Mark. I'm glad you made it. We're in the backyard right now, enjoying the sun."

He had no inclination to give her a hug in greeting, as he had Alana. But he didn't know her well yet.

Harry stepped away from Mark and snuggled his hand into his mother's. Mark lifted the gift and stood.

"Hello, Damaris. It's nice to see you. Thank you for inviting me. My GPS gave me good directions." The two standing in front of him shared the same shade of bright blonde hair and blue eyes. "How have you been since the accident?"

Her demeanor remained friendly, but no spark jumped between them.

"Let's go to the back," Damaris said. Harry skipped in front of them as Mark fell into step with Damaris. "We're fine. My bruises are gone. Harry had a couple of bad dreams at first, and he became anxious in the SUV for a while, and the SUV required some major repairs, but insurance took care of most of it."

"Good."

Harry ran off to play with some children. Damaris introduced Mark to her parents, Harry's father's parents, and other party guests. Interestingly, Harry's proper name, Harrison, had been Damaris's last name before marriage.

Although he'd just met them, he felt comfortable and accepted, like he belonged. The feeling continued during the picnic meal and while watching the children play the games Damaris planned for them.

When the sun descended toward the horizon and the air cooled, Mark joined Harry's family and friends as they went indoors to watch Harry open gifts.

Harry dove into his gifts, but his mother pulled him back and settled him on the living room floor.

"Dylan, will you hand Harry his gifts, please?" A teen boy, introduced to Mark as Harry's cousin, sat between Harry and the pile of gifts.

Harry tore the paper from each gift, paused long enough to hold it up so everyone could see, then asked for the next gift.

Mark chuckled. Blythe had opened her birthday and Christmas gifts with the same gusto. The usual pain that accompanied memories of Blythe didn't happen.

Mark chatted quietly with Damaris's parents. He didn't regret accepting Harry's invitation to the party, but did he belong with this family, with Damaris and her small son?

Harry tore the balloon birthday paper off the long box containing Mark's gift to him.

"Firetruck!" Harry looked at Mark with a huge smile. Damaris smiled, forming "thank you" with her lips. Mark smiled and nodded. He'd chosen the right gift for Harry.

Dylan helped Harry pull the firetruck out of the box. Immediately, Harry attempted to run the truck over the gift-strewn floor, imitating a fire siren. Mark chuckled. Maybe it wasn't such a good gift after all.

"Harry, it's time for your birthday cake. Why don't you park your truck in the corner next to the chair? You can play with your truck and other gifts later."

Damaris handled the situation well. She didn't scold, but she introduced something else that caught his attention.

The little boy's lips formed a pout at his mother's words. Dylan whispered something in his ear Mark couldn't hear. Whatever he said worked.

"Okay!" Harry jumped up and pushed the truck into the corner. He followed Dylan into the dining room where a big, purple and green dinosaur birthday cake sat in the middle of the table.

Of course, a dinosaur cake. Where was Purple tonight?

Harry's eyes glowed as they sang Happy Birthday.

Soon after Damaris served the cake and ice cream, guests began to leave. Harry gave Mark a hug and hurried to play with the fire truck.

Damaris walked out to his car with him. Now, away from the other guests, would be a good time to ask her for a date.

"Thank you for coming, Mark. Harry was thrilled to see you, and the firetruck has already become a favorite toy."

"Thank you for inviting me. I enjoyed the time with your family, and I'm glad Harry liked the fire truck." He turned to face her and took a deep breath, his heart pounding. "Maybe we can go out sometime. I'd like to spend more time with you and Harry, get to know you better." He held his breath.

She hesitated, then shook her head. "We're moving next month. Harry and I need to be closer to my mom and dad. I'm sorry, but I'm selling my house."

"Oh, I didn't know." Disappointment deflated him.

"I appreciate your friendship and your kindness, Mark, but I believe this move will allow my son and me to get a new start. I'm sure you understand. I want to move forward with my life, a new home, a new job, and maybe sometime in the future, someone to love and cherish."

She wanted to move forward, but she would move forward without him.

Well, okay. He took a chance asking her. Nothing had indicated she was interested in him. Surprisingly, her rejection, if he could call it that, hurt nothing but his ego.

When she offered her hand, he clasped it. "Thank you for inviting me today. I've enjoyed getting to know your family."

"I'm glad you came. Harry was thrilled to see you. You made quite an impression on him on the day of the accident." She gently pulled her hand from his. "I wanted to tell you in person about our move. You're a wonderful man, and I wish you happiness in your future."

"Thank you, Damaris. I wish you the same." He got into his car and waved as he drove away.

He'd tried to open a door, and it had swung shut right away. Better to know now, before his ties to them strengthened. After losing his father, Harry didn't need another man disappearing from his life.

Maybe he'd tried to open this door on his own, without asking God.

CHAPTER TEN

The sun made its first appearance for the day on Friday evening as Alana pulled into the Chambers' driveway and parked behind her sister's van.

She lifted the foil-covered, glass dish containing mixed berry crisp from the passenger seat and got out of her car. Kate had assured her she had vanilla ice cream in her freezer to go with Alana's blueberry, raspberry, and blackberry dessert.

Where was Mark's car? Surely, they'd invited him for dinner tonight too. She'd seen him in church, but they hadn't spoken since their impromptu meeting outside the pastor's study. For a reason unknown to her, he was avoiding her. Why didn't he want to talk to her? They were friends, right?

Maybe he was on his way. Or maybe he had something else to do.

"If Mark doesn't come, so be it." She'd enjoy her evening with some of her favorite people, anyway. However, it would be even better if Mark showed up.

She'd cuddle with Ian if she could wrestle him away from the other adults. Jack and Kate should have a baby so Ian could have a playmate and there'd be another baby to hold.

Perhaps one day she'd have a home and family of her own. What fun if she and Ellie and Kate all had babies that grew up together.

She approached the door and knocked.

Kate opened it immediately. "Lanie, come in! How are you? Dinner's almost ready, and everyone else is here."

Stepping into the kitchen, Alana set the container with the dessert on the counter and gave her friend a hug. "I'm fine. Thank you for inviting me." She laid her hand over her hungry stomach. "It smells wonderful in here!" She didn't ask about Mark, although she wanted to. "Anything I can do to help?"

Kate lifted the corner of the foil from the berry crisp. "This looks yummy." She turned back to Alana. "Why don't you go into the living room and greet everyone? Then ask Ellie to come back here with you, and you can help get the food on the table. If Ellie's busy with Ian, that's okay, but I know she has a couple of willing babysitters in there."

"Ben and Jack." She joined Kate in laughter. Ben was, of course, a loving father who enjoyed spending time with his son, and Jack never refused an opportunity to entertain the baby.

In fifteen minutes, the food was ready.

"Come and get it!"

At Kate's invitation, the five adults sat around the dining room table. Ian lay asleep in his portable crib. Jack prayed, and they passed around the food.

Alana inhaled the aroma of the meat loaf. "Mm, this smells good." Her appetite had improved, and her digestive tract tolerated a greater variety of food. She took small portions of meat, mashed potatoes, vegetables, and one of Ellie's homemade rolls.

"This meatloaf is delicious, Kate." Ben pointed at his plate with his fork. "It tastes like Ellie's."

"That's because I used Ellie's recipe."

"Kate and I exchange recipes," Ellie said. "Meatloaf is one of Ben's favorites."

"My brother is going to be sorry he missed this," Jack said. "He likes meatloaf too."

Kate shrugged. "I think Mark likes most food. He never refuses to eat anything."

"He knows you're a good cook, honey. And, as he says, 'What single man will refuse a home-cooked meal?'"

Ah, the perfect opportunity to ask about Mark. "Where is Mark tonight? I know he eats with you often, and I thought he'd probably be here."

"He planned to come at first, but he got an invitation from a friend to attend her son's birthday party." Kate sipped her iced tea.

"Oh." Alana buttered a section of her roll. So, he had somewhere else to go.

Jack took another slice of meatloaf and passed the plate. "A few weeks ago, Mark helped a woman and her young son after they had an accident. The boy wanted Mark to come to his third birthday party, and Mark couldn't say no."

Damaris Cook. I should have guessed. Alana chewed the last bite of her roll.

Kate nodded. "He said it was a good opportunity to make sure they were all right, and he didn't want to disappoint little Harry. So, he made his apologies and went to the party instead."

"Remember the red SUV we saw in the ditch on your first day back, and we stopped to see if we could help?" Ellie set her fork against her plate.

"Yes, I remember. Her name is Damaris Cook." Alana patted her lips with her napkin and lowered her eyes to her plate so no one would see her disappointment.

"Mark didn't mention you were there," Jack said.

Alana shrugged. "We didn't stay long. He probably just forgot."

She finished her meal and folded her hands in her lap. She'd been right about Mark and Damaris, and it hurt.

"You have your appointment at the clinic soon, don't you, Lanie?" Kate began to collect the dinner plates, and Alana rose to help, glad for something to do.

"Yes, next Friday."

"Are you going alone, or is someone going with you?"

"I think I can do it by myself, although having a friend along would be nice."

"I'll go with you." Kate looked at Jack, who nodded. "That is, if your sister doesn't want to go and will give me the day off."

"Of course! I'd go, but it would be hard with Ian." Ellie stood. "I think it's wise for you to have someone with you, Lanie. It's a three-and-a-half-hour drive, and it may be too much for you alone."

Ian fussed.

"Ben, will you get Ian while I help clear the table and get the dessert?"

"Sure, honey." Ben retrieved his son.

Alana laughed as Jack leaned toward Ben, and the men had a contest to see who could make the baby smile the most. She carried empty serving dishes into the kitchen.

Ellie looked up from loading the dishwasher. "What are you laughing about?"

"You should see those men trying to make Ian smile."

"It's not hard to do. He's a happy baby."

Kate took the ice cream from the freezer and handed a spatula to Alana. "Why don't you serve the crisp, and I'll scoop the ice cream?"

Alana cut the dessert and placed the pieces on small, glass plates Ellie took from the cupboard and set on the counter. Alana wanted to ask more about Mark's relationship with Damaris and her son, but she didn't want to explain why she was interested. She had to get her mind off Mark.

"How is your painting going, Kate?"

Kate pushed the scoop into the ice cream. "It's been steady. I have a couple of commissioned landscapes nearly finished, and I've been asked to do a portrait of a businessman's wife in Break-a-Bean, someone Jack knows."

She placed a scoop of ice cream on top of each serving of crisp, the juicy berry mixture oozing out from under the crumbly top.

"You stay busy." Alana was happy that Kate was living out her dream of being an artist.

"Jonathan Weeks in Mountain View sells my paintings to tourists in his gift shop. I'm teaching a children's class at the community center again, and I've been asked to do a painting party with a women's group."

Ellie closed the dishwasher door. "Kate has been a great help to me since I've had Ian."

"Oh, it's been my pleasure." Kate laid the ice cream scoop in the sink.

"Well, now that Ian's a little older, I'm getting back to my usual schedule at the shop, and you'll have more time to paint."

"I see Jack is quite comfortable with Ian. Do you have any plans for starting a family yet?" What fun it would be to have another baby around, one who could play with Ian.

Ellie's gaze danced between Kate and Alana.

"I'm sorry, Kate." Alana covered her mouth. "I had no business asking that question. That's between you and Jack."

Kate's cheeks turned pink. "It's okay, Lanie. Maybe soon. We wanted to have a little time for just the two of us before having a baby."

"You and Jack will make wonderful parents. I'm glad that you and Ellie are both so happy." Alana meant it, but she wanted the same happiness for herself.

As though reading her mind, Ellie placed her arm around her and squeezed. "Your time will come."

She hoped so, but when would that be?

Until her illness brought her home, until she held Ian, until she saw Mark again and her attraction to him grew stronger, she'd been content with her singleness and her work. Was her desire for a family just her own want and not God's will? *Rest in the Lord,* the Bible says, *and wait patiently for Him.*[*] Patiently waiting—was that possible for her?

Alana rested the spatula against the serving dish. "Do you think Mark might like a piece of the crisp? There's enough for one more serving."

Kate returned the package of ice cream to the freezer. "He won't refuse. I'll make sure he gets it." She and Ellie each lifted two plates of dessert from the table.

"Thanks, Kate." Alana claimed the remaining plate and followed Kate and Ellie into the dining room.

Alana had many compliments on her dessert. When they finished, Kate announced, "Jack and Ben are doing clean-up tonight. We women get to talk and play with Ian."

Men's laughter from the kitchen filtered into their living room chat about Kate's painting, Ellie's experiences as a new mom, and Alana's stories about some refugees she'd met. Alana and Kate each had their turn cuddling Ian until he insisted that only his mama would do.

Jack and Ben came in from the kitchen.

"Who's ready to play UNO?" Jack pulled a small box from a bookshelf stacked with board games.

She would store this fun family evening as a good memory of home for when she returned to work in a few months, completing her contract with the IAS.

---

[*] Psalm 37:7

CHAPTER ELEVEN

*M*ark pulled his toolbox from his kitchen utility closet. The church trustee board, with Pastor Clary's recommendation, had asked him to build shelves for several Sunday school rooms at church. Mark stored his power tools in a section of Pastor Clary's garage at the parsonage now because Kate's painting supplies filled his workshop at the cottage.

The shelves comprised the first wood project he'd worked on since Blythe's death. Not only did he enjoy building things with wood, a skill learned from his father, but it relieved stress. Today he'd cut the boards and sand them. If all went well, he'd fully install the shelves by the end of next week.

Gravel crunched as cars drove into the parking lot at JC Computers. Time for Jack to open. Good, he wanted to touch base with his brother this morning because he hadn't seen him all week. Leaving his toolbox at the foot of the stairs, he entered the store through the back door. His brother's employees greeted him, and he headed for Jack's compact, well-arranged office.

"Hey, Mark!" Jack looked up from his desktop computer. "We missed you last night. Did you have a good time?"

"I did. Damaris planned a fun party. Harry was excited I came, and he liked the fire truck I gave him."

"Great. But you missed out on Kate's meatloaf, Ellie's homemade rolls, and Alana's mixed berry crisp with a scoop of vanilla ice cream."

Mark leaned against Jack's desk. "You're trying to make me feel bad." His brother knew he liked Kate's meatloaf, or anything else she made.

Jack smirked.

He refused to fall for Jack's ribbing. "Damaris made a purple and green dinosaur birthday cake and served it with ice cream."

"A purple and green dinosaur cake?" Jack chuckled. "Kate saved you a plate of food, and Alana left a piece of berry crisp for you, but I forgot to bring the food with me this morning. Kate's painting at home today, so if you have time, you can stop at the cottage and get them."

Alana must still consider him a friend if she saved him a piece of her dessert. The thought warmed him.

"I'm on my way to Pastor Clary's garage to cut and sand Sunday school shelves today. I'll try to find time later."

He pushed away from the desk. He'd make the time to get the leftovers.

"Will you be seeing Damaris again?" Jack glanced at his computer screen and moved his mouse.

Mark shook his head. "Damaris and Harry are moving away next month, closer to her parents. She let me know her plans don't include me."

"I'm sorry it didn't work out."

Jack had never met Damaris and knew only what Mark told him.

"Damaris is an attractive woman, and she's the mother of an adorable little boy who needs a father. I'm lonely, I'm still young, and I'd like another family. Honestly, I didn't know if she was the one, but I wanted to explore the possibility." Mark shook his head. "Her refusal didn't bother me as much as it would have if I really loved her."

Jack's gaze held Mark's for a few seconds. Evidently, he accepted Mark spoke the truth because he nodded and leaned back in his chair.

"How's your job hunt? Any responses to your résumé yet?"

Mark shook his head. "Not even one. It's been three weeks and hard not to become discouraged."

"Have you thought of applying for a different kind of work?" Jack rested his elbows on his desk. "I don't have a place for you in my store, but another computer store might hire you. Or what about house building or carpentry?"

"I use computers, but I'm not into set-up and repairs like you. I enjoy working with wood, but I don't think I have the skills to pursue that line of work professionally." He was still young enough to learn a new type of work, though. "I'm not unwilling to work in another occupation, but I'm not ready to pursue that yet." He tapped the top of Jack's desk.

"God has something in mind for you. Maybe He'll surprise you."

When Jack's telephone rang and a customer entered the store, Mark said goodbye and left. He was qualified for the jobs he applied for, so why did no one want him? And with the door shut on a relationship with Damaris, what was his next step?

He looked forward to the project that lay ahead, a practical and enjoyable use of his time that would keep his mind off his problems. He grabbed his toolbox and placed it in his car trunk, then drove to the church. Yesterday, he thought about Blythe without self-pity and tears. Today, he talked about Damaris without regret. He'd mourned at the beach, and he expected he'd have more sad times, but God was restoring his joy and giving him hope. His Heavenly Father would provide what he needed.

～

83

WHEN MARK DROVE into the church parking lot, the Clarys's van and car were parked outside the garage, so Mark had easy access to his power tools and plenty of workspace.

By mid-afternoon, he finished cutting and sanding. He removed his protective face mask and goggles, cleaned up the sawdust, and moved the power tools and cut boards to the side. Pastor Clary came out of the church, hands in his pockets, and sauntered toward Mark.

"Hey, Mark, how are the shelves coming along?"

"They're all cut and sanded." Mark showed him the shelves stacked together. "I'll get the paint on Monday. The teachers were specific about the colors they wanted for the shelves in their rooms."

"When do you think you'll finish?" The pastor rubbed his hand along one smooth board.

"Hopefully, by next Friday. If I get them installed, the teachers will have time to arrange their supplies on them and be ready for Sunday school."

"If you need help, be sure to ask."

"Sam said he and his wife will help." Sam did a lot of maintenance work for the church.

"That's true. They both like to paint." Pastor Clary gazed around the garage.

"I just have to let them know when I'm ready."

"Good. You're set then." The pastor followed him to the car door. "There's something else I want to discuss with you."

"What's that?" Mark faced his pastor.

"Ever since you came to talk to me a couple of weeks ago, something has been on my mind. I believe God put it there."

Mark nodded. He'd often benefited from the pastor's sound advice.

"Have you ever considered attending seminary to prepare full time as a pastor or a missionary?" Pastor Clary leaned against the car. "I think you would do great in ministry."

"Y-you do?" Mark stared.

"Yes. You have Bible knowledge and a servant's heart. Now may be a good time to consider it, while you're between jobs."

Mark couldn't speak.

"Have I surprised you?"

Mark rubbed the back of his neck. "You have. I haven't had any success in my job search. Just this morning, Jack said maybe God would surprise me."

"When you're ready, we can talk about it more."

"I'd like that. I'm going to give it some thought and prayer." He pulled out his car key. "I have to get going. My sister-in-law saved some food for me I want to pick up."

Pastor Clary stepped back as Mark got into his car. "I'll pray for you to have wisdom and discernment as you think your next steps through."

WHEN MARK ARRIVED at the cottage, Kate had just come in from her studio.

She greeted him at the door. "Hi, Mark. Did you have a good time last night?"

"Yes, I did. I'd forgotten how much fun it is to watch a child opening gifts. Harry liked the fire truck I gave him."

Kate washed her hands at the kitchen sink.

"You have yellow spots on your face." He pointed to her cheek.

She lowered her face to the faucet and scrubbed her cheek with her hand, then dried it with a towel. "How's that?"

"You got it." He waited as she hung up the towel. "Jack said you have some food for me."

"Yes." She pulled a foil-covered, Styrofoam plate and a second, smaller one from the refrigerator and handed them to him. "Here you go. We missed you last night, but I'm glad you could go out and enjoy yourself."

"I'll be sure to join you guys next time." He lifted the corner of the foil covering Alana's berry crisp and sniffed. "I can't wait to try this. The thought makes my mouth water."

"It was delicious."

"Thanks again, Kate. I'm going for a run on the River Walk before I eat, so I have to take off."

"Have fun!"

MARK RAN around the outskirts of town, then headed toward the River Walk in the park, a place popular with joggers, hikers, and bikers. As he ran, he recalled the pastor's words.

Did God want him to be a pastor? He knew God might have a different career in mind for him, but this? *God, can I do it? Is this why You allowed me to be unemployed?*

There was a difference between working for a company involved with building and working in ministry where he'd be responsible for the spiritual well-being of the people in his congregation. He loved the church and had been involved with his all his life. He loved teaching Sunday school and men's Bible studies, but a pastor's responsibilities were even greater.

He respected Pastor Clary's spiritual leadership, so he took the pastor's suggestion seriously. But this was a bigger step than he'd considered when applying for new employment.

I'm willing, if that's what You want, Lord. But I'm scared I'll fail. Please give me an extra dose of Your power to do what I need to do.

But it would take time to find a seminary, apply, and be accepted. In the meantime, he needed a job.

Leaving the park, he jogged through the part of Millvale with new homes. A man in blue jeans and a denim work shirt with rolled-up sleeves stood beside a truck in one driveway. He placed tools in a large toolbox in the truck's bed. Mark slowed to a walk as he read the words on the side of the truck: *Eastman's Cabinetry*.

The business had been in the area for a long time. The man nodded at Mark. "Nice day." He wore a gray cap and looked to be in his late forties to early fifties.

Mark stopped. "It is." Although he'd never been inside Eastman's Cabinetry, he'd passed the shop on the other side of Break-a-Bean, about forty-five minutes from Millvale.

"These are nice homes." Mark gestured with his hand. "Do you work here?"

The man closed his toolbox and shut the tailgate of his truck. He turned to Mark. "Yes, the contractor hired me to build and install the kitchen cabinets." He smiled and held out his hand. "Dennis Eastman."

Mark shook his hand. "Mark Chambers."

"Any relation to Jack Chambers?"

"He's my brother. Do you know him?" Jack had never mentioned knowing him.

"You look like him. He helped us get computers when he worked for Clint in Break-a-Bean." He lifted his cap and resettled it on his head. "How's his new business going?"

"Quite well." Mark was proud of his brother's success. "He learned a lot working for Clint, but Jack's dream was to have his own store. It was a gamble to open one in a small town like Millvale, but he's done well."

"Glad to hear it. Do you work with him?"

Mark shook his head. "I'm not into computers like my brother. In fact, I'm between jobs right now." That was probably more than this stranger wanted to know.

"I'm sorry to hear that." The cabinetmaker rested his hands on his hips. "Before I started my company, I went through something like that—hard times."

"Yeah. I worked for Engineering and Building Concepts for eight years." Mark ran a hand through his hair. "They merged with Maxwell Corporation recently, and they let the employees in my division go." Why was he telling Dennis Eastman this, and why would he care?

"I'm sorry to hear that. Are you looking for another job in the building or engineering field?" Resting his arm along the top of the cargo bed, he leaned against the truck.

"I have my résumé out, but no bites yet. I'd consider other options."

"Do you have an interest in carpentry?"

Mark hesitated, unsure where the conversation was heading. "My dad taught me woodworking when I was a boy. I enjoy it."

"If you're interested, you can apply for a job with me."

Mark rocked back on his heels. "That's awfully nice, but—"

"Before you decline automatically, I honestly have more work than I can handle alone, and my wife has been bugging me to hire another worker. She keeps the books, and she comes into the shop to help me when I need her." He handed Mark a business card. "She's right. I'm working too hard. We haven't had a vacation in two years."

Mark read the card. Dennis wanted him to apply for a job although they'd just met, and he had no idea about Mark's skill level. Was this God's answer to his prayer?

"Thank you." Cabinetry was a useful trade. "Can I get back to you about this?" He wanted time to find out what Jack knew about Dennis Eastman and check out the Eastman's Cabinetry webpage.

"Sure. I'll be waiting to hear from you." Dennis got into his truck.

"Thanks." Mark waved and started jogging again, his step lighter, a weight lifting from his chest. *Thank you, God.*

He passed through an older residential section of town,

where the Somers's house was located, with Alana's apartment in the basement. He slowed, then stopped in front of the house.

The draperies were pulled back from the upstairs picture window. The notes of a piano filled the air, accompanied by a lovely voice singing "How Great Thou Art." He'd forgotten that Alana used to sing in church with Ellie. She also played the piano quite well.

He stood for a few minutes, letting the melody sink into his mind and heart as the words reminded him of God's greatness and love.

The song ended, and Mark moved on, not wanting Alana to catch him standing in front of her house.

Would there be any harm in talking to her as he would with any friend, to compliment her on her music that he enjoyed, or to ask about her health? He longed to talk in person with her as they had with emails because he had enjoyed it and missed it. He missed her.

ARRIVING HOME, Mark stepped into Jack's store, instead of going straight to his apartment, to ask his brother to see him before Jack went home after work.

He'd already devoured his meal when Jack knocked at his door a few minutes later. "Thanks for coming up."

Jack sniffed. "It smells like a meatloaf dinner in here. You must have stopped at the cottage for your food." He laughed.

Mark patted his stomach. "Excellent cooking all around."

"You have something on your mind?" Jack asked.

Mark indicated a chair for Jack and poured a mug of coffee for each of them before he sat across the table from him. "Yes. I met Dennis Eastman today."

"Where did you see him?" Jack pulled his mug closer.

"He's building cabinets in some of the new homes near the

park. I stopped to talk to him after he'd finished with one of the jobs. He said he knows you."

"Yes."

"I enjoyed speaking with him. He said he's overwhelmed with business right now and needs help, and he asked me to apply for a job."

"Really?" Jack's hand, holding his coffee cup, stopped halfway to his mouth. "Are you interested?"

Mark shrugged. "Maybe God's telling me there is something else He wants me to do. I haven't had responses to my résumé yet. You know how much I enjoy working with wood, and I'm sure Dennis, with how skilled he is, can teach me anything I need to know."

Jack nodded.

"What's your opinion of Dennis Eastman?"

"He's an honest businessman who produces quality work. He and his wife are a nice couple."

Mark turned his coffee mug around. "I told him I needed a little time to consider his offer." He pointed to the business card lying on the table. "I think I'd like to do this."

Jack finished his coffee. "Kate and I will be praying, Mark. This sounds like a great opportunity for you." He checked the time on his phone. "I'd better get home. Kate will have supper ready, and I don't like to keep her waiting." He stood and pushed in his chair.

Jack meant he wanted to see his wife.

"Thanks for stopping by. I'll let you know what happens." He'd send Dennis his résumé and set up an appointment for an interview ASAP.

CHAPTER TWELVE

*A*lana checked her purse. She had her phone, food journal, a list of questions for the doctor, and a book to read if she had to wait. Kate had offered to drive her own car, but Alana wanted to drive her grandmother's car. If for some reason she couldn't, if she became tired or ill, she'd let Kate drive it.

The clock on the wall indicated eight forty-five. She'd agreed to pick Kate up at nine. The queasiness in her stomach might be from anxiety about her appointment or the residual effects of the malaria, which she still experienced from time to time.

Alana pulled into the Chambers's driveway, thrilled at the puffy, white clouds drifting lazily across the blue sky and the sun shining. A perfect day for a road trip. The wildflowers in the meadow showed off their bright colors.

"Right on time." Kate slid into the passenger seat and closed the door.

"Good morning. I like to be on time. Thank you for going with me." Alana waited for Kate to buckle her seatbelt before backing out of the driveway.

"Thank you for asking me. It's been a long time since we last went anywhere together."

"It was in college, and we went to an art show our senior year."

"I think you're right." Kate nodded. "I was an art major and bought two tickets at half price."

"Didn't we take a bus?"

"Yes! Remember, we almost missed our ride home that night." Kate settled her bag in her lap.

"I hadn't thought of that in a long time." She'd missed hanging out with Kate.

Kate ran her hand gently across the bag in her lap.

"I see you've replaced your quilted bag with an embroidered one. It's beautiful. Where did you get it?" Kate usually carried her tote bag so she'd have her sketchbook and pencils with her.

"I found a website in my artists's network. My quilted bag was getting shabby, and when I saw the beautiful ones this woman made, I couldn't resist. They're expensive, but we traded: I painted a portrait of her parents from a photo, and she made a tote bag for me. She hand-embroidered the wildflowers design. Doesn't it remind you of the meadow outside the cottage?"

"It does." Alana put on her blinker to merge onto the inter-state. "Ellie would love one, don't you think? And maybe I could get one as a gift for my mother. I won't be here for Christmas, but I can order them and wrap them before I leave." Christmas at home would be wonderful, but it wouldn't happen this year. She missed spending the holidays with her family.

"I'll send you the link when we get back."

"Thank you, I'd appreciate that."

Halfway between Millvale and the doctor, Alana pulled off at a rest area to use the restroom, take a walk, and have a snack. Alana's stomach remained unsettled, but she wasn't ready to give up driving yet.

On the road again, traffic grew heavier. With an hour left

before reaching their destination, Kate's voice broke into Alana's thoughts.

"Mark wanted me to tell you your berry crisp was delicious."

"I'm glad he liked it." She smiled. He'd sent her the message, even though it was through Kate.

Alana hadn't talked with Mark recently. Their paths hadn't crossed in church, although she'd seen him there. She suspected he was avoiding her, but she didn't know why.

Kate took a deep breath. "Forgive me for being nosey. You don't have to answer if you don't want to."

"O-kay." Alana prepared herself. Kate wanted to know about her and Mark. "What's the question?"

"Is there something going on between you and Mark?"

Alana waited for a van to pass them. Nope, she didn't want to answer Kate's question. "I'm not sure what you mean."

"I thought … well, he invited you to lunch at the diner, and you seemed excited to go."

On the one hand, Alana preferred to keep her thoughts about Mark to herself. She didn't want to inflate her hopes, nor did she want people like Mrs. Matthews or her sister to become involved with a matchmaking scheme doomed to fail. On the other hand, talking about Mark might ease her mind. Kate was a good listener and kept confidences.

"I don't know how to answer you, Kate. I've known Mark most of my life."

Kate nodded. "Jack told me most of the girls in his class swooned over his big brother."

"Jack said that? Swooned?" Alana laughed with Kate. "Just like the entire jr. high, I had a schoolgirl's crush on him."

"Then, I'm right. You do like him."

"Back then, he was older, and by the time I graduated, he'd married Rachael."

Kate frowned. "So?"

Alana rubbed her hands on the steering wheel. "Mark is one of the nicest men I know."

"Agreed." Kate smiled encouragingly.

All right. She'd tell Kate everything. "He and I started an email correspondence after your wedding."

"Awe! I love that our love inspired your—" Kate stopped when Alana raised her eyebrows.

"Communication." Alana finished for Kate, keeping things in a safer, more comfortable category. "It was nice because he prayed for me and my work with the IAS, and I learned a lot about his struggle with grief after Blythe died. When I came home, and he asked me out for lunch, his invitation nearly blew me away. I hoped it meant he was interested in a deeper relationship." She shook her head. "But I guess it's not to be."

Alana braked for a slow-moving vehicle ahead and waited for a car to pass her before pulling into the passing lane.

"Why not?"

"I don't know exactly. We went to the diner and ordered our food. Suddenly, it seemed like a wall came down between us. I started feeling ill, and our conversation became stilted and uncomfortable."

"What did you do?"

"Nothing. We talked briefly the day I went to see Pastor Clary, but we haven't spoken since."

"I'm sorry. That sounds frustrating." Kate took a sip of her water.

"I think Mark has been avoiding me. And I know he's interested in his friend Damaris. So, no, I can't say there's anything going on between Mark and me."

"Oh. Well, in case you're interested, Damaris told Mark, who told Jack, that she was moving away, and he wasn't included in her plans."

"Really?" Alana glanced at Kate. A seed of hope swelled within her. "Poor Mark. He must be devastated."

"No, he has accepted it and is moving on."

To what or to whom? "I'm returning to work in a few months anyway, so I guess it's best to remain just friends."

"Maybe." Kate's one word contained an edge of doubt. "Jack and I have been worried about Mark. He's so lonely. He needs someone, and I think that someone could be you."

Could Alana become Mark's someone? She wanted Kate to be right, but Mark's behavior left that in question.

Time to talk about something else. "I hear Jack's business is thriving."

Kate had much to say about that. "Yes, Jack loves what he does and is good at it. He has good business sense too." She paused. "He knew it would be hard to run a computer store like JC Computers in Millvale, that he might not get enough business. But he and his two employees stay busy." She sighed. "The only drawback is that he works a lot of overtime. But he's happy."

"I'm glad for him, and for you."

After taking the exit for the Tropical Disease Clinic, Alana stopped at a family restaurant that served homemade meals. The chicken soup and crackers Alana chose eased the quivering in her stomach.

Her GPS directed them to the clinic, where she parked in front of a large, red brick building surrounded by well-manicured lawns, flower beds, and shrubbery.

In the clean, open waiting area, Kate found a seat while Alana checked in. She sat beside Kate while she filled out a health history form.

A door across the waiting area opened. "Alana Somers," a nurse called.

When she glanced at Kate, her friend smiled and patted her arm. Taking a deep breath, she stood. What would the doctor tell her?

Thirty minutes later, Alana emerged from her examination.

She caught Kate's eyes and smiled, then turned to the receptionist to set up her next appointment.

"Thank you. See you next month." She turned away from the reception desk. "I'm ready to go."

Kate stood and lifted her bag to her shoulder. "Everything good?"

"I'll tell you in the car." She exited and pulled the keys from her pocket. "Will you drive home? I'm exhausted."

Kate took the keys. "Of course. Are you okay?" Her brow wrinkled with concern.

"I'm fine, but I'm tired. It's been a long day." She yawned. "I saw a Dairy Freeze on the way in. Let's stop and get milkshakes."

"Okay."

After stopping at the Dairy Freeze, Kate followed the GPS directions back to the Interstate, heading home. "Did you like your doctor?" Kate lifted her shake from the cup holder and took a sip through a straw.

"Yes. Doctor Cole was patient while he explained the progression of recovery. I'm grateful I'll probably see him each time I come." Alana stirred her shake with the straw. "They took six vials of my blood and asked a myriad of questions. Dr. Cole said I need to put on weight, and he'll send me the blood test results in a few days, but I seem to be progressing through recovery as expected."

"Did he say how long it will be until you can go back to the field?"

"He said the blood test results should show I'm cured. However, if I go back before I'm ready, I could have a relapse or catch something else because my immunity's been compromised."

"Are you disappointed?"

"Not really. I'd been told up to six months." Would Mark be pleased when she told him? Would it make a difference in their relationship? Alana took a long draw of the milkshake. The coolness refreshed her. "I'm sorry in a way because my IAS team needs me. I'm not indispensable, but when a team member is unable to work, the burden goes to the other team members. They're looking for a temporary replacement for me."

"Are you close to the other aid workers?"

"I'm close to my tent mates and a few others, but we're all like a family." Alana stirred her milkshake with her straw.

"What about the refugees?" Kate glanced at her. "You once told me they were so lost and needy when they arrive at camp."

"Some of the refugees haunt my dreams, the children especially—the starving ones with distended stomachs, the ones carrying physical and emotional wounds of war, those suffering from diseases that ran rampant through their villages." Alana swallowed back tears.

Kate frowned. "I don't know how you can handle the pressure and stress of that. It would break my heart. Those poor mothers."

"The mothers, when they know you care, reach out for help and friendship, which is a blessing I never expected. You're right though, you have to be careful not to let your heart become too entangled because the relationships are only temporary. One of you will probably be leaving soon." Alana yawned.

Kate's eyes rested on her for a moment before returning to the road. "Why don't you take a nap? I'll wake you if I become drowsy. We'll stop at the rest area about halfway home."

Alana took one last sip of her milkshake and set her cup in the cupholder. "Thanks, Kate." She laid her head back against the seat.

"Remember in college how I had considered the mission field and talked about becoming a missionary nurse? I signed up with the IAS instead to see the world while helping people in Third World countries."

"I was surprised when you joined the IAS. You always talked about being a missionary."

Alana shrugged. "I know." She hadn't realized signing with the IAS, a secular organization, would limit her opportunities to share her faith and help hurting people find hope in Jesus.

"You can still work for the IAS if you became a nurse, right?"

"Yes, definitely. They need more people with medical training. I'd have to take time off to get my RN."

With less than a year left on her present contract with the IAS, now was the time to consider a career change, before signing another five year contract. A nursing degree would open new doors for her to work almost anywhere.

What would it mean for her and Mark if she lived in the U.S. rather than thousands of miles away?

IN HER APARTMENT, Alana leaned against the back of the sofa. Pulling her legs up, she dialed her mother's cell number.

"Hi, Lanie. Are you home?"

"Yes, I just got here. I ate at Ellie's." She stifled a yawn as she told Mama about the appointment. "Mama, may I come to see you this weekend?" She longed to see her parents and grandmother and was sure she could drive to Grammy's house in Kellersville by herself.

"We'd love to have you. Your grandmother will be so happy to see you."

If Grammy even recognized her. "How is she?"

"Well, she almost got away from me this morning. I forgot to lock the door, and she decided to go for a walk by herself. A neighbor spotted her and called me."

Poor Mama. She sounded tired. "It must be so hard for Daddy to see this happening to Grammy." It was time to step in and help them. "I plan to leave here tomorrow afternoon, and I'll stay with you until Tuesday morning. Will that work for you?" She could rest at Grammy's house if she needed to.

"Oh, yes. It will be good to have you with us for as long as you can stay. Your father and I have been wishing you'd come."

"Okay, Mama. See you soon. I love you."

A warm shower relaxed her. In her pajamas, she turned on a CD of classic hymns and sat on the sofa wrapped in a quilt to read her book. She finally gave up after reading one paragraph three times. Laying her book beside her, she tried to reconcile how she remembered her grandmother with how Ellie and Mama described her now and shook her head. From the reports given her, the bright and active individual she'd known as Grammy made only occasional appearances, and no one knew when that would be. Splinters of fear and sadness pierced her heart.

CHAPTER THIRTEEN

hen Alana walked through the door at Mill Valley Florist the next morning, her sister handed her a fussy baby. Kate, busy with a customer, nodded to Alana. In Ellie's office, away from the noise of a shop full of customers, Ian stopped crying, stared at her, and grinned.

"You little charmer. I'd take you home with me, but I'm going away." She hugged him. When she returned from Kellersville, she'd talk to Ellie about setting up a babysitting schedule. She'd waited until she was physically strong enough to care for him, and now was the time.

Ten minutes later, Ellie came in, inhaled deeply, and blew out her breath. "Thank you for rescuing me." She pushed hair back from her face. "You came at just the right time. A lot of people want flowers for their gardens, and Mother's Day is next week, one of our busiest times of the year. The crowd has thinned out for now."

"My pleasure." Alana kissed her nephew's cheek. "I came to tell you that I'm heading to Kellersville this afternoon. I'll probably return on Tuesday."

"I know you were waiting to get your strength back."

"I thought I might relieve Mama a bit. And I'd like to see Grammy again before she entirely forgets who I am." Alana's voice broke. Some of her happiest memories were of summers with Grammy.

Ellie nodded. "Probably wise. She seems to be losing her grasp on reality more and more." She shook her head. "It's sad, isn't it."

"Oh, Ellie. What if she's forgotten me already?" Tears filled Alana's eyes. "When I remember Grammy, I think of a funny, vibrant woman, who made life so special for us." She sniffled and wiped away tears with her fingertips. "She taught me how to play piano."

Ellie's arms came around her, and they wept together, Ian sandwiched between them.

"Will I have to say goodbye to her when I go back to work? I don't want to say goodbye."

"Me either." Ellie's voice shook. "I want Ian to know his great-grandmother and what a wonderful person she is."

Ian squirmed, and Ellie stepped away. "Sorry, sweetheart." Ian grinned at her. "I'm glad they agreed to come for dinner on Mother's Day." Ellie sniffled. "I can't get away from the shop until late on Saturday, so it would be hard for Ben and me to make it to Kellersville."

"You're a wonderful cook, but let me help you more with our dinner." This would be her first Mother's Day home since she started with the IAS four years ago. She wanted it to be special.

"Are you sure? I don't want you to overdo it." Ellie yawned.

"I can do it. I know my limits, and right now, you have more responsibilities than I do."

"All right. When you get back, we'll decide who will do what." She yawned again. "I appreciate your offer to do more. I'm feeling a little overwhelmed." Ellie reached for her son. "I think my employees can handle business for a while. You need to get ready for your trip. I'll nurse and change Ian, then I'll put him down for a nap."

Alana kissed Ian's cheek and handed him to his mother. He watched her over his mother's shoulder as Alana walked away, and she blew him a kiss.

Choosing six pink roses from Ellie's supply, she said to Kate, "Mama and Grammy will love these roses."

"Let me box them for you." Before Kate placed the roses in a box with tissue, she inserted each stem in a vial of water. "This will keep them fresh."

"Thank you." Saying goodbye to Kate, she drove home to pack for her trip, excited yet dreading what she'd find when she arrived at her destination.

～

"IS ALANA SICK TODAY?" Mark asked Kate on Sunday. They stood side-by-side at the church door, waiting for Jack to finish talking to Ben. "She wasn't sitting with the Jakobs."

He'd seen her in church last week, and a few times, he caught her looking at him. Her smile and wave made his heart skip a beat. He'd acknowledged her with a smile but made no move to meet up with her. Today, he wanted to see her, talk to her. He had a lot to tell her.

The corners of Kate's mouth twitched. "Alana? She went to Kellersville to visit her parents and grandmother."

"She's not sick. Good." What did Kate's little smile mean? "You went with her to her appointment with the tropical disease specialist, right?"

Kate nodded.

"Do you know what the doctor told her?"

"The doctor said she was doing well but needed to put on weight. He said she wasn't ready to go back yet."

"That's good. I mean, she shouldn't go back before she's

fully healed." Good that she was doing well and that she wouldn't be leaving right away.

Jack called Kate over to join him and Ben.

Alana had to go back to work, but Mark didn't want her to leave yet. He needed more time to sort out his feelings for her. She'd been a younger friend for many years, a kid, who'd suddenly appeared as a lovely adult woman at Jack and Kate's wedding. He might not be ready to be a couple, but how would he know if they could become more than friends if he avoided her?

ON MONDAY MORNING, Mark met Dennis Eastman for a nine o'clock interview at Eastman's Cabinetry.

Dennis's well-equipped shop, with top-quality tools and machines, and his gracious, business-savvy wife, Grace, impressed Mark. The kitchen cabinets on display indicated craftmanship, beautifully designed and finished. Grace showed him the photo album of cabinets they'd sold and installed in homes, which they kept in the showroom for prospective customers. The photos and shop samples convinced him that Dennis had a well-earned reputation.

"I've been hoping he'd hire someone to help him." Grace said. About Alana's height, she wore a yellow T-shirt tucked into jeans, her brown hair with streaks of gray pulled back in a ponytail. "He loves his work. We both do, but he's not getting younger. He's had good employees in the past, but the last person he hired didn't work out." Her eyes connected with her husband's. "I'd like to take a vacation, or even a day off, from time to time."

She smiled at Mark. "I'll leave you to your interview. "It looks like we have customers already," she said as a car pulled up outside. She greeted the couple who came in.

Mark followed Dennis into the office.

"Have a seat, Mark." Dennis indicated a chair in front of his desk. He sat and lifted his copy of Mark's résumé. "I've read this through and contacted your references. I have a few questions to ask you."

Mark responded to the cabinet-maker's inquiries about his carpentry experience and knowledge of terms and tools of the trade. He showed Dennis photos of his recently completed shelves in the Sunday school rooms at church and the studio he had built for Rachael and invited him to see them both in person.

Dennis leaned forward. "The job is yours, if you want it."

Caution followed Mark's rush of excitement. "I have one thing to tell you before I give you an answer."

Dennis nodded. "Go ahead."

"As a Christian, I'm actively involved in my church. Sundays are my day for worshipping God, and I'm committed to taking Sundays off from work." Would Dennis rescind his job offer?

Dennis folded his hands on his desk and looked down at them. "To be honest, we started out that way. Grace and I always attended church, and we took our kids. But as I got busier, I began to work on Sundays, and it became a habit."

Mark prayed as he waited for Dennis's response. *Please, Lord, I think I'd like learning cabinetry and working for Dennis, if it's Your will. And I can be a witness to him.*

"I appreciate your being up-front about this." Dennis looked up. "I like what I've learned about you, Mark, and I'm still offering you the job. With you assisting me, Sundays shouldn't be necessary. Maybe Grace and I will start attending church again."

He had the job. *Thanks, Lord.* "You're always welcome to come to my church, Valley Community in Millvale."

"Thank you. I'll keep that in mind." Dennis stood and held out his hand.

Mark got up from his chair and shook hands with his new employer. "Thank you. I'm looking forward to working with you."

"I'll be glad to have you helping me. I'm still installing cabinets in the new development. Will you meet me over there at eight o'clock tomorrow morning? I'll text you the address."

"I'll be there."

When the men stepped out of the office, raised voices drew Mark's attention to the opposite side of the showroom, where a young man in jeans and a T-shirt spoke with Grace. Her lips were set in a firm line as he waved his hands. Mark couldn't hear what he said.

Dennis tensed and gave them a grim glance, then walked outside with Mark. "My son, Carter. I'll introduce you another time."

Dennis's body language indicated something amiss between father and son. Carter appeared old enough to help his father in the business, but a son doesn't always want to follow the family's line of business. Or perhaps the trouble went deeper than that.

"I'll email you some forms you'll need to fill out and send back to me," Dennis said.

"I'll get them back to you ASAP."

Dennis reentered the Eastman's Cabinetry building, and Mark started his car and drove away. "Father God," he prayed, "it's obvious something's wrong between Dennis and his son. Please let them work things out and come to a peaceful resolution."

After parking his car at home, Mark walked into JC Computers to find Jack there alone. Good. He wanted to talk to his brother about his new line of work and his other potential career path.

Jack looked up from the front counter when Mark entered. "Hey Mark, what's up?"

"I came to let you know Dennis hired me, and I start work tomorrow morning."

"That's great!" He clapped Mark on his shoulder. "Want a cup of coffee? There's a fresh pot in my office."

"Sure, as long as it doesn't keep you from your work."

"Scooter's on break, and Misty had a doctor's appointment and will be in later. The morning has been slow."

Mark settled in Jack's office with Jack seated so he could watch the door for customers.

"I'm impressed with Dennis's shop and his products, and I met Grace. I think I'll enjoy working for them." Mark rested his right leg across his left knee.

"They're a nice couple, and people compliment his craftsmanship. It's a different line of work for you, but you look happy about it."

"I'm excited. It's not what I expected, but God often surprises us with His answers to our prayers." Taking a deep breath, he prepared to tell Jack about seminary. "But there's another change I might be making." Mark sipped his coffee.

"Another change?" Jack set down his mug.

"My work with Eastman's may be temporary." Mark leaned forward. "I'm considering studying for a seminary degree in pastoral studies."

Jack stared at him, and for a moment, he seemed speechless. Mark watched Jack's face, trying to read his brother's thoughts.

"You mean you want to be a pastor?" Jack tapped his desk.

"Maybe." Mark sat back, waiting for Jack to finish what he had to say. To hear his insights.

Jack twisted his mug. "Does Dennis know? Maybe he won't want to hire you."

"Not yet. I'll tell him when I'm sure. He needs someone now, and I need a job now." He could start saving up for school expenses.

"This thing about seminary is rather sudden, isn't it?" Jack frowned.

Was he opposed to the idea or just taking time to process the news?

"Perhaps." Mark gazed at his hands folded on the table. "When I was laid off, I thought God had deserted me, but that wasn't true. Although I don't understand why everything happened as it did, there's a verse in Romans where Paul reminds us that God uses everything in our lives for good if we're faithful to Him." His eyes returned to Jack's face. "You said God might want me in a different line of work. Then Pastor Clary told me I should consider going into ministry."

"Huh. That's interesting." Jack slumped back in his chair.

"I don't think our pastor would tell me that unless he prayed and is convinced it's the direction I should go." What else could he say that would assure Jack that it was all right for him to consider a profession that would change the course of his life?

"Which seminary will you attend?"

"The school Pastor Clary recommended to me yesterday is Summit Hills Seminary, about three hundred miles from here. I'll take my classes online and make a campus visit each semester. I can keep working for Dennis and do the courses in the evening and on weekends."

Jack rubbed the back of his neck. "You surprised me." He looked up with a smile. "I think it's great, Mark. If you know God wants you to do it, go for it. I'll be one hundred percent behind you, and I'm sure Kate will be too."

"Will you pray for me? I want to do the right thing."

"You know we will."

When Scooter and a couple of customers entered through the front door, Mark left by the back door and climbed the stairs to his apartment.

While sipping a glass of milk and munching a sandwich, Mark turned on his laptop. He reviewed the Summit Hills Seminary online catalog to learn the requirements for pastoral studies and then scanned through the application. He'd have courses on books of the Bible, Christian counseling, leading a church, and many others that interested and excited him. Could he do this? Should he do this?

A run usually helped clear his mind. Now it would give him time to think and pray and use the nervous energy that was building within him.

After changing his clothes and shoes, he set out on his usual running route past the cottage and the River Walk.

Lord, is this excitement about going into ministry from You? I've been considering it for only a couple of days, but more and more I want to be a pastor. I know it won't be easy forging a new path in life, but I want to honor and serve You.

He continued his run through the new development and past the older homes, slowing in front of the Somers's house. According to the drawn drapes on the picture window and closed windows she usually opened upstairs, Alana still hadn't returned.

She'd be glad to know he had a job, but he wondered what she would think of him preparing for vocational church ministry.

CHAPTER FOURTEEN

Grammy hummed as she stared out her living room window and rocked in her antique rocking chair, knees covered in Mama's crocheted blanket. Alana hardly recognized this woman as the vivacious person who'd played an important role in most of her life.

Daddy took Alana's suitcase out to her car while she said goodbye to Mama and Grammy. Her mother's hair had turned entirely gray, and there were dark half-moons under her eyes and lines around her mouth.

"I'm worried about you, Mama. You're tired. Daddy too." She sat beside her mother on the love seat and grasped her hand.

"It's hard work, Lanie, but it's a labor of love. We'll do this as long as we can. Your grandmother is comfortable in her own house. If she goes into a nursing home, she may become lonely and confused." Her voice held no resentment, and she gave Grammy a loving look.

Alana agreed Grammy was better off at home, but her grand-mother was already confused most of the time. She wandered around her house at night, and at times, she stared at them with empty eyes, not to mention how much weight she'd lost.

"Your aunt and uncle each come on a Saturday every month to give us a respite. One of your grandmother's friends from her church, a retired nurse, comes to stay with her if we have an appointment and must go out. Thankfully, she's not belligerent. She just has to be watched because she wants to cook by herself or go for a walk alone."

"I'm glad she still likes to take walks. The exercise is good for both of you." As far back as Alana remembered, Grammy took walks. When Alana walked with her, she'd share her love of nature and her love for God.

Mama nodded. "Her house is on a cul-de-sac, and traffic is light. The neighbors know her and watch out for her."

"I'm really surprised at how much weight she's lost." Alana fidgeted with the throw pillow.

"Yes, my biggest concern is her nutrition. She enjoys food, but she forgets to eat. Sometimes I can coax her, but other times she can't be convinced." Mama sighed.

"She's eaten well since I've been here." She ate smaller portions, but she finished everything put on her plate, and that comforted Alana. She'd witnessed the awful effects of starvation on the refugees.

"Your grandmother likes having you here." Mama squeezed her hand. "I haven't seen her smile this much since we took her to see Ellie's baby."

"Ian has that effect on people."

Hopefully, Alana's presence relieved some of her parents's concern for her health as well as giving Grammy joy. They'd baked cookies, taken walks, and looked at old photos together. Grammy laughed and talked about the photos. But much of her memory was missing, and there was little she remembered about today or yesterday.

"Do you think she knows who I am?" Alana swallowed past the lump in her throat.

Mama touched her cheek. "Sometimes she does."

"But does she know I'm her granddaughter?" Tears filled Alana's eyes. "I hate it when she says my name, then suddenly her eyes become blank."

"She's comfortable with you here. Last night, she sang her heart out when you played the hymns." Mama smiled.

"We used to sing and play together a lot. She made almost everything fun. Mama, I hate seeing her like this now." She laid her head on her mother's shoulder.

"I know." Mama hugged her. "It's very hard for all of us."

Daddy came in the back door. "Your suitcase is in the car." His gaze turned from them to the elderly woman in the rocking chair, and his expression showed he understood what was happening.

"Thanks, Daddy."

"Before you go, Lanie, will you play again for your grandmother? She hasn't sung like that for a long time."

"Of course."

As Alana opened the piano and sat on the bench, Grammy stopped rocking. By the time Alana played an introduction to "Jesus Loves Me," her grandmother stood beside the piano and sang her heart out in a crackly voice. Alana's vision blurred. Grammy always loved singing about her Jesus. Mama's voice shook, and Daddy struggled to get the words out. Alana played the last chord, and the song seemed to echo in the silence. Daddy squeezed her shoulder.

She closed the piano and stood facing her grandmother. The old woman cupped Alana's cheek in her soft, wrinkled palm. "Thank you, dear." Her hand dropped away, and she hobbled back to the rocking chair.

Tears filled Alana's eyes again. For a moment, it seemed Grammy remembered her.

Daddy wiped his reddened eyes with his knuckles and sniffled as he clung to Mama.

Alana leaned over and kissed her grandmother's forehead. "'Bye, Grammy. See you again soon. I love you."

Grammy rocked and stared out the window.

Daddy's arms felt as safe and secure as ever to Alana when he held her close.

"We're still planning to come to Millvale next Sunday so we can celebrate Mother's Day together. We probably won't make it for church, but we'll see you at Ellie's afterward."

"Your house is always ready if you decide to stay overnight—I've been airing it out occasionally so it doesn't get stuffy with you gone. And if Grammy's having a bad day next Sunday, maybe Ellie and I can come here for a quick visit." With church and dinner and Ian, Alana wasn't sure how that would work.

"I think we'll try to do it all in one day this time. Grammy can sleep in the car, and there's a little restaurant where we can stop if necessary for her to use the restroom or if she needs a break. We've been there so many times, the owners know us, and they love your grandmother."

"That's nice." Alana hugged her mother. "Perhaps Ellie and I will come with Ian to visit you during the summer."

"We'll look forward to it." Daddy opened the door and followed her out.

Mama watched them from the doorway. She blew Alana a kiss, and Alana blew one back, tempted to run back and give her another hug.

One more embrace from her father. "You're probably looking forward to getting back to work."

"Yes. I'll have a little over six months on my contract when I go back." She hadn't made her final decision, but more and more she favored not staying with the IAS. Even if her heart and Mark's didn't connect, her former desire to be a nurse drew her.

He kept his hand on her arm. "Then what?"

She faced her father. "Why do you ask?" Her father always read her well.

"Are you having second thoughts? You mentioned the time left on your contract. Are you going to sign another contract with them?" His gaze didn't waver.

"I don't know. My work is rewarding because sometimes I can make a difference in someone's life, but few of my team members have been with the IAS for over five years. It's hard to witness so much suffering day in and day out. Many leave to work in other fields, spend time with their families, or get married."

She waited for him to comment, but he didn't. He only nodded.

"I want to be able to tell the people I work with how to find hope in Jesus. Two other women and I are allowed to have a Bible story time for the children twice a week, if we have the time, and we hold a weekly church service with singing and Bible reading for those who want to attend. We have to be careful. If people of other faiths are offended, we could lose our jobs, or the IAS might be told to leave the country."

"I'm sure your attitude and example display your faith, but sometimes words are important, and it's hard not to speak out." He leaned against her car with arms and legs crossed.

"Yes." She took a deep breath. "I've been thinking about getting my degree in nursing. I like being independent, and I've enjoyed my travels and benefitted from my experiences, but the more I think about it, the more I'm convinced I might need some change."

"Nursing?" His forehead wrinkled as he raised his eyebrows.

"Before I joined the IAS, I thought about nursing. Remember? But then when the opportunity to work for the IAS fell into my lap, I grabbed at it instead."

"You wanted a challenge, and you wanted to help people, but you didn't want to get stuck in a small town like Millvale." He spoke without resentment. He'd never tried to change her mind.

"I did say that. I love Millvale, and I love you, but I wanted to see the world. When I contracted malaria, and I had to come home, I discovered it's not so bad. I don't want to stay in Millvale, but I ..."

"Go on."

She licked her lips. "Ellie has a husband, a baby, and a business. I want a home, a family of my own. My co-workers are like family, yet it's not the same as what Ellie has. I'm not jealous. She deserves what she has. I just want something different from what I have now."

"Have you prayed about this?" He had taught her the importance of prayer.

"Not until recently. I've had a lot of time to think in the past month." She'd had time to reconsider her life's priorities.

"A career in nursing would open new doors of opportunity for you." He stuck his hands in his pockets. "I can personally recommend the benefits of a home and family. Do you have a young man in mind?"

"Huh?" Her sister wouldn't have said anything to their parents about her lunch with Mark, especially since nothing else had happened.

Her father's brown eyes twinkled, and he grinned. He was teasing.

"Dad!"

He laughed. She loved his hearty laugh and joined in.

"You'd better get on your way." He pulled her into a side hug. "I'm glad you came and that you're healing. May I share with your mother what you've told me about nursing?"

"Of course, so long as you promise to pray. I'm not ready to decide yet. I have a few months before I go back."

"You know we will." He glanced at the house and shook his head. "Your grandmother was a real prayer warrior. I miss hearing her pray."

Her throat constricted. "I know, Daddy. I'm so sorry." She rubbed his back, wishing she could wipe away his pain. She hated seeing her grandmother zoned out from the world and the people she loved. She could only imagine how hard it was for her father to live with her every day. "You pray for me, and I'll pray for you. I'm glad I'll have time with Grammy while I'm home."

"Your mother and I are both glad you came, and I know your grandmother is too."

"Thank you."

The hardest thing about living overseas was being so far from her family. If one of her loved ones were ill or dying, could she get home in time to say goodbye?

"I'd better get going."

As she backed out of the driveway and drove away, her father watched her, his hands in his pockets. He'd always been a strong man, loving God, providing for his family. Her heart ached for his vulnerability as he witnessed his mother's decline.

Alana drove the 175 miles back to Millvale and arrived in time to make lunch. Then she checked the house.

She opened the drapes at the picture window to let in some light and a couple of windows to let in the fresh air. The beds were already made. Later, she'd dust and run the vacuum cleaner. In case Mama and Daddy decided to stay overnight, she'd make lasagna and store it in the freezer.

Some photo albums lay on a bookshelf. Making herself comfortable on the sofa, she paged through them. Lots of pictures of her grandparents. Grammy and Grampy laughing, Grammy diving into the swimming pool, Grampy taking Alana for a driving lesson. Thanksgiving, Christmas, family dinners, and Grammy's mouth-watering food. What a change to the frail woman she was now!

Yawning, Alana rested her head against a throw pillow and closed her eyes. She could almost smell Grammy's delicious pot roast dinner and hear family laughter around the table.

Thud! She jumped.

She'd dozed off and let the photo album drop to the floor. One day soon, she'd have the stamina to avoid a nap in the middle of the day.

After closing the windows and drapes, she returned downstairs to her apartment. With her house key and phone in her pocket, she headed for Mill Valley Florist.

Grammy might not be around another year, and she had some ideas she'd like to share with Ellie to make this Mother's Day extra-special.

CHAPTER FIFTEEN

The next evening, Alana turned the corner on Main Street, and a man's voice called out to her. She peered over her shoulder, and her stomach flip-flopped as she turned.

Mark waved as he jogged toward her. His shorts and t-shirt revealed fit muscles, and his wind-blown hair and good looks made her stomach spiral.

"Hi, Mark!" Her schoolgirl crush was growing into something stronger, and no matter what she said she'd do, she couldn't seem to stop it.

He paused a few paces away from her, breathing hard. "Are you out for a walk?"

His direct gaze sent a zing down to her toes. A wild desire to brush the lock of hair from his forehead washed through her, but she looked away and forced her hand to remain at her side.

"I'm on my way to get my Ian fix. I haven't seen him since Saturday."

He chuckled. "I think your nephew has you wrapped around his fingers."

"Ellie told me you can't spoil a baby with love."

"I agree." Something about him was different than the last

time they'd met—happier, more confident. His smile reached his eyes, and he didn't hurry away.

Remembering she had a destination, she turned and walked again, and he fell into step beside her. *Surprise!*

"I missed you in church Sunday. Kate said you went to see your parents and grandmother. How are they?"

Did he say he missed me? Oh, he asked me a question.

"Mama and Daddy are tired, but otherwise, they're all right. Grammy is … well … Grammy isn't herself. I had a good time with them, though."

"I'm glad you could go." Mark waved to a bicyclist riding along the street. His hand brushed her arm when he lowered it. "I always wished I had a grandmother like yours."

The spot he touched tingled. "I think she knew who I was, at least sometimes. She mostly sat in her rocking chair and looked out the window." Alana pushed back the sadness that threatened to take over and smiled instead. "They're coming here on Sunday."

"For Mother's Day?"

"Yes." She explained her family's plans.

"Jack and Kate are leaving Saturday afternoon to go to Mountain View to be with her parents. Kate's brother and his family will be there as well." He sounded downcast.

Mark shouldn't be alone on Mother's Day. Alana opened her mouth to ask him to join them for Sunday dinner, then closed it. She had to make sure it was all right with Ellie first.

"I have a new job." She heard his excitement.

"You do? I'm happy for you." Probably the reason for his more relaxed and cheerful attitude. "What is it?" Would he have to move away? No, he couldn't do that.

"I'm working for Dennis Eastman, a local cabinetmaker just beyond Break-a-Bean. Today was my first day installing kitchen cabinets in the new development by you."

"Good for you!" Eastman's Cabinetry. She knew the place,

and it wasn't far. She laid her hand on his forearm. Her heart flip-flopped at the contact with his skin, and she dropped her hand. "I think that's a good job for you. You did a great job on the Sunday school shelves. The teachers love them."

"Thank you. I enjoyed making them." His warm glance set her insides a-flutter. "I learned a lot from Dennis today, although I mostly watched, handed him tools, and helped him carry and place the cabinets."

She waited for him to ask about her doctor's appointment, disappointed he didn't. She said, "The doctor told me it would be a while before I can return to work for the IAS." Did he care?

He nodded. "Kate told me. Does that upset you?"

Oh, he already knew. "Not really. I mean, I like my work, but I'm enjoying time with my family. And I love springtime in Millvale." *And I want time for our friendship to grow and become so much more.*

She'd like to continue their talk, but they'd arrived in front of Mill Valley Florist.

Did he mean to walk this far with me?

Mark had initiated their meeting today, and he walked and talked with her all the way to Ellie's shop. Had she only imagined he'd avoided her before?

She greeted someone who came out carrying a flowering plant.

Mark glanced over his shoulder. "Oh, are we here already?"

"You can join me inside, if you'd like to." She knew he wouldn't, dressed in his running shorts and sweaty T-shirt, but she couldn't resist inviting him.

"Thank you, but I have to go home." He pulled at the bottom of his shirt and grinned. "And I'm not exactly dressed to be seen in public."

She chuckled. "I think you're right." He looked good to her, though. And he made her feel wanted—at least as a friend—by taking time for her.

"Please say hello to Ellie for me, will you?" He ran his fingers through his hair. "It was great seeing you." He glanced down, then lifted his eyes to her face. "I'm glad you're back and you'll be around for a while longer."

"Me too." Their gazes connected and held for an electric moment. Her heart raced.

Wow, that hadn't happened before, and the moment left her dazed.

He touched her hand. "You'd better get in there for your Ian fix before Ellie closes her store."

"You're right. But this has been nice. Thank you for taking time to walk with me and tell me about your job." They were back on track as friends, at least. Maybe more.

"I'll see you in church?"

"Of course." If she had her way, it would be sooner than that.

He turned and jogged back the way they came.

Alana watched him as she opened the door to Mill Valley Florist.

"Excuse me, please."

"Oh, I'm sorry, Marcy." Alana held the door, allowing Ellie's college student employee to exit. She stepped into the shop and let the door close behind her. Ellie came out of her office carrying a bank night deposit bag and a key.

"Hi, Lanie. I see you got home safely." She hid a yawn behind her hand.

"Yes, I did. Mama and Daddy send their love." She leaned her arms on the counter. "I'm glad I went. Grammy is so frail, and I'm not sure she knew me."

"It's sad, isn't it? My heart aches for her." She laid the bag on the counter. "I'm glad Mama and Daddy can care for her at her home."

"Mama calls it a labor of love. Grammy joined right in when I played the piano, and we all sang hymns and other songs. Her singing voice is still strong." Such a wonderful memory.

"I'm glad she met Ian before ..." Ellie shook her head. "He won't remember her, but I can take pictures, and it's so sweet to see them together."

"And she'll see him again when they come to Millvale on Sunday for dinner. And he'll give her joy like he does everyone else." She pushed away from the counter. "Can we go over our menu and make sure we have everything?"

"Sure. Do you want to eat with us tonight?" Ellie yawned again.

"Not tonight, but thank you. You need family time with Ben and Ian, and I can see you're tired." She didn't want to wear out her welcome at her sister's house. "I'll call you this evening, and we can talk about it. Or maybe you should call me when you have the time."

"If you don't hear from me by nine o'clock, you'll know I fell asleep. Ian doesn't wake up during the night as often as he did, and Ben helps me a lot, but I'm working full time now."

Alana gently grasped Ellie's arm. "Let me take care of Ian for at least part of each day you work. I want all the Ian time I can get in the next few months. We can work out a schedule."

"I'll pay you." Ellie played with the key in her hand.

"Let me do this for you, Ellie. I don't expect you to pay me. I know Mama would love to have grandma time with him, but she can't."

"All right, but I still intend to pay you." Ellie checked her phone. "It's time for me to close the shop. Ian's asleep."

"Need any help?"

"I'm good. I have to lock up and get the money ready for deposit."

"I'll go so you can do that. I love you." She embraced her sister and stepped back. "Is it all right if ... I mean, Kate and Jack are going to Mountain View, and Mark will be alone on Sunday. Should we invite him to dinner?"

Her sister stared at her for a moment. Alana's cheeks

warmed. Did her sister see Alana's request as more than a friendly gesture? How would she answer if asked?

"That's fine with me." Ellie smiled. "Mama and Daddy know him, and Grammy might remember him." She followed Alana to the door. "He shouldn't have to be alone."

"Thanks, I'll let him know." She started out the door, then turned back. "Oh, I forgot to ask you. Remember how we used to sing duets in church?"

"Uh-huh."

"Do you think we could sing on Sunday?"

Ellie's eyebrows rose. "Do we have time to practice?"

"Let's make time, okay? We can sing one of our old favorites. I've been playing Mama's piano nearly every day. I know it's late to be planning this, but I'll call Pastor Clary when I get home to see if there's a place for us in the service."

"All right. I'd love to sing together again. If Pastor Clary says yes, we'll make time to practice."

"Great. Talk to you later." Ellie closed the door, and the lock clicked.

Alana hurried home. Calling Pastor Clary was an easy task. Figuring out the right way to invite Mark for dinner on Sunday was something else entirely.

CHAPTER SIXTEEN

From his apartment's living room window, Mark watched Alana pass by on her way home and tried to think how he could step out and stop her without it being awkward.

He'd just finished his run when he saw her walking up the street this afternoon. Despite his sweaty jogging clothes, he ran to catch up so he could talk to her. Her smile welcomed him. They walked and talked together comfortably as friends. Relieved he hadn't spoiled their friendship by avoiding her, he came home with the distinct impression they were on their way to more than a friendship.

He'd ask her for a date, just a dinner out. But he remembered their lunch at the diner and didn't want a replay of that uncomfortable experience. He'd been in an emotional tailspin that left him empty. Then God renewed his hope and filled his future with exciting possibilities—a new occupation, a new calling, and maybe a new love?

He shook his head. He'd been out of the dating pool for a long time, and his first attempt to return had been rejected by

Damaris. Asking Alana to go on a date with him was no easier than asking Rachael that first time years ago.

Alana turned the corner and disappeared.

The oven timer dinged, and he returned to the kitchen to remove the pizza from the oven.

He'd call her tonight.

Laying his phone beside him on the table, he stared at it as he ate the tossed salad and pizza he didn't taste. He debated whether he should call, and practiced what he would say, changing his mind several times.

Hi, Alana. Will you go on a date with me?

Hello, Alana. This is Mark. I'd like to take you out to dinner. Will you go?

Hey, Alana. I had a good time with you this afternoon. Do you want to go out with me?

He'd have to come up with something better.

After washing the dishes, wiping down the table and counters, he headed for the living room to turn on his computer.

He halted. "You're procrastinating, Chambers."

Scrolling down to Alana's number on his phone, he hovered his thumb over the call button. He sat in his recliner, then stood and looked out the window. It shouldn't be this hard to call someone. Alana was a good friend and a former pen pal via email.

Finally, he pressed call, and his heart thudded against his ribs as he listened to her phone ring and waited for her to answer.

Was she ignoring his calls? It was ringing forever.

"Hello." She answered on the third ring.

"Hi, Alana, it's Mark."

"I was thinking about calling you."

"You were?" He liked the sound of that.

"Yes. Um … you said Kate and Jack are going to Mountain View this weekend to visit Kate's family."

"Yes, to celebrate Mother's Day with her family." And he'd be alone again.

"Would you like to join us for dinner on Sunday at Ellie's house?"

He longed to say yes. After losing his mother and then his wife, celebrating the holiday had been difficult for him. He attended church and said, "Happy Mother's Day" to the women, but was grateful when it was time to leave. Mother's Day was sad for Blythe, too, after her mother died. When Jack married Kate, and he learned they'd spend the day this year with Kate's family in Mountain View, he expected to be alone all afternoon.

Pleased with the invitation, he said, "I don't want to intrude on your family's Mother's Day celebration." Still, the thought of spending the afternoon with Alana and her family lifted his spirits.

"It won't be an intrusion. My parents know you, and Grammy might remember you. Of course, we don't know how Grammy will be on Sunday, so you have to be ready for anything. But I'd … we'd like for you to come."

Mark stilled, hardly breathing, and his mind whirled. Alana said *she'd* like him to come. She wanted him there. Maybe one day he wouldn't have to borrow a family for Mother's Day, but being included in the Somers family gathering this year appealed to him.

He took a deep breath. "Then I will gladly accept. What can I bring?"

"Ellie will call me later to talk about who will provide what. You know she loves to cook, but she's got a lot to do right now, so I told her I wanted to help more. I'll tell her you offered to provide something, but don't feel you have to. May I call you back when we've decided?"

Her melodious voice enlivened him. "I'd love that. Thanks for inviting me."

"You're welcome."

Was this invitation more than a friendly gesture? He hoped so. The conversation paused as he thought about what to say next.

"Mark?" Her voice was soft and tentative.

"Yes?" He leaned back in his recliner and pictured her soft, brown curls and expressive hazel eyes.

"Didn't you …? Oh, never mind."

What did she want to say? "Are you sure? Did you want to ask me something?" He let the footrest on his recliner down.

"No, it's okay."

"Well, all right, if you're sure. Don't forget to let me know what I can bring for Mother's Day."

"I won't forget. Goodnight, Mark."

"Goodnight, Alana."

He pressed *End* and leaned forward. He should get an appropriate hostess gift for Ellie. Flowers. Scratch that. Ellie had lots of flowers. He could buy flowers for Alana's mother and grandmother. Maybe.

Oh, no! He clapped his hand to his forehead. "I forgot to ask Alana on a date, but she ended up asking me for Sunday dinner." Did that count? Would she consider Sunday a date too? "I can't believe I forgot to ask her." Should he call her back? "I'll talk to her on Sunday."

Now he was talking to himself and procrastinating again.

ALANA HELD her phone and stared at it. Mark had called her! That made it easier for her to invite him for dinner on Sunday. But why did he call her? Reminding him may have been rude, but she should have done it anyway. Maybe he'd remember and call her back.

She laughed and hugged a throw pillow. By Sunday, her

secret would be out. Daddy would know the answer to his question, and she could see the twinkle in his eyes already.

Her mother might be shocked, but she and Daddy knew and liked Mark.

Heat rose into her face.

She shouldn't hope for more than friendship if she didn't intend to stay in Millvale. She still had to fulfill her responsibilities to the IAS for a few more months. His life had always been in Millvale. His wife and daughter were buried here. He'd never leave.

God, what should I do? Is it selfish to set aside work that helps desperate people because I want to get married and have a family? Do you want Mark and me together? I want to do the right thing.

ON THURSDAY MORNING, Mark took charge of the showroom when Dennis had a meeting with a potential client and Grace had a doctor's appointment. He answered a phone call and then greeted a couple who entered. They wore business attire, the man's hair short and the woman's pulled back into a bun. They appeared to be around his age.

"Hello, welcome to Eastman's Cabinetry. May I help you?"

"No, thank you. We'd just like to look around." The man rested his hand on the woman's waist.

"That's fine. Please let me know if you have questions."

They walked to a nearby set of cabinets and paused.

The door opened, and Mark turned.

Carter Eastman, Dennis's son.

The young man, probably around twenty-one, stood at the door for a moment and glanced around the showroom before letting it shut behind him. He stood with his hands on his hips as though waiting for someone to notice him, then glanced at the couple with a scornful expression. Because of what Mark witnessed on Monday, he prepared for a confrontation.

Standing near the office, next to a stand that held the shop's photo album and some business cards, he said, "May I help you with something?"

"No." Carter wandered around, running his hand over counter tops and opening and closing cupboard doors. "Just looking." He wore his hair short and brushed upward. His blue jeans, probably designer, fit snugly, and a short-sleeved plaid shirt revealed muscled arms, the arms of someone who lifted wood and used a hammer.

The couple walked toward the door. "Thank you." The man nodded to Mark.

"Thank you for coming in." Mark stepped up to them and glanced at Carter. He didn't want the potential customers to witness a scene if Carter caused trouble.

The woman paused and turned to Mark. "I love your cabinets. We're having our kitchen remodeled, and a friend told us about this place."

"I'm glad you stopped by. Is there something I can help you with today?" Mark had worked with potential customers at the BEC. These two were interested but not yet committed to purchasing Eastman's cabinets.

The man glanced at the woman. "Not right now, but we may be back." She smiled and nodded.

"In the meantime, if you have questions, here's our business card with our telephone number." Mark handed them a card, and they left.

When the door closed, Carter turned to Mark. His icy blue eyes looked Mark up and down. "Is Grace or Dennis here?"

"No." Although Mark knew him to be Dennis's son, Carter probably didn't know him. "I'm Mark Chambers. I just started working for your father." He held out his hand.

Carter shoved his hands in his pockets. *Wow.* He lacked his father's manners and congeniality.

Mark dropped his hand to his side. "Your parents aren't here. May I help you with something?" He tried to maintain a cool exterior despite Carter's irritating attitude.

Carter narrowed his eyes. "I know you. You're the computer guy."

Mark smiled. "No, I'm his brother."

"Didn't know he had a brother." He made his way around the showroom and came back to the office door. "When will they be back?"

Mark checked the time. "Within the next half hour."

Carter reached for the doorknob and jiggled it. "Have a key?"

Dennis had locked the door earlier, saying Mark would have no need to go into the office. He didn't know enough to conduct business yet. And perhaps his employer expected Carter to show up and cause trouble.

"I'm here in case customers come in." He didn't tell Carter that Dennis had left a set of keys with him. "Dennis wants the office locked while he and Grace are out. One of them will be back soon." The sooner the better.

Mark didn't offend easily, and he didn't pick fights, but Carter looked ready to start one. His last fight had been in elementary school when he'd stood up to the class bully. And he didn't want to revisit that event.

Carter pulled himself to his full height, about an inch shorter than Mark. His mouth cut a tight, straight line. "I work with my dad. You can let me in."

"I can't do that."

"Let me in, or I'll …"

"That's enough, Carter. You're to respect my employees." Carter spun around at his father's voice. Dennis stood just inside the door. "What are you doing here anyway? You're supposed to be job hunting."

Carter's face turned red. He glared at Mark and then back at his father. "I work for you."

Dennis shook his head. "Not anymore, remember? You're a good carpenter, but you're unreliable. I don't know when you'll show up for work, and you're careless about what you do. You need to work for someone else. I told you that last week."

"Mom will hear about this!" He stomped across the floor and slammed the door behind him.

Mark flinched, then sighed with relief.

"I'm sorry about that." Dennis ran his hand through his hair.

Mark nodded. He inhaled and blew out. "I'm glad you came in when you did."

Dennis unlocked the office door, and Mark followed him in.

"I saw and heard enough to know what happened. He's probably after money. He spends a lot. He doesn't want to work, and I'm afraid some of his friends are a bad influence. Carter is getting out of control."

Mark hadn't known or worked for Dennis long enough to establish a confidential relationship with him. But relating his experience with Jack might help. He prayed silently for the right words.

"I was eighteen and my brother, Jack, was thirteen when our parents died. It was incredibly hard because the state wouldn't let me have custody, so our great-uncle lived with us, which allowed us to stay together."

Taking a breath, he continued.

"Jack turned into a handful, angry and rebellious for a couple of years. We had always attended church, and our uncle made sure we continued. Probably the best thing he did for us—that and helping us stay together. I'm thankful that Jack and I have a great relationship now. Anyway, I believe the love of God and our church family was the exact thing that broke through to Jack when he was struggling most."

The older man sat on the corner of his desk. "You think going back to church will help Carter?"

"It might. I believe when a person recognizes his need for Jesus Christ and receives the gift of salvation through Jesus, it will make a big difference in his life. Church is one place we can learn how to be saved and how to live as a follower of Jesus."

"Sunday is Mother's Day." Dennis brushed his hand across the surface of his desk. "I wonder if Grace would like to go to church before we take her out for dinner. Maybe I can convince Carter and Nova, our daughter, to go with us because it's Mother's Day."

"You're welcome to join me at Valley Community Church in Millvale. I think you'll enjoy it." He looked forward to Sunday. He'd see Alana in church and spend the afternoon with her and her family.

"I'll talk to my wife and kids."

The door opened, and Grace walked in.

"Hello, Grace." Mark turned to Dennis. "I'll wait for you outside." His employer might want to talk to his wife now about her appointment or church on Sunday or their son, and they didn't need an audience.

He leaned against Dennis's truck that was backed up to the loading dock. He didn't know what he could do, but he wanted to reach out to the Eastman family. "God, help me be up to this task."

About five minutes later, the loading dock door rumbled open. "Okay, let's get these cabinets loaded into my truck." Dennis didn't look angry, but he didn't say much as they transferred the cabinets to the truck and fastened the gray canvas tarp over them. Mark followed in his car to their worksite.

If Carter only understood the importance of a father/son

connection and how much he'd benefit from a good relationship with Dennis, then he could use Carter's help with the business.

CHAPTER SEVENTEEN

*D*addy phoned. "This looks like a good day for your grandmother. We'll be leaving for Millvale in a few minutes."

And Mark was coming for dinner too.

Last evening, Alana had set Ellie's table with their mother's fine China and etched crystal glasses they used for special occasions, adding the freshly polished silverware and their grandmother's linen napkins folded into origami butterflies. She did what she could in the kitchen so Ellie would have less to do this morning. Before she left, she'd crossed everything off her list.

Alana's heart sang as she thought through her day, beginning with church and a duet with her sister, followed by dinner with her family and Mark. The sunshine outside matched her mood. She drove to church and parked in the already half-filled parking lot.

Mrs. Clary approached her as she walked down the church hallway to the adult Sunday school class. The pastor's wife wore a pastel pink, below-the-knee dress and a pink rose corsage.

"Good morning, Alana! You're just the person I must speak with." She didn't look or sound angry, but her business-like manner reminded Alana of a few times when Mrs. Clary had corrected her as a teen.

"Happy Mother's Day, Mrs. Clary. Is something wrong?" Already the thought of singing in front of the church congregation had her stomach quivering. And she wanted everything to be perfect for dinner.

"No, dear." The pastor's wife laughed and hugged Alana. "Laura Betts will be going away in two weeks. Are you willing to teach her middle grade girls's class that Sunday?"

"I'd be glad to." *Whew, what a relief!*

"Good. I'll let her know." Mrs. Clary scribbled a note in the notebook she carried with her Bible. "Laura will make sure you have what you'll need to teach. Maybe next Sunday you can sit in on her class and let the girls meet you."

Alana nodded. "That's a good idea. I'll plan on it." They walked together toward Alana's classroom. "Pink is your color, Mrs. Clary. And your corsage is beautiful."

Mrs. Clary bent her head and sniffed the roses. "Thank you. My husband ordered it from your sister's florist shop. She's such an artist with flowers."

"She sure is." Alana hugged her music book and Bible. "God has truly blessed her, both with a family and work she loves. I hope one day I can find the love and contentment she has." She bit her lip. She didn't want the pastor's wife to think she was jealous of her sister. But being a mother would be such a blessing.

Mrs. Clary patted Alana's arm. "God has a plan for you, dear. And whatever it is, you can trust that His plan is best."

Alana entered her classroom. *Proverbs three, verses five and six, says to trust in God with my whole heart and He'll direct my way.*

Alana greeted Nate Betts, Matt and Kelly Sampson, and a few others and chose a seat in the circle of chairs. She counted three visitors this morning, and her eyes returned to one she recognized, Burkley Maines.

She'd had a secret crush on Burkley during high school, but it passed quickly when he ignored her. He graduated the year before her, and she hadn't seen him since. Wasn't he married? He looked the same, blond hair, blue eyes, except he'd gained a few pounds, and he wore a navy-blue suit that fit him to perfection.

To her surprise, he aimed his smile at her. "Hello, Alana."

So, he knew her name. At one time, that would have been important to her.

"Hello, Burkley."

Burkley had moved away from Millvale when he went to college. His presence at Valley Community Church surprised her, awakening her curiosity.

Nate Betts called the class to order and asked for prayer requests. Alana asked for prayer for her family's safe travel today. *They should reach Millvale soon.*

Burkley raised his hand. "Will you pray for my mother? She's been ill recently, and she's waiting for the results of some medical tests."

Alana wrote down Mrs. Maines's name and other prayer requests so she'd remember to pray. During prayer and the teaching and discussion that followed, her mind kept reviewing the list of all she had to do this day, including singing with Ellie during the worship service. She knew the music and loved to sing and play, but performing in front of people made her fingers shake and her throat tighten.

Hurrying out of the room after class, clutching her Bible and song book, tension radiated through her. She peeked in the window on the door of the nursery as Ellie handed Ian to the nursery attendant and headed for the door. Alana stepped back and greeted her sister with a hug.

"I nursed Ian just now. I'm hoping he'll be satisfied until we get home. I don't want to be called out of the service in the middle of our song."

Alana fell into step with Ellie. "I'm nervous. Are you?"

"A little. We haven't done this for a long time, but Grammy always told us it was good to be nervous because it made us trust God more to help us through."

"I wish Grammy and Mama and Daddy could be here." Alana turned on her phone.

"I do too. At least we'll see them after church."

"Mama wrote a text. 'Trip going well. Be there soon.'" Alana changed her ringtone to vibrate and returned her phone to her purse. Vibrate would warn her in case of an emergency with her parents.

A familiar baritone voice spoke behind them. "You didn't tell me you girls were singing today."

Alana whirled around and nearly crashed into Mark. When he grasped her shoulders to steady her, a current of warmth threaded through her. He held an open church bulletin in one hand.

Ellie smirked as she looked from one to the other. "Good morning, Mark. I'm meeting Ben in the sanctuary. See you in a few minutes." With a knowing glance at Alana, she walked away.

Mark lowered his hands, and Alana stepped back. *He is so good looking.*

He wore a brown suit with a French blue shirt and a brown and blue tie. When his blue eyes focused on her face, she could hardly breathe. The fluttering in her stomach double-timed. Pressing her books against her abdomen, she tried to still the quivers.

"I wanted to do something to make Mother's Day special. I haven't celebrated with my mother for several years, and Ellie is a new mother."

"Ah, that makes sense. Lovely idea." He folded and unfolded the paper in his hand.

"I only wish my parents and Grammy could be in church to hear us. That would be so special."

"I'm sorry they can't be here to hear you." He held up his bulletin. "I am ushering today, so I'd better get in there, but I'm glad I bumped into you. I know you'll do well, and I'll be praying." He gave her a broad smile.

Alana's nerves settled. "Thank you. I'm headed your way."

Alana turned with Mark toward the sanctuary and fell into step beside him.

"I remember when you and Ellie used to sing." He glanced at her.

"You do?" Pleasure swept through her.

"I do, and I have something to confess."

They paused before entering the auditorium.

"What's that?" He'd awakened her curiosity.

"I've stopped outside your house a few times to listen to you play the piano and sing."

Her cheeks heated. "Really?" Mark had heard her? Embarrassing. How many of the neighbors had also heard? She hadn't had any complaints.

"You have a musical gift, Alana. Have you thought of using music as ministry?"

A ridiculous thought, except it came from Mark. "Oh, no. I don't play that well, and performing in front of an audience makes me nervous, well, it's okay in my home church, but not on a stage or in front of strangers."

"Weddings? Nursing homes? Maybe not fulltime but for special events?"

He really meant it. She shrugged. "Maybe."

He waited for her to precede him through the door into the half-filled auditorium.

She turned to him. "Since Jack and Kate are away, will you sit with us today?"

"I'd love to, but I have to keep my eye open for people coming in, especially visitors. I have a chair by the door."

Alana's heart sank.

As if sensing her disappointment, he said "I'm looking forward to dinner today, though."

"It will be a feast." She inched closer. "I have a question."

He tipped his head, and a smile played at the corners of his mouth.

She almost forgot her question. Teasingly, she asked, "Can you really make éclair cake?"

He chuckled. "My mother's recipe. Wait and see." He wiggled his eyebrows.

She laughed as a zing passed through her.

He headed for the back of the church auditorium as she took her place with Ellie and Ben.

The room filled quickly, the time for service drawing closer, and Alana's stomach quivered. Ellie talked quietly to Ben beside her. How could her sister be so calm? Maybe she made a mistake when she volunteered to sing today, but it was too late to back out now.

The Matthews family, children and grandchildren, filled an entire pew. The Clarys's son and daughter sat toward the front with their families. Burkley nodded to her from across the auditorium, but where was his wife?

When Mark escorted two middle-aged and two young adults to a seat in the center aisle, her eyes connected with his for a moment, and her lips curved into a smile she couldn't prevent. He smiled back.

The music began, and the congregation rose to sing, followed by a choir anthem and the welcome and prayer led by Pastor Clary. After the Scripture reading, Ellie touched her arm and nodded.

Alana's legs wobbled like jelly as she made her way to the grand piano and sat, with Ellie standing beside her. She took a deep breath, placed her fingers in position on the keys, breathed a quick prayer for God's help, and began to play. As their voices blended in notes and words of praise, joy filled Alana, and she forgot her fear.

"Be Thou my vision, O Lord of my heart …"

When the last notes faded away, reverent silence filled the auditorium. Alana gathered her music and stood. Ellie grasped her hand, and they started for their seat.

"My girls!"

Alana and Ellie both gasped when the crackly voice called out. Many of the congregation turned in their seats to see who had broken the silence.

"Grammy," Alana whispered. Their grandmother sat in the back pew with their parents. Mama patted Grammy's shoulder. Tears filled Alana's eyes. "Thank you, God."

Ben put his arm around Ellie when she sat. Alana fumbled in her purse for a tissue to wipe her tears and nose. Her arms and legs trembled, and she took deep breaths to steady herself.

Pastor Clary stood behind the pulpit and opened his Bible. "Thank you, Ellie and Alana, for singing for us today. What a special performance. And that, by the way, is the girls's grandmother who called out her approval from the back." Laughter met his words. "Welcome, Mr. and Mrs. Somers and Grandma Somers."

Daddy waved.

Alana opened her Bible to follow the Scripture for the pastor's Mother's Day sermon. Her body stopped trembling, and taking sermon notes kept her mind off her dinner to do list.

After the service, Ellie said, "Mama and Daddy texted they've already taken Grammy to our house. Ben and I will get Ian, and we'll go home. You come when you're ready."

"I won't be long. I'll wait for Mark." She spotted him talking to the family she'd seen him seat earlier.

"That was very nice singing, Alana."

Startled, she turned. Burkley stood beside her. "Thank you." *Why was he being so friendly today?*

"I thought you'd be overseas. Don't you work for the IAS?"

He probably read it in the newspaper, or he heard it via the small-town grapevine. "Yes. I'm home on medical leave for a few months."

Burkley didn't invade her personal space, and she couldn't read more than friendly interest in his eyes. But why all the questions?

Mark shook hands with the Clarys's son. Did he see her talking to Burkley? What would he think?

Burkley persisted. "Are you staying with your parents?"

Why did he want to know? "I'm at my parents's house."

Mark now spoke with the Matthews family. He probably wanted to wish Mrs. Matthews a happy Mother's Day. How sad he couldn't say it to his own mother.

"I was wondering if we could go out for coffee sometime, you know, for old time's sake."

What?

Stepping back, she crossed her arms in front of her with her Bible and songbook clasped against her. She raised her eyebrows. "I'm sorry your wife missed the church service today."

"My-my wife? Oh, she's with my mother and the baby." He had the grace to blush. "Mother planned to come with me, but she's not feeling up to it today. Elise decided to stay back with the baby. We have a girl, three months old."

"Congratulations."

"Thank you." He folded his church bulletin into quarters and stared at the floor. "When I asked you to go for coffee ..." He looked up. "I mean, I love my wife. It's just that, when I saw you in Sunday school class, I thought maybe you could answer some questions I have about God and life. I know you and your family are lifelong church goers."

Mark stood by the door as the church emptied, his gaze drifting to Alana as others from the congregation departed, saying an occasional goodbye.

"If you have questions, I know you could make an appointment with Pastor Clary or talk to someone like Mark Chambers. Pastor Clary has been a huge help to me when I've struggled." With her hand, she gestured toward the pastor then Mark.

He nodded once as his eyes met Mark's. He turned back to Alana. "I might do that." He shifted his feet. "I wondered if you'd do me a favor and visit my mother sometime. Her house is in the same neighborhood as yours."

Alana bit her lip. "I know where she lives, but why do you think she'd want me to visit?" The wealthy Maines family had their own exclusive set of friends that didn't include Alana's family—or Mark's either.

"Mother doesn't get out like she used to, and we don't get here to visit often enough. I know she'd appreciate company."

"Why me?" Mrs. Maines would probably shut the door in her face.

Mark walked between the pews, picking up discarded bulletins and straightening hymnbooks.

"You live close by." Burkley glanced at Mark. "Most of her friends have moved away or are too busy to take time for her now that she's ill."

Mark turned off the lights.

Alana didn't want to be rude. If it weren't Mother's Day and the time allowed, she might introduce Burkley to Mark so they could talk.

"I'm sorry your mother is unwell, and I'll pray for her. I'll try to visit her sometime, but I have to go now." She moved toward the door. "My family is waiting for me at my sister's."

"Thanks, Alana. I should get back too, before my sister and her family arrive." He stopped long enough to shake Mark's hand, and he went out the door.

"Isn't that Burkley Maines?" Mark slid her Bible and songbook from her hands and tucked them under his arm along with his Bible.

"Yes. I'm sorry you had to wait for me."

"I didn't mind. He was in school with you and Jack, wasn't he?"

"He graduated the year before us. I don't remember ever seeing him in church before today." She stepped through the doorway, giving Mark a brief rundown of Burkley's request.

Should she be flattered or worried that he sought her out? If he sincerely wanted to talk about faith, had she missed an opportunity to share hers?

"We'd better go. Grammy might get impatient if she has to wait too long before eating. And I'm supposed to be helping Ellie."

Mark locked and closed the church door behind them. "Would you like to ride with me? We can leave your car here and pick it up later, on the way back."

"That's a great idea. There'll be one less car to park at Ellie and Ben's." And she'd get more alone time with him on the ride to Ellie's and back to the church. Win-win.

"That's one good reason." The warmth in his eyes convinced her of a second reason: he liked being with her as much as she liked being with him.

CHAPTER EIGHTEEN

hy had Burkley talked to Alana? Alana's facial expressions and body language indicated her discomfort. A bit of protectiveness kicked in just before Burkley left.

Mark had little contact with the Maines family. Widowed Mrs. Maines, Burkley's mother, lived on a street not far from the Somers. To his knowledge, Alana and Burkley had never dated, and he believed Burkley had married.

"Is everything all right, Mark?" Alana's voice brought him out of his thoughts.

"What? Oh," he cleared his throat, "everything's fine." Now that she was here with him. "Thank you for inviting me to join your family today. It will be nice not to be alone."

He opened the car door for her.

"Is Mother's Day hard for you?" He read sympathy and understanding in her eyes, and when she laid a comforting hand on his arm, he covered it with his own.

"Always." He took a deep breath. "You don't know how tempting it is to stay home and sleep in instead of attending church where I see all the families with their mothers and wishing the mothers Happy Mother's Day." Until now, only Jack and Kate knew how much Mark dreaded Mother's Day, when loneliness weighed heavily on him.

Closing her door, he walked around the car and slid into the driver's seat.

He fastened his seatbelt. "Jack and Blythe and I used to take flowers to the cemetery. We tried to answer Blythe's questions, but it was hard talking about my mother and my wife. After Kate came, she encouraged us to talk about them more so we could heal from our losses. It's still hard."

His church family had stood with him through his times of sorrow, and Kate's family had embraced him at the time of Kate and Jack's wedding. But Alana's invitation to join her family for Mother's Day was like a salve over the wound that remained in his heart.

"I'm sorry. I remember your mother as a sweet, kind person. You probably have many wonderful memories." Her words gave comfort.

"Yes, many." One day, he'd tell her more about his mother. He started the car.

"You and Rachael were the perfect couple, and she loved being a mother."

She wanted to talk about his wife? Her smile encouraged him to respond.

"Yes, she did. She wanted more children, but her illness ..." He swallowed and squeezed the steering wheel. "We wanted a large family."

The touch of Alana's hand on his arm sent a spark to his midsection. Her gentle gaze offered comfort like a warm hug.

She folded her hands in her lap. "I'm glad you can join us for dinner."

"I'm looking forward to this afternoon with you and your family."

After parking along the street in front of the Jakobs's house, he said, "Wait." He got out and hurried around the car to open her door.

"Thank you, Mark."

He loved the way her smile lit up her eyes and created dimples in her cheeks. "My pleasure."

Mark removed his éclair cake from a cooler on his back seat, along with two boxes of chocolates wrapped in pretty paper, one for Alana's mother and grandmother, and the other for Ellie. He hoped Alana wouldn't mind he'd bought them only for the mothers and not for her.

As he approached the front door beside Alana, his stomach clenched. Should he be here today? What would her parents think when he entered with their daughter?

Alana, apparently unaware of his discomfort, opened the door and called out, "We're here!" She took the éclair cake from Mark. "I think you know everyone. I'll be back in a minute."

As she disappeared through the dining room into the kitchen, Mark turned to the people in the living room. Mr. Somers and Ben each sat in a recliner with Alana's mother and grandmother across from them on the sofa.

Yes, he knew these people, but the circumstances were different because he came as Alana's guest. Her sudden disappearance left him uncertain.

"Welcome, Mark." Ben stood and shook his hand. "You remember my in-laws, don't you?"

Relieved by Ben's welcome, he remembered the gifts in his hand. "Yes, of course. Hello, Mr. Somers. Mrs. Somers, this is for you and Grandma Somers." He handed Alana's mother a box of chocolates. "Happy Mother's Day."

"Thank you, Mark. This is kind of you." She turned to her mother-in-law. "Mark brought us a gift, Mother."

The elderly Mrs. Somers stared at Mark for a minute. A smile slowly lit her face. "Why, hello, Noah. I haven't seen you for a long time." She held out her hand. "Isn't Eden with you today?"

Mark gasped. She'd mistaken him for his father. He glanced at Alana's mother, then took the grandmother's thin, wrinkled hand gently in his. "Hello, Mrs. Somers. It's so nice to see you again. It has been a long time."

Alana's father stood. "It's good to see you, Mark. I'm glad you can join us today." He shook Mark's hand then turned to his mother. "Mama, this is Mark, Noah's son."

She blinked. "Noah's son." Her smile faded, and she began plucking at her pant leg.

"Please take the recliner, Mark." Mr. Somers indicated the chair where he'd been seated, then he settled beside his mother on the sofa and clasped her hand.

Mark sat and placed Ellie's gift on the end table beside the chair.

When Alana returned, tension drained from Mark's body. He soaked in the warmth radiating from her smile and her family.

"Hi, Mama. Happy Mother's Day. Hi, Daddy." She gave each of them a hug. "Hi, Grammy." She bent toward her grandmother.

At her voice, the old woman turned her head and blinked. "You are …" Her voice faded.

Did Mark feel worse for Alana or her grandmother?

"I'm Alana, your granddaughter."

"Alana." Life sparked in her eyes, and she smiled. "My granddaughter. You sang in church this morning." She held her hand against Alana's cheek. Alana covered her grandmother's hand with her own, a tender gesture that touched Mark's heart.

"Yes, Grammy. You were there."

"Yes, you played the piano, and you and Ellie sang beautifully. I'm so proud of you. And Ellie has a beautiful baby."

"That's right, Grammy. I'm so glad you came today. Happy Mother's Day!"

Her grandmother pulled her hand away and began to pluck at her pant leg again.

Alana stepped back. Her troubled gaze briefly rested on Mark. He gave her what he hoped was an encouraging smile. Her heart and that of her family must break each time her grandmother retreated into her own world.

"I have to help Ellie." Her smile returned. "I hope all of you are very hungry. We've prepared a feast." Her eyes rested on him for a moment, sending sparks through him.

"Do you need some help?" Mrs. Somers started to get up.

"No, Mama. This is your special day. Yours and Grammy's. You have enough to do."

She disappeared into the kitchen. Mark prepared to volunteer for kitchen duty, but Ben stopped him with a question.

"How do you like working for Dennis Eastman?"

"I like it so far. He's a good carpenter and a patient teacher. I've learned a lot from him in just a week." He'd like to be with Alana, but Ben's interest in his work made him feel included in the men's circle.

Mr. Somers leaned forward. "I was sorry to hear that Building and Engineering Concepts let you go. You were with them for quite a while."

"Yes, eight years. It was a shock at first." God had a different plan.

"Sometimes we don't understand the road God leads us along." Mr. Somers held his mother's hand between both his hands. "You've had many hairpin turns in your road."

Mark nodded. "I confess I've often asked God why. It's like receiving confusing GPS signals. I'm not sure which turn I'm to take."

The Somers family would probably be happy for him if he told them about his call to ministry. But he hadn't told Alana yet and wanted her to know first.

Ian fussed, and Ben left the room to check on him. At the

baby's cry, Alana's grandmother began to whimper, and Mr. and Mrs. Somers turned their attention to her.

The aroma of food wafted into the living room, and Mark's mouth watered. He'd be more useful now if he joined Alana and Ellie in the kitchen.

Walking through the dining room, he stopped to admire the festive and inviting table.

When he entered the kitchen, the scent of turkey teased his sense of smell. He could already taste the delicious food.

Alana glanced over her shoulder as she whipped potatoes with an electric mixer on the counter beside the stove, where two pots he assumed contained vegetables steamed. Her sweet smile sent a current to his toes.

"It smells wonderful in here. How may I help?"

Ellie finished scooping stuffing from the hot, golden turkey on a cutting board and looked up at him.

Without pausing, she said, "First, you may take the gelatin salad out of the refrigerator and put it on the dining room table. The serving spoon is already out there. Then you may come back in here to carve the turkey. I planned to call Ben, but since you're here—."

"Ben is caring for Ian. I'll be glad to take his place." He placed the pretty molded salad made with lemon gelatin, grated carrots, and crushed pineapple in the dining room and returned to the kitchen.

Picking up the carving knife and fork lying beside the turkey, he cut the meat, slightly distracted by Alana's every move as she filled serving dishes with vegetables and covered them and the stuffing with foil.

Working as a team, the three of them soon had everything ready. Mark helped Alana carry dishes to the table as Ellie invited her guests to be seated. Ian cooed from his baby swing. The seating arrangement had been carefully planned to accommodate the needs of Alana's grandmother, with the elderly woman between her son and daughter-in-law. Alana sat beside Mark, with Ellie on her other side.

This was so much better than spending the day alone. He said his own silent prayer of thanksgiving as Ben prayed over the meal from the head of the table.

"You surprised us by being in church today, Daddy." Ellie served herself, then passed the bowl of whipped potatoes to Alana.

Mr. Somers placed a spoonful of peas on his mother's plate before passing the dish to his wife. "We thought Mama might enjoy hearing you girls sing, and we wanted to hear you as well. The service had already begun when we came in."

"Being together today, hearing you girls sing, and enjoying this lovely dinner you've prepared … my heart is full." Mrs. Somers smiled across the table at her daughters. "Thank you."

"We wanted this day to be special for all of us." Alana scanned her family seated at the table. "I haven't celebrated Mother's Day with you since college, and I wanted to include Grammy because …" Her voice broke, and she bit her lip. No one spoke, but they all nodded in understanding—except the elderly woman intent on her food.

When Alana's moist eyes settled on Mark, his heart clenched, and he wanted to reach over and wipe the tears away. Time on earth was running out for Alana's grandmother.

"Mark helped us get everything ready. And he made dessert." The pride in Alana's voice warmed him.

Mark rested his fork against his plate. He didn't want to drop food on himself with the whole family watching him. "My mother believed all men should know how to cook, and she taught me. I wanted to do my share to honor the mothers here."

"Thank you, Mark." Mrs. Somers beamed at him.

Ellie touched her sister's arm. "I couldn't have prepared this meal by myself this year. Alana and I worked out the menu together. We know how much Grammy loves turkey dinners. We wanted to celebrate the love of our family and show how much we appreciate you, Mama and Grammy."

"The food is delicious, and your grandmother is eating well." Mrs. Somers wiped her mother-in-law's chin with a napkin. The elderly woman rocked and hummed tunelessly as she chewed her food.

Being with Alana's warm and welcoming family filled his heart with joy and gratitude.

Ian, who'd fallen asleep in his swing, let out a wail that startled Mark from his thoughts. Alana's grandmother whimpered.

Alana whispered in his ear. "While the others are busy with Ian and Grammy, will you help me clear the table? Then we can serve your dessert."

Her breath against his ear sent tingles through his body, and he liked the sound of *we*. When he turned his head, her face was only inches from his. He gazed into her hazel eyes with their dark lashes. If he leaned forward just a bit, her lips were close enough to kiss. Mark's breath caught as temptation assaulted him. She didn't pull away. Another wail from Ian reminded him they weren't alone.

"Be glad to." Yield not to temptation.

Alana's cheeks glowed pink, and his ears felt hot. Everyone else appeared occupied with other things. He stood and pulled Alana's chair out for her to stand.

Mark cleared the serving dishes, mostly empty, as Alana collected the plates, and they carried them into the kitchen. He loaded the dishwasher as she placed the few leftovers in containers and left them on the kitchen table to cool. How easy it would be to step over and plant a kiss on her lips. But he didn't want witnesses to their first kiss, should someone enter the kitchen unexpectedly.

Alana removed the dessert from the refrigerator and placed it on the counter with dessert forks and small China plates, then lifted the coffee carafe.

"Why don't you cut the éclair cake while I see if anyone wants coffee? I'll help you serve it when I get back." Dark half-moons curved beneath her eyes, but she smiled, again tempting him to kiss her.

"I can do that." He couldn't resist brushing back a stray curl from her forehead. "Are you all right?"

She sighed. "Just a little tired."

He touched her cheek. "You've worked hard today." He picked up the knife lying beside the dessert.

"Yes, but it's been worth it. I'm not sorry."

He wanted to remove the carafe from her hand and hold her in his arms. "Okay, you go serve the coffee. I'll take care of dessert. We make a good team, don't we?"

"We do." She turned and left the kitchen.

His eyes followed her retreating figure. Did she ever wish for a home and family? *She's the one, isn't she, Lord?*

He cut the cake and discovered a cake server hanging on the wall with other utensils. After placing pieces of dessert on plates, he found a can of whipped cream in the refrigerator and shook it. He turned when Alana came through the doorway.

"Mark, if you want extra whipped cream for the dessert, it's in the ..." She set down the nearly empty carafe. "I see you found it."

"I guess we think alike. I hope Ellie won't mind I helped myself. I forgot to bring a can with me." He squirted a small dollop of whipped cream on each piece.

She shook her head. "Ellie won't mind at all." She pulled a large tray from the back of the counter. "I think this will hold all the dessert plates, and it will be easier than carrying them in our hands."

She held the tray while he set the seven plates on it, then gently removed the tray from her hands. "Let me carry this." Following her into the dining room, he held the tray as she gave each person their dessert.

Mr. Somers's eyes widened. "Éclair cake. One of my favorites. Did you make this, Lanie?"

"No, Daddy. Mark did." Of course, Daddy had a lot of favorites.

Self-conscious as all eyes turned to him, Mark said, "My mother's recipe."

"I asked him if he could really make éclair cake. Now we'll find out for sure." She threw him a glance.

"I assure you, you won't be disappointed. My mother's recipe is fail proof." This was one of his favorite desserts and easy to make.

"With extra whipped cream." Ben placed a forkful in his mouth and closed his eyes. "Mm! Ellie, we'll have to have Mark over again so we can have another éclair cake."

"I'm sure that can be arranged." Ellie glanced at her sister. Mark couldn't see Alana's face. Ellie winked at him. "Mark is really handy in the kitchen. He'll be quite a catch for any woman."

Mark nearly spit out the cake in his mouth. Heat climbed his neck into his face. A few snickers passed around the table. He swallowed his mouthful of cake and took a drink of water.

Mr. Somers's eyes twinkled, and the corners of his mouth twitched as he lifted his fork to his mouth. Mark had been accepted by the family as Alana's beau.

"This is very good. Is there any more whipped cream?" Everyone stared at the elderly woman, then chuckled at her unexpected question.

"I'll get it." When Mark started to get up, Alana pressed his arm.

"I'll do it." She avoided his eyes and quickly left the table.

She returned with a serene face and squirted more whipped cream on her grandmother's dessert. "Anyone else?"

She handed the can to her father and returned to her place at the table without looking Mark's way. If she did, Mark would certainly burst out laughing.

CHAPTER NINETEEN

Grammy's sudden request for whipped cream gave Alana an excuse to escape to the kitchen to compose herself. The air from the refrigerator cooled her face.

Should Alana be amused or upset by her sister's words? Ellie couldn't have chosen a worse time to hint about her relationship with Mark. The snickers from her family indicated they knew exactly what Ellie implied, and the twinkle in Daddy's eyes convinced her he remembered their conversation last week. She didn't dare look at Mark to see his reaction, although he'd emitted a strangled cough.

When she returned to her chair, Ellie nudged her arm.

"Sorry," she whispered.

Alana shrugged. "Apology accepted." She gave her sister a quick smile and picked up her dessert fork. Ellie hadn't spoken directly about her and Mark, and everyone there already figured Mark was special to her.

Time to test Mark's dessert. She placed a forkful in her mouth and forgot her embarrassment. "This is delicious, Mark. You *can* make éclair cake."

"You doubted me?" He raised his eyebrows, his lips twitching.

"Well, I was mildly curious." She rolled her lips between her teeth to keep from laughing.

He chuckled. "I've never heard doubt described that way before."

She licked the last little bit off the fork. "Yum."

"Told you." He tipped his head and grinned. A powerful arc sizzled between them as he held her gaze.

"Okay, everyone. It's time for family pictures." Ellie stood. "Let's get them done before Grammy gets tired or Ian gets crabby. Alana and I will clean up later."

Her stomach fluttering and her heart beating double time, she broke her gaze. Mark appeared as shocked as her when she left him at the table to join her family.

Settling Grammy on the sofa, Ellie placed Ian in her arms. Grammy spoke to the baby, held his tiny fingers to her lips, and smiled. How precious. Ian studied his great-grandmother. Several cell phones flashed. Daddy and Ellie joined them on the sofa for a four-generation photo. Photos of Ellie and Alana with their parents and grandmother came next, then one of the Jakobs family.

All Alana's efforts to make this day special, all the fatigue now creeping up on her, was worth it to have this time with her family.

When they wanted a group photo of the entire Somers family, Ben suggested Mark be the photographer.

Alana looked for him and frowned. *Where did he go?* "Maybe he's in the kitchen. I'll get him." They'd been celebrating family and left him out. She had to apologize.

The dining room table had been cleared, and she heard the refrigerator door close.

When she entered the kitchen, Mark looked up from wiping

down the table. The dishwasher hummed, hand-washed dishes and pans filled the drainer, and the counters had been cleaned.

"Mark, you didn't have to do all this." What a wonderful man.

"I wanted to. You were needed for photos."

"I'm sorry. I didn't think—"

He stepped up to her and took her hand, sparking a wave of electricity through her.

"It's all right, Lanie." She smiled at his first use of her nickname. "You invited me here, and your family allowed me to be part of their celebration, so I didn't have to spend the day alone. I had a delicious, home-cooked meal prepared by someone other than me." He kissed her hand. Her knees almost gave way. "You have nothing to apologize for."

A burst of laughter from the living room reminded her of her mission. "Will you come take a photo of my whole family? Actually, you'll probably have to take a half dozen with different cell phones."

"I'd be glad to." He didn't let go of her hand until just before they entered the living room, where she handed him her cell phone.

Four other cell phones lay on the coffee table. He used each one, and the family broke formation. Alana paused and smiled while Mark took her picture with his phone.

"Mark," Ellie said. "Stand beside Alana so we can get your picture too."

Alana's heart galloped when he stepped to her side and winked at her. Between them, Mark's hand folded over hers. Did anyone else notice? Her feelings for this man raced past the friendship mark.

Five flashes went off. "All set. Thank you." Ellie lowered her phone, and the group spread out.

Overcome by a floating sensation, Alana checked to be sure her feet still touched the ground.

Mark squeezed her hand, winked at her, and joined the men when they called him over to join their chat.

Ellie nudged her, distracting her from Mark. Mama sat on the sofa holding Ian with Grammy beside her, a sweet, heart-squeezing scene. Ian's little fingers were wrapped around Grammy's index finger, and she cooed at him. They both took pictures.

Tears filled Mama's eyes. "Ellie and Alana, thank you for making this day special for all of us. Before we go, let me help you with clean-up."

Alana shook her head. "No, Mama. Mark already finished it."

"What?" Mama's and Ellie's eyes widened.

Alana knelt on the floor by her mother, relieved to get off her feet. "Yes, while we were taking family pictures, he cleared the table and cleaned up the kitchen. There's not a thing left for us to do except put dishes away." She hoped Mama wouldn't notice her weariness.

Mama shook her head. "Mark's like his father in more ways than one. Noah was a man with a servant's heart." Yes, Mark had a big heart.

"Mother's Day is lonely for him since Rachael died. He appreciates being asked to spend the day with us, so he didn't have to be alone."

"And it gave you an excuse to invite him for dinner." Ellie smirked.

"Yes." *So what if Ellie knew the truth and wanted to tease.*

Mama grasped Alana's hand and squeezed. "He's a fine young man who has traveled a difficult road. You can invite him to our family gatherings any time you wish."

"Thank you, Mama." Her mother's words confirmed Mama's approval, making her glad.

"We need to head home." Mama stood and handed Ian to

Ellie. "Your grandmother has been doing well today, and we don't want to push her too hard."

The day had been long and busy and worth every minute of toil. Alana's energy level demanded recharging, but she hated to see them go.

"I hope you will join us again, Mark." Daddy shook hands with Mark and laid a hand on his shoulder. "Perhaps you can come with Alana to visit us."

"Thank you, Mr. Somers. I'd like that."

Daddy approved. Alana stepped forward and gave her father a hug.

He whispered in her ear. "So, this is the young man you referred to."

"I didn't refer to, Daddy, you did."

He chuckled. "Just want you to know he has my approval."

"I know. Thank you." She gave him an extra big hug.

Out loud, he said, "We'd like to stop at the house before leaving Millvale, just to check on things. Is that all right with you, Lanie?"

"Of course. It's your house. I think I'll go home as well." She felt as limp as a cooked noodle. She bent to hug her grandmother. "I'll see you soon, Grammy, okay? I love you." Grammy responded only with a smile. "Will you take me to get my car, Mark?"

"Of course. Thank you, Ellie and Ben, for letting me join you. And, Ellie, this is for you." He picked up her gift from the end table. "Happy Mother's Day."

Ellie kissed his cheek. "Thank you, Mark."

"You're welcome here any time." Ben shook his hand. "Especially if you bring more of that éclair cake." Everyone laughed.

Mark followed Alana out the door.

As Mark drove her to her car, she leaned her head against the seat, her eyes closed, fighting the now familiar nausea. A warm hand covered hers. She opened her eyes.

"Are you all right?"

"I'm tired, that's all." It couldn't be malaria again.

"Do you want me to drive you home? You can pick up your car another time, or I can drive it to your house later."

She sat up. "No, thank you. I'll be all right. It's not far, and Mama and Daddy will be there. I'll be fine." Mark's gaze mirrored his doubts, but she didn't want him to worry.

He pulled into the church parking lot next to her car. Releasing his seat belt, he turned toward her. "I had a wonderful time today with your family. Thank you for inviting me."

"Thank you for accepting my invitation." She still floated a bit.

He lifted her hand and intertwined their fingers, his touch leaving her breathless. Ensnared in the blue depths of his eyes, she closed her eyes as he leaned toward her and touched his lips to hers, and she stopped breathing. She'd been waiting for him to kiss her all afternoon.

He pulled back quickly. Why? Didn't he like kissing her? When she opened her eyes, his tender gaze made her heart puddle. He kissed the back of her hand, but he offered no explanation for his previous action. Maybe he thought it was too soon to kiss her.

There'd be other days, maybe even a lifetime. A girl could dream, right?

"I have to go, Mark," she whispered, wishing she didn't have to.

He released her hand. "I know." He cupped her cheek with his hand before he opened his door and got out.

Alana remained silent as he walked her to her car.

He leaned into her car as she inserted her key into the ignition. "Will you go out with me, Lanie, on a date?"

His eyes pleaded for her to say yes.

"I'd like that." Were they officially a couple now?

"I'll call you tomorrow, after you've had time to rest." She nodded, and he closed her door.

Kiss or no kiss, her heart belonged to Mark Chambers.

~

MARK HUMMED as he walked up the stairs to his apartment and unlocked the door. His fingers still tingled from the softness of her hand and the memory of her sweet scent when he kissed her. If she hadn't been so pale and tired, he would have deepened his kiss. The next one would be memorable. After all that happened today, he was sure there'd be a next one.

He chuckled. If Blythe were alive, would she give him permission to marry Alana Somers like she had for Jack to marry Kate? He hoped so. He wanted to marry again, and he wanted to marry Alana. And if he read her reactions correctly, she had similar thoughts.

Changing into running shorts and a T-shirt, he headed out for a run on the River Walk. Although he'd love to be with Alana, she needed rest. He'd be on his own for the rest of the day, with memories to keep him company.

Alana played a large part in making the day special. She'd worked hard with her sister, to the point of exhaustion, to give her mother and grandmother and the rest of the family a memorable Mother's Day. And she'd invited him to be a part of it all.

He pictured her as his wife, raising a family with him and facing the challenges of ministry with him when he became a pastor. But could he ask her to give up the work she loved helping refugees who needed her to join him? And did she even want a family of her own?

~

When Alana arrived home, Grammy had already fallen asleep in her parents's car. At their request, she slid into the back seat, leaving the door open to wait with Grammy.

Her grandmother leaned peacefully on a pillow propped against the opposite door, snoring lightly through an open mouth. Her bones protruded from her arms and hands, and blue veins appeared through transparent skin. Grammy had become feeble since Ellie's wedding nearly three years ago, and Alana's heart clutched.

Grammy probably wouldn't be with them many months longer. Once she returned to her work with the IAS, she might not make it home again to say goodbye. Grammy would join loved ones in heaven, which comforted Alana, but she'd still miss her.

"Thank you, Lanie." Her mother's voice startled her from her thoughts. Mama leaned down and peered into the car. "Is everything all right?"

Alana nodded and yawned. She slid out of the seat and stood, her hand resting on the car for support. "All is quiet. Grammy's still sleeping."

"I think you need a nap as well." Mama's hand cupped her cheek. "You worked hard today, and I appreciate all you and Ellie did. And Mark too."

Daddy put his arm around her. "You girls did a fine job today, and you've taken good care of the house, Lanie. Is your apartment comfortable for you?"

"I like my apartment. It's just the right size for me. And I'm glad I can look after your house while you're away. It's the least I can do." She could never repay her parents for all they did for her.

"Well, I guess we'd better go." Mama hugged her then examined her face. "You make sure you get some rest now." She kissed her cheek and slipped into the seat Alana vacated.

"I will. Have a safe trip, and thank you for coming." Her

nausea and weariness reminded her of the effects of malaria. She didn't want to be alone and almost asked her parents to stay, but Grammy needed them more. And she wasn't alone—God was with her.

Daddy grasped her shoulders. "We approve of Mark as your beau. He's a man of faith and integrity. It's obvious you care for each other."

Mama leaned toward her. "Remember, I'm always available to talk. Come and see us sometime and bring Mark. He's already like family."

"'Bye, honey." Her father kissed her and got in the driver's seat. She waved as they drove away.

"'Bye." Their approval gave her joy.

As she turned to go in, she swayed with dizziness and paused to restore her balance. Her efforts to make the day special had been rewarded, but now she had to pay. She had to rest.

Indoors, removing her sandals and dropping them on the closet floor, she replaced her red dress with a blue knit lounge dress for greater comfort as she napped.

She lay on her bed under a light blanket, the impression of Mark's kisses lingering on her lips and hand. With a smile, she closed her eyes and slept.

The message tone on her phone sounded, and her eyes popped open. *Mark?* She grabbed her phone from the bedside stand. No, a text from Mama.

> We're home. Grammy didn't wake up, so we drove through. Thanks for the wonderful time!

> Love u.

The shadows outside her window indicated that the sun hung low on the horizon. The fuzziness in her brain tempted her to lie back down. Hopefully, this weakness would be gone by tomorrow.

She stumbled toward the kitchen, holding on to the furniture and walls to maintain her balance. She made a cup of green tea with honey first. Soup, a slice of wheat toast, and applesauce settled easily in her stomach along with her supplements.

What a wonderful day with her family. *Thank You, God.*

When she invited Mark, she didn't know how well he'd fit with her family. How well he'd fit with her. The day soothed those worries.

However, she still had a commitment to fulfill with the IAS. And if the doctors determined she couldn't return because of her health, Mark shouldn't have to be responsible for her. He'd already suffered enough.

God, I think I love Mark. If You want us together, please show me.

CHAPTER TWENTY

Mark whistled as he prepared for work early the next morning, his life filled with new purpose and passion. He had a job he liked, God's calling to vocational ministry, and Alana.

Alana. Her hair felt like silk to his fingers, her skin so soft. Her eyes with their dark lashes filled with life and laughter. He chuckled over her reaction to his éclair cake, and his breath caught as the memory of her gaze filled him with sparks once again. Her beauty went deeper than the physical. He admired her faith, her heart for people, her musical gift, her willingness to work hard, and how much she valued her family.

Longing to hear her voice, he picked up his phone and scrolled to her number. No, she might not be awake yet. He'd text.

> I had a great time with you and your family yesterday. I'll call you after work.

She'd agreed to go on a date with him. It had to be something special. Since Blythe's death, he'd become mostly a home body.

His time at the beach had been his only excursion except for his travel for work. What did Alana like to do?

As he ate breakfast, he checked out restaurants and events on the Internet.

A balloon festival advertisement caught his eye. He'd taken Rachael to the festival once, but her fear of heights prevented them from going up in a balloon. It was still on his bucket list. He'd invite Alana to go with him, an adventure for them both.

One balloon adventure didn't mean a lifetime together. *What if* Alana didn't want to give up her work with the IAS? *What if* she didn't want to marry him and preferred to remain single? *What if* she refused to be part of his call to ministry?

He had to talk to her soon.

ALANA AWOKE IN THE MORNING, aching all over, shivering and feverish.

After seeing the Somers family doctor and stopping at the pharmacy for a prescription, Alana plopped on the sofa in her apartment, her energy spent. She arranged a throw pillow under her head. "Thanks for taking me," she said to Kate, whom she had called to drive her because she was too weak.

"You know you can call on me anytime." Kate handed her a glass of water to take with her pills. "What a relief it's not a recurrence of malaria or a virus you can give to others."

"I'm under quarantine." Alana moaned. "Two days of rest and minimum outside contact."

Kate sat on the arm of the sofa. "I hope you had a good time with your family yesterday since you managed to wear yourself out."

Alana pushed herself up. "A perfect day!" She told Kate all about it. "And everyone raved about Mark's éclair cake."

"Mark made éclair cake?' Kate's eyes widened.

"Yes, his mother's recipe." She licked her lips. "And it was delectable."

"Hmm. I'll have to ask Jack about his mother's recipe."

"You should have seen him, Kate. He pitched right in and helped Ellie and me serve the food, then he cleaned up while we were taking family pictures." She was so proud of him.

"Wow."

"There's not much about him not to admire." Alana pulled the pillow into her lap and squeezed it. The heat in her face didn't come from a fever alone.

"True." Kate nodded. "I love my brother-in-law dearly. After Blythe died, Jack feared Mark would give up and die, so he could be with his family. The grief group helped him, then he lost his job. He's lonely. We hope he'll one day find someone else to love." Kate held out her hand. "You may be the one."

"A girl can hope." Mark would make any wife happy.

"I'd better go." Kate stood. "I have some errands to run and a painting to finish. Ellie doesn't need me today." Kate put up her hand when Alana started to stand. "No, don't get up. I know my way to the door. If you need anything, just call me."

"Thank you." Alana dropped back as the door closed, leaving her alone.

I don't want to be alone, sick and stuck in my apartment.

Yesterday, she got back into life, but today, she paid for it. *Unfair!* Throwing the pillow aside, she pushed herself up and shuffled into the kitchen.

Seated in a chair at the table, she texted Ellie and her mother that, although she was sick, it wasn't contagious, and today, she'd be resting. She texted Mark that she looked forward to his call but said nothing about her illness.

As she reviewed yesterday's events, she felt ashamed. Why should she grumble and complain about the unfairness of life just because she experienced a slight setback today, when yesterday God blessed her so much?

"Please forgive me, Father God. The refugees in the camps have lost almost everything, and they depend on strangers to provide basic needs and health care. You've given me all I need, including my family and good medical care. How can I offer hope to others when I forget to be thankful for what I have?"

She'd follow the doctor's orders and stop griping.

CHAPTER TWENTY-ONE

Mark placed his tool belt in the trunk of his car.

"We'll be finished here on Wednesday." Dennis leaned against his truck. "Thursday we can start work on the next project. I wish I'd hired you sooner."

"I haven't done much, but I'm learning a lot."

"Just having you here to hand me tools and hold the cabinets in place saves me time." He looked past Mark as though something caught his eye, his jaw clenched. "I had hoped Carter would become my partner, but that hasn't worked out."

"When he matures a little more, maybe he'll be ready to join you." Mark prayed for his employer's son, so self-centered and defiant he couldn't see his father's pain.

Dennis shrugged and lowered his eyes to the ground.

"I'm glad your family came to church yesterday." Including Carter.

Dennis raised his head. "Grace and I enjoyed it. We'll probably go again."

"You're certainly welcome."

"Nova said it was okay, and she might go with us again, but Carter only went because Grace begged him for family time. He wasn't impressed. Although he was quite interested in the pretty young woman who played the piano and sang."

"Alana? She and her sister both have nice voices." Mark wanted to see Carter in church again, but unless Carter's attitude changed, he'd prefer to keep him away from Alana.

"Grace and I enjoyed their music." Dennis straightened. "Well, I have a meeting with a potential client this evening, so I'd better go. I'll see you tomorrow."

"Bright and early." Mark nodded and walked to his car. Mark wanted to help Carter, but so far Carter had rejected all Mark's attempts to befriend him.

As Mark turned into the parking lot at home, someone exited the front door of JC Computers. Carter Eastman. The young man stomped along the sidewalk, his face red and contorted with anger. He passed the parking lot without a glance in Mark's direction.

Mark got out of his car and walked to the edge of the parking lot. Carter turned at the street corner and disappeared.

The tense atmosphere in the store when Mark entered warned there'd been a confrontation. Jack stood at the front counter with his employees. When they saw Mark, Scooter hurried into the back storeroom, and Misty busied herself with something at the cash register.

Mark glanced around the store and back at Jack. No sign of violence. "What did Carter Eastman want?"

Jack shrugged. "A job."

"What did you tell him?" His harsh tone made him cringe. He was overreacting.

Jack frowned. "What's eating you, Mark?"

Misty stared at him.

Mark leaned both hands on the counter and took a deep breath. "Sorry, Jack, Misty. I saw Carter leave, and he was angry. He doesn't impress me as someone to be trusted."

"I told him I didn't need anyone else right now, so I couldn't hire him. He said a few choice words and left in a huff. I take it you don't think much of your boss's son."

"He's a hard person to like. But you have the right to hire who you want." Mark relaxed. Enough about Carter. "Did you have a good time with Kate's family yesterday?"

"Misty," Jack turned toward his employee, "I'll be in the office if you need anything."

"Okay, Jack."

Following Jack into the office, Mark took a seat.

"We had a great time at church and with Kate's family." Jack sat at his desk. "How did Mother's Day go in Millvale?"

Mark described the service at Valley Community Church.

"What was it like having dinner with Alana's family?"

Mark smiled at the predictable question. "Like coming home and having a family to welcome me."

Jack nodded in understanding.

"Alana and Ellie worked hard to prepare the dinner, and it was delicious."

"Can we consider you and Alana an item now, since she invited you to her family's Mother's Day celebration?" Jack grinned.

Mark laughed at Jack's question, then became serious. "An item—I suppose so. Yesterday was the best day I've had in a long time. I enjoyed being with her family, but the best part was being with her. I'm falling in love with her, Jack."

"My wife's been hoping you two would get together." Jack got up and poured himself coffee. He held out the pot toward Mark, and Mark shook his head. "Kate said the doctor told Alana today she had to take a couple of days off to rest." He returned to his chair with his coffee mug.

"The doctor?" Mark tensed and leaned forward. "Alana saw a doctor? She was tired yesterday afternoon, but I didn't know she was sick! Is she okay?"

"She just did too much, I guess." Jack leaned his elbow on

his desk and rested his cheek in his palm. He smirked. "You've got it bad, big brother."

Mark leaned back and rubbed his hands against his pant legs. "It's been five years, Jack. I didn't know if I'd ever find another woman to love."

"Not even Damaris?"

He shook his head. "I never felt a real spark between us. Not like I do with Alana." *With her, it's more like I put my finger in an electric socket.*

"Do you think Alana's interested in a serious relationship with you?"

"Yesterday, I think she felt the connection as strongly as I did." He rested his right foot on his left knee. "The problem is, she has a commitment to the IAS, and she doesn't know yet that I'm planning to go into the ministry. She likes to travel. If I become a pastor, I may live in the same town for many years. Plus, I don't know if she wants to get married. Maybe she'd prefer to remain single." He couldn't put their talk off much longer.

"What are you going to do?"

Mark thought a moment. His mouth stretched into a smile. "I guess I'll have to convince her to marry me."

Jack grinned and held up his hand for a high-five. "Go for it!"

∾

By late afternoon, Alana no longer ached, although she didn't feel ready to run a footrace.

Her phone dinged. An IAS teammate sent her a photo of her replacement. She sighed and bit her lip. She'd been supplanted.

She shrugged, oddly okay with the fact. They did what they had to do. And she had to get well before going back. A fact proven by Mother's Day.

Refreshed by a shower, she dressed in a T-shirt and sweatpants.

Did she want to sign a new contract with the IAS? Or would she finish out her year, then go to nursing school?

And what about Mark?

Yesterday was wonderful. She hugged herself. Mark fit in with her family, like he belonged there with her. Maybe she was Mark's someone.

Opening the sliding glass door in the kitchen, she stepped out into the backyard, wishing Mark was here with her now.

And that was it. She wouldn't sign a new contract with the IAS when her present one ran out. She'd start researching nursing schools and find out the requirements for a nursing degree and license. Her heart's desire, though, was a family of her own, a husband and children to love and care for. *Trust in the Lord.*

The faint outline of her parents's garden, left fallow since they went to Grammy's, reminded her she still had time to plant one of her own. If she asked Ben, he would till the ground for her the next time he came to mow the lawn. Or maybe she'd ask Mark.

Mark said he'd call her after work, and she'd left her phone inside. Fearing she'd missed his call, she retrieved her phone from the kitchen. Nothing yet—surely soon. As she dropped a tea bag in a mug of water and placed it in the microwave, her stomach growled. She checked the cupboards and the refrigerator for something to eat. Ugh, nothing appetizing.

A knock on the front door startled her. Probably Ellie checking up on her. She hadn't asked her to do that, but a little company right now sounded great.

She opened the door. "Hey …" Her breath caught.

On the other side of the screen door, stunning even in blue jeans and a work shirt, and holding a large white paper bag, stood a smiling Mark.

Butterflies danced in her stomach.

"A dinner delivery for Miss Alana Somers." He held up the bag.

"What are you doing here? You said you'd call." She bit her lip, regretting her blunt words.

His smile disappeared. "I can still call, if you'd prefer." He pulled out his phone and scrolled.

She shook her head. "No, don't. I'm sorry. I thought you were my sister checking up on me." She'd been wishing for him, though. She opened the screen door, and he stepped in. "You brought me dinner?"

"A little bird told me you went to see the doctor this morning, and he prescribed a couple of days of rest. If you're resting, you shouldn't have to fix yourself a meal. You have to eat, so I brought you a dinner from the diner." He held out the bag.

When she took the bag, their fingers brushed, and her pulse raced.

"A little bird, huh? Kate or Jack?" She peeked in the bag.

"My brother mentioned it. How are you feeling?"

Alana couldn't avoid his warm, caring gaze. If she had known he would be on her doorstep, she'd have taken time to dress a little nicer.

"Much better, thank you. I've been asleep for most of the day." She hid a yawn behind her hand. "My fever's gone, but I'm still tired."

"I'm glad you're getting better." He stepped forward and pulled her into a hug. She leaned against his warm, solid chest. Just what she needed.

He kissed her forehead and let her go too soon, but she understood. Laying his hand on the knob of the screen door, he said, "I'll call you later." He started to open the door, then turned back. "If you're well by Wednesday, will you go out with me after Bible study and prayer meeting? For just a little while."

His eyes shone with anticipation.

"I'd like that, Mark." She had to be well by then. Holding up the bag, she said, "Thank you for bringing me dinner."

"You're welcome. If you need my help with anything, please let me know."

"I will." Mark made her feel so special.

He turned and waved once as he headed for his car parked along the street. She blew him a kiss. He grinned and got into his car.

Heat rushed into her face, along with surprise at her spontaneous action.

The aroma from the bag in her hand enticed her to eat. Chicken with mashed potatoes, carrots, and applesauce—so good, and she didn't have to fix it herself.

After eating, she settled on the sofa with a romance novel. That fit her mood exactly.

Her phone rang. "Hi, Ellie." She laid her book down.

"Hi, Lanie. How are you feeling?"

"I'm much better. Still tired though." Every time she thought about being tired, she yawned.

"Well, be sure to rest. I'm bringing dinner over to you tonight. I prepared extra because I knew you wouldn't feel like fixing your own."

"Um, I appreciate that, Ellie. But I've already eaten." Thanks to Mark.

"You have? Oh." Was she disappointed or surprised?

"Yes, Mark brought me a dinner from Mill Pond Diner." She pulled off her sandals, stretched her legs out on the sofa, and waited for her sister's reaction.

"Mark did? I think you have a serious boyfriend, Little Sis. As I said yesterday—"

Alana shook her head. "Yes, I know. You said he'd be a catch for any woman." She agreed, wanting to be that woman.

She really didn't mind that Ellie teased her about Mark. Not now. However, she and Mark still had wrinkles to smooth out before they could settle into a serious relationship.

Too late. She was already serious about Mark.

Ian fussed in the background. "Sorry, Lanie. Ian is demanding my attention. I'll bring your dinner tomorrow, if that's all right with you."

"That will be helpful. Thanks for calling and checking up on me. Love you."

"Love you back." Ian's fussing became crying. "'Bye."

She scrolled on her phone to a photo of her and Mark taken yesterday. Was that dreamy-eyed woman really her and the handsome man beside her Mark Chambers?

CHAPTER TWENTY-TWO

*T*ime to celebrate. After two days confined to the house, Alana wanted out.

The bright reds, oranges, and yellows of her skirt with soft pleats reminded her of a fiesta. She checked her hair and make-up one more time.

Laying her sweater and purse on the sofa, she checked the lock on the back door.

A knock on the front door sent her scurrying to open it. Mark must have come a few minutes early, but that was all right. She was ready.

"Hello, beautiful."

Stunned, she blinked. Six-one, slender, with blonde hair and gray eyes, the man standing at her door with a big grin on his face was not Mark Chambers.

He wasn't a stranger, either. "Nicholas Ames? What are you doing here?" She'd last seen him in the IAS camp about six weeks ago and hadn't heard from him for a month.

"Surprise!" He spread his arms out. "I came to see you."

"Yes, I'm surprised to see you." She smiled as she stepped

outside. She positioned herself to give him a side hug then moved away.

He kept his hand on her shoulder and faced her. "You're looking well, but you've lost weight."

"You don't have to assess my health, Mr. P.A. The doctor already told me I had to put on weight." It was great to see him, but why was he really here? "You didn't come all the way across the ocean just to see me."

A day's growth of whiskers shadowed the lower part of his face, and his eyes reflected fatigue.

He dropped his hand. "No, I returned to the States to take some refresher courses and update my physician's assistant license. I hoped we might spend some time together." He grasped her hand.

"Oh." What exactly did he mean? She and Nicholas had spent many hours working together. His calm manner and sense of humor often eased tense moments, and his kindness and caring for the refugees had impressed her. She would love to talk to him about her teammates and what was happening with the refugees, and she'd like him to meet Mark. But was he implying there was something more? She stepped away. "I'm sorry, Nicholas. If I had known you were coming, we could have arranged lunch or something. But I'm going out. My ride will be here any minute." What would Mark think if he found another man on her doorstep?

He placed his hands on his hips. "I thought you'd be glad to see me and offer some hospitality to a traveler from afar." He probably referred to the biblical admonition about entertaining strangers and offering hospitality. Although not a believer, Nicholas knew the Bible.

His words pricked her conscience. "I am glad to see you, but I didn't know you were coming, and I've made other plans. I can offer you a bottle of water if you're thirsty."

"No, thank you. I have some in the car." He looked around

the front yard. Mark's car turned the corner and pulled into the driveway.

"Here's my ride now." Alana's stomach twisted. "Nicholas, if I've ever done anything to make you think I wanted to be more than friends, I'm sorry." God forgive her if she had.

Mark got out of his car, wearing a light blue dress shirt and navy slacks. As he confidently strode toward her, her stomach fluttered.

"Now I see why you're trying to get rid of me," Nicholas muttered.

Alana chuckled. "I treasure your friendship. I've known Mark for most of my life, and we've become close since I returned home." Very close.

Invite Nicholas to church. "We're going to a Bible study, if you'd like to join us. And getting something to eat afterwards."

She didn't expect him to accept the invitation. However, if Nicholas became a believer through their Bible study and prayer meeting tonight, she'd be glad, even if it disrupted her date with Mark. God often worked in unexpected ways.

Mark drew near, and as always, her heartbeat raced.

"Good evening, Alana." His eyes told her he was glad to see her. He turned to Nicholas and, with a smile, offered his hand. "Mark Chambers." Mark's gracious manner relieved her fear of confrontation.

Holding out her hand toward Nicholas, she said, "Mark, I'd like you to meet my friend Nicholas Ames, one of my teammates from the IAS."

Nicholas shook Mark's hand.

"Hello, Nicholas. I'm glad to meet one of Alana's co-workers."

"Nice to meet you, Mark. Alana told me you've known her for a long time. You probably have some stories to tell." Nicholas grinned at her.

Alana blushed. What kind of stories would Mark tell Nicholas? She held her breath.

"My lips are sealed." Mark made a zipper motion across his lips. Alana breathed again.

"Aw, I'm disappointed." Nicholas shook his head. "I'm always interested in a good story." His wink assured her he was teasing.

Mark stepped closer to her. "So, what brings you to Millvale, Nicholas?"

Nicholas crossed his arms. "I had to return to the States to update my physician assistant's license and stopped by to check on Alana's health."

Is that all, Nicholas?

"I'm sure you meet with a lot of challenges as a medical worker in a refugee camp," Mark said.

"There's always someone needing help. It's quite interesting, though, as Alana can tell you."

She nodded. A thread of tension stretched between the men, likely because of her. Under different circumstances, they probably could be friends.

"What do you do for a living, Mark?" Nicholas dropped his arms to his side.

"Right now, I work for a cabinetmaker."

"A good trade."

"Yes, I enjoy working with wood, and my employer is a craftsman."

Alana remained silent, uncertain what to say.

Nicholas pulled his phone from his pants pocket. "Do you have any recommendations for overnight accommodations?"

Alana started to answer, but Mark spoke first. "There's a B&B on the other end of town. And a motel about three miles east of town."

"Thanks." Nicholas entered the locations into his phone.

Alana touched Mark's arm. "Mark, we'd better go, or we'll be late. I've asked Nicholas to join us."

Mark nodded and turned his gaze to Nicholas. "You're welcome to come."

He shook his head. "No, you go ahead."

His refusal, although expected, disappointed her.

"Well, I'd better go." Nicholas waved his hand toward his car. "I'll be leaving early in the morning for a six-hour drive to my parents's house." He held out his hand to Mark. "Good meeting you, Mark." He turned to Alana and clasped her hand. His eyes met hers briefly. "Take care of yourself, and I'll see you in a few months." He looked from Alana to Mark and back. "If you're planning to return to the IAS."

"I still have a contract with them. I'll be back when the doctor releases me." But only temporarily.

"Good. Have a nice evening." He held up his hand and walked to his car.

"'Bye, Nicholas. Thank you for stopping."

Mark's arm came around her, and she relaxed against his side with a sigh, breathing in his clean scent.

"Are you all right?" His arm tightened.

"I'm fine. It's just that I didn't expect to find Nicholas on my doorstep." She didn't want Mark to think Nicholas was any more than a friend. "We'd better go."

He released her and gazed down at her. "You're right. We'll talk later. That is, if you're up to going out after church."

"I'm looking forward to it."

"We'd like two cups of green tea and one order of chocolate chip cookies, please." Mark told the waiter, glad to oblige Alana's request for refreshment at the diner.

The waiter wrote on his pad. "I'll bring your order shortly."

Alana blushed when Mark caught her staring at him. She ducked her head and fingered the edge of her placemat. "You like tea?"

"I do. I learned to drink tea with Rachael. She kept many kinds." He preferred coffee, but enjoyed a cup of tea from time to time.

Alana pulled a napkin from the table dispenser. "Do you still miss her?"

Miss Rachael? Yes, in a way. He reached for Alana's hand and held it between his. He'd loved his wife, but she was in heaven now, with Jesus. He'd said his final goodbye to her. He'd never forget her, but he no longer felt bound to her.

He gazed into her eyes. "Please understand, Rachael will always be a part of me." He rubbed his thumb over the back of her hand. "But if God allows me to love and marry again, my devotion will be to my wife, not to my memories." *Do you want to marry me, Lanie?*

He squeezed her hand. "Do you understand what I'm trying to say?"

She nodded, and her eyes remained focused on his. "You won't let your memories of Rachael replace your commitment to someone else you choose to marry."

Mark nodded and kissed her warm, soft palm. His gaze traveled to her lips, then back to her eyes. Kissing her the way he desired wouldn't be appropriate right now.

Taking a breath, he opened his mouth, but before he could say more, the waiter returned and placed their tea and cookies on the table. "May I get you anything else?"

"This is fine, thank you." Mark hoped the waiter would leave so he could tell Alana what he needed to say.

Still holding her hand, he thanked God for their time together and their refreshments, then squeezed her hand. He let go only because he needed both hands to eat.

He laid his napkin on his lap. *How will she react when I tell her about the big changes coming for me? And maybe for her?*

Pulling her teacup toward her, she poured a packet of sugar into her tea and stirred. She bit into one of the cookies and closed her eyes. "Mmmm."

She doesn't know how beautiful and alluring she is. He forgot about his tea as he observed her—her lovely face, her soft brown curls, her long, slender fingers that played the piano so well. When she opened her eyes and discovered Mark studying her, she swallowed and pushed the plate with the remaining cookie toward him. "It's best when it's warm."

He broke the cookie in two and took a bite, savoring the taste.

"I didn't expect Nicholas to appear on my doorstep." She fingered the curls around her ear. "I didn't know he'd returned to the States."

"You don't have to explain." She really didn't. He accepted Nicholas was her friend.

"I think I do. He and I often worked together when new refugees arrived. My job was to maintain a record of who came into camp, and his job was to assess their health needs and see they got proper medical care. In his free time, he organized soccer matches and other games for boys, many of whom didn't have fathers." She sipped her tea and set the cup on the saucer. "In some ways, he reminded me of you."

He licked a bit of chocolate off his lips. "Is that good or bad?"

"You're a kind person, Mark, and you care about people. Nicholas is like that too. He's a good physician's assistant, and the IAS is fortunate to have him."

Mark nodded and took another bite of cookie. Her explanation gave him a clearer picture of Alana's life with the IAS.

"I enjoyed working with him." She broke off a piece of her cookie and popped it in her mouth. "I valued his friendship and still do, but I'm starting to suspect he thinks of me as more than a friend." She shook her head.

Propping his elbow on the table, he rested his cheek in his palm. When he leaned close enough that their noses almost touched, her eyes got big. "You don't give yourself enough credit for being the person you are. You're committed to what you do, and you follow through. You have an inner and outer beauty that is attractive to men, including Nicholas. Including me."

She smelled like chocolate and the sweet scent of a light fragrance she wore. His eyes moved to her lips. With increasing difficulty, he resisted them. He shifted back and finished his cookie.

She took another sip of tea and met his eyes over the top of her teacup.

His stomach knotted, and his heart raced. He rested his arm on the back of the booth. "Alana, Jack and Pastor Clary know this, but I want you to hear it from me." What he shared with her now could decide their future together.

Her forehead wrinkled in a tiny frown.

"God has called me into the ministry, to become a pastor."

Again, her eyes widened, and she set the cup on the saucer with a click. "A pastor?" She stared at him. "But you just took the job with Eastman's, and I thought you liked it. When did this happen?"

He expected her surprise. "After BEC laid me off, my world fell apart. Pastor Clary told me he thought I should attend seminary and go into vocational ministry." He folded his napkin and set it beside his teacup. "It surprised me, but the more I thought and prayed, the more I knew that's what God wants me to do. I'm really excited about it."

She clasped her hands in her lap, her eyes focused on the table in front of her. She probably needed time to process what he'd said.

"I'm happy for you." She turned her teacup around on the

saucer. "You love God and have a heart for people. And you are a teacher and spiritual leader in our church. If God has called you, it's what you should do."

He gently pulled her hands into his, but she kept her gaze down. "I know you want to travel and like working for the IAS. It's only fair for you to know where God is directing me. What you think matters a great deal to me because I want a future with you, and I can't say no to God."

She finally met his gaze, her expression troubled. "When will you go?"

"Go?"

"To seminary."

"Oh, I'm not going anywhere right now. I'll keep working for Dennis and take classes online. I'm only required to go to the seminary for a week every semester."

"That's good." She took a deep breath. "I can't stand in the way of God's call on your life."

Her response left him a bit deflated. He'd hoped she would be excited for him, but there was something evasive in her words.

She pulled her hands away and curled the edge of her place-mat. "After I complete my present contract with the IAS, I won't be signing a new contract."

"What will you do?" He sat up, surprise and anticipation coursing through him. Did he influence her decision?

"Over the past four years, I wished I had more medical knowledge so I could help more people." She glanced at him. "Before I went with the IAS, I thought about a career in nursing."

He nodded. "Nurses are needed, and you'll be able to work almost anywhere. Will you then go back to the IAS?"

"No, I'm ready for something different. I've loved returning to Millvale, and I think I can be content wherever God leads me."

God, are You directing us to go different ways, or will we meet at the crossroads and travel together?

Mark held out his hands. Alana hesitated only a moment before she placed her hands in his. "Will you pray with me, Lanie? We both have a lot to consider." He needed God's guidance more than ever.

CHAPTER TWENTY-THREE

The next morning, Alana headed outdoors, accepting the invitation of the sun and warm air.

Mark's announcement about his call into ministry shocked her. She'd fallen in love with this man she'd admired all her life, and she wanted to marry him and raise a family with him. But was she qualified to be the wife of a pastor?

His compliment about her inner and outer beauty warmed her heart. She'd always wanted to emulate Grammy, Mama, and Mrs. Clary—loving, gracious women whose faith wove through their words and actions like a sweet melody. Yet, she in no way lived up to their example. If Mark knew all the ways she'd failed in her life as a Christian, he might change his mind.

The overgrown and weedy flower beds in front of the house caught her eye. She needed something useful to do while she processed the changes that might enter her relationship when Mark became a pastor.

With the key she found hanging on a nail by the back door upstairs, she unlocked the shed. The garden rake, hoe, and spade hung along the wall. Mama's trowel and gloves sat on a shelf.

Alana dumped out wood scraps from a bushel basket to use it as a container for weeds.

Until she started college, she'd helped Daddy plant his vegetable garden every year. The moderate exercise and fresh air from tending a garden would be good for her, and fresh vegetables would enhance her diet. But she'd start with Mama's flower beds.

She dug out the weeds and worked the soil with the hoe and rake. To encourage the new growth on the rose bushes, she cut back dead branches. Was that what God was doing in her life, weeding and preparing the soil of her heart for ministry? Cutting out of her life the things she did that kept her from following Him fully?

The daffodils and tulips had finished blooming. She'd separate the bulbs and replant them before leaving in October.

Moaning, Alana stood and stretched the stiff muscles in her back. The beds lay ready for new annual flowers.

"Do you want a kitten?"

Alana whirled around, surprised but not frightened by the child's voice behind her. In the refugee camps, children had often approached her with sudden needs.

Perhaps nine or ten years of age, the girl had brown skin, multi-braided black hair, luminous, dark eyes, and an infectious smile.

Brushing her hands together to get rid of loose dirt, Alana pulled off her gloves and smiled at the girl. "Do you have kittens?" Did she want one?

"Well, Mother Cat does, and Mama says we can't keep them." The girl wasn't at all shy.

Alana held out her hand. "I'm Alana. What's your name?"

"I'm Carolyn." She shook Alana's hand. "I live over there." She pointed to the white ranch house three houses down and across the street. Carolyn's family must have moved in after

Alana left Millvale. "Do you live here? Isn't this Mr. and Mrs. Somers's house?"

"Yes, I'm their daughter. I live in an apartment in the basement, and they're away, taking care of my grandmother." Alana liked this girl.

Carolyn nodded. "It's nice to meet you."

"It's nice to meet you too. Now, about those kittens, how many do you have?"

"We have four, but only one isn't promised. She's gray with white feet, and her name is Mittens." She put her hands behind her back. "We won't let them go all at once. Mother Cat will get lonesome."

"I imagine so." Carolyn seemed to know a lot about cats.

A kitten would be company for Alana, and she had plenty of time to take care of it now. But what would she do with a cat when she returned overseas? Would Ellie take it? Or Kate?

It wouldn't hurt to at least see the kitten, would it? And meet the neighbors, something she hadn't done yet. "May I come to meet Mittens before I decide?"

"Yes, you can come now. My mother's taking a break."

A break from what? And why was this child not in school at this hour of the morning on a weekday? Did her mother know she had left their yard? And would an unexpected visit from a stranger be welcome?

"Shouldn't you be in school?"

Carolyn nodded. "I am. I'm taking a break, too. When I came outside and saw you, I came over to ask about Mittens."

"Oh." Realization hit like the sun bursting from behind a cloud. "Do you homeschool?"

"Yes, Mama's my teacher."

Alana nodded. "I'll tell you what. Why don't you go home so your mother doesn't worry? Let her know I'll be over in a few minutes, if it's all right with her."

"Okay. See you." Carolyn skipped back to her house. Alana watched until the girl reached her yard.

After brushing dirt off her clothes, Alana went inside. She washed her hands and checked for dirt on her face. Her hair looked fine. She locked her door and pocketed the key.

Despite her illness earlier in the week, Alana felt stronger and more energetic today. She gazed with satisfaction at her morning's handiwork. She'd get Ellie's advice on which flowers to choose and get them planted, hopefully before the end of the day.

Three bicycles and a soccer ball lay on the lawn of the white ranch. She climbed the red brick steps and put up her hand to knock, but the door whooshed open.

Carolyn stood before her, beaming. "Hi! Come on in." The girl opened the door wide, and Alana stepped into the living room.

Colorful throw pillows accented the brown furniture and beige walls. A landscape painting of an orange and pink sunset with an acacia tree silhouetted in the foreground hung on the wall over the sofa. She'd seen a sunset like that in Africa.

Children's voices and a woman's soft tones drew her eyes to the doorway across the room. The slender woman who entered shared Carolyn's skin tone and facial features. She smiled at Alana. Her black hair was styled in an attractive pixie, and she wore a bold-patterned blue, green, and gold tunic over leggings.

Alana's eyes fastened on the two tiny kittens in the woman's arms.

Two boys younger than Carolyn, with dark skin and short, curly black hair followed her, each cuddling a kitten in his arms. The gray tabby mother cat trotted behind them, meowing softly as she watched the humans with her babies.

Setting the four kittens on the living room floor, the boys sat with them. Mother Cat sniffed each kitten, a gray one with white paws, a white one with orange patches, a gray tabby, and an orange tiger. Carolyn sat on the floor and stroked the cat.

The kittens fell over each other, batting each other with their paws and crawling on the children.

The charming scene made Alana laugh. "They're so cute."

"Yes, they are, and that makes it harder to let them go. But we can't keep them." The woman extended her hand. "I'm Lucinda Woods."

"Alana Somers." She clasped Lucinda's hand. "Thank you for letting me come on so short a notice."

"You're welcome. Carolyn is anxious to find a good home for Mittens." She turned to the boys. "These are my sons, Samuel and David." She laid a hand on each one's shoulder as she said their names.

The boys looked up at Alana and grinned.

"Hi, Samuel. Hi, David. It's nice to meet you." She waited for their response.

"Boys, say hello to Miss Alana."

They glanced at their mother, then at her. They were perhaps shy of strangers.

"Hello, Miss Alana."

"Hello, Miss Alana."

Why had she waited so long to meet this family?

"This is Mittens. She's a girl." Carolyn lifted the kitten fitting Mittens's description and cuddled it in her arms. The kitten purred, seeming content.

Lucinda turned her eyes to Alana. "Carolyn said you're interested in adopting Mittens."

Alana dropped to her knees and held out her hands. Carolyn placed Mittens in them. The kitten sniffed her hand and looked up at her with blue eyes. Alana fell in love.

"I want to." Alana stroked the soft fur on the kitten's back. "I live alone, so Mittens would be good company." She rose to her feet. "However, I must be honest."

Lucinda indicated the sofa, and the two women sat.

"I'm here for only a few months. I'm with the International Aid Society, and I'm home on medical furlough because I contracted malaria."

Lucinda nodded. "Oh, I'm sorry to hear you've been ill."

"I'm much better now, thank you."

The boys giggled as they played with the other three kittens under the watchful eye of Mother Cat. Carolyn scooted over to Alana on her knees and scratched Mittens between her ears.

"I'd love to adopt Mittens, but I'll have to find someone to care for her while I fulfill my contract with the IAS, which will be up next year. If I can find a friend who will take care of her for me when I leave in October, I'd still like to have her."

"I see." Lucinda ran her fingers over Mittens's soft fur.

Carolyn sat back on her knees. "Mittens really likes you."

"She's beautiful, Carolyn. I like her too." *I want her.*

The other three kittens lost interest in play and nuzzled against their mother. With a soft meow, she lay on her side, and the kittens began to nurse. Alana set Mittens down so she could find her way to Mother Cat.

"I have some friends who might be willing to take Mittens. Will you save her for me for a couple of days so I can ask them?" She prepared herself in case Lucinda refused.

Lucinda looked at Carolyn, who nodded. "I think we can do that. They won't be ready to adopt for another two weeks. They have to be old enough to be separated from Mother Cat and eat solid food well. If someone else asks for Mittens, we'll tell them you have the first choice."

"Thank you." Alana stood. "Carolyn said you homeschool, so I don't want to keep you any longer."

"Yes, they have to get back to their schoolwork." She looked at her children, who got up quietly and left the living room, taking the kittens with them. "I'm glad you came over. I've seen you go in and out, and I wanted to meet you. How are your parents and grandmother?"

"Mama and Daddy are well. My grandmother has dementia, but she is as well as can be expected. They came on Sunday, and we had a Mother's Day dinner at my sister's house."

"It's wonderful they could come. We've missed them since they've been away."

An argument broke out in the next room. Lucinda frowned. "I'd better see what's going on in there."

"Thank you. I'll let you know about the kitten within a couple of days." Alana let herself out.

Alana hummed on her way home. She'd known some of her neighbors since childhood, but several new families now occupied homes along her street. She'd remained aloof from her neighbors during the past six weeks because she was convalescing, and she didn't want to become attached to them and Millvale.

Maybe falling in love with Mark Chambers had opened her eyes to the people around her, to living where God wanted her.

Hmm. Maybe Mark would like to have a cat.

THE BELL on the door at Valley Florist jingled when Alana opened the door. Only Ellie was there with Ian.

"Hi, Ellie."

Ian lay cooing and squealing in his portable crib while Ellie put together an arrangement at the work counter.

She glanced up. "Hi, Lanie."

"Are you alone today?" She didn't see Ellie's employees or any customers.

"Kate has the day off, and Marcy's at lunch." Her arrangement included carnations and lilies, with a single red rose in the center.

Alana looked down at her nephew. He didn't notice her at first. On his side, he reached for a soft, squishy ball. He swiveled to his back with the ball between his hands. Then he spotted her. With a big smile, he waved his arms and kicked his legs with excitement.

"Go ahead and pick him up," Ellie said. "I'm almost finished here, and he's kept himself entertained for quite a while."

Without hesitation, Alana lifted Ian to her shoulder. He cuddled against her, then lifted his head and smiled at her. He reached up and poked her nose and touched her lips. She laughed and kissed his cheek. How wonderful it would be to have a child like Ian.

Ellie finished the arrangement and placed it in the cooler. She turned to Alana. "Did you have a good time with Mark last night?"

"Of course!" How much should she tell Ellie? "We had tea and chocolate chip cookies at the diner. And we talked. He told me he's going to become a pastor."

Ellie's eyes widened. "Mark is? That's wonderful! Will he continue to work for Dennis Eastman?"

"He plans to do seminary classes remotely and continue to work. It should take him about two years.

"What do you think?"

"If Mark is following God's will for him, it's fine with me." *What's your will for me, God?*

Ellie pushed pieces of stems and leaves into a barrel beside the counter. "Have you heard again from your co-worker who showed up on your doorstep?"

She shook her head. "No, Nicholas said he'd be going home this morning." She didn't expect him to contact her before leaving. However, she came here for another purpose today. "Can we talk about flowers?"

"You came to the right place." Ellie rested her hand on the counter.

"I want some suggestions about annuals for Mama's flower beds. They're ready for planting."

"I'll show you what I have, and we can decide what will be best."

When Alana followed Ellie into the greenhouse filled with flats and hanging baskets of brightly colored blooms, Ellie made recommendations. Alana chose petunias, marigolds, begonias, and other annuals in a variety of colors as Ellie waited on another customer. Marcy returned, and Ellie rejoined Alana.

"Ian's asleep now." Alana rubbed his back as he snuggled against her neck. How she loved him, so sweet and soft.

"I'm thankful. He's awake more, and that's not a problem unless he's fussy." She touched her son's cheek. "It's time we set up a schedule for you to take care of him."

Alana could hardly wait. "Why don't you and Ben come over for dinner tomorrow night? We can talk about it then."

"That sounds wonderful, as long as it doesn't tire you out." Ellie rested her hand on Alana's arm.

"I've wanted to ask you over, and making dinner won't be a problem. I have lasagna in the freezer and a loaf of Italian bread. I'll fix a tossed salad and cut up some apples."

"Do you want me to bring a dessert?" Ellie pinched a dead flower off a petunia.

"Thanks for offering, but I'll take care of it." Brownies would be quick and easy to make. "You've had me over so many times to eat with you. Let me do this for you."

"All right. I'll check with Ben tonight, and I'll let you know if we can make it." Ellie tipped her head. "Are you inviting anyone else?"

Alana face warmed "Well, probably Mark." He'd be working late tonight, but she'd text him.

"Thought you might." Her sister smiled.

"Kate and Jack as well. Maybe the men will till the vegetable garden for me while we discuss a babysitting schedule." Would they think she'd invited them for dinner so they could work for her?

"Ah-ha, you have ulterior motives. We wouldn't want them to get bored." Ellie laughed, and Alana shrugged.

Alana laid the sleeping baby in his crib and covered him with a light blanket. "Bye, Ian." She kissed her hand and pressed it to his cheek.

After she paid for the flowers, Ellie helped her carry four flats of annuals and five bags of cedar mulch to her car.

"Thanks." Alana closed the trunk. "Oh, there's another thing."

"What's that?"

"Have you ever thought about getting a pet, like a dog or a cat?" She clasped her hands and held them against her chest. She wanted Mittens an awful lot.

Ellie shook her head. "Ben and I discussed it, and we decided that, with both of us working and now having a baby, it would be better for us to wait. When Ian gets a little older, we'll get a puppy."

"Okay." Alana twisted her mouth. One down, two to go.

"Is there a reason you asked?" Ellie placed a hand on her hip. "You weren't planning to get Ian a puppy, were you?"

"No, I wouldn't do that without your permission." That wouldn't be fair to Ellie. "Do you know the Woods family who live in the white ranch down the street from Mama and Daddy's house?"

"I've met them." Ellie picked dead blossoms from a basket hanging beside the door.

"Their daughter Carolyn came over this morning and asked me if I wanted a kitten. It's the cutest thing, gray with white paws."

"You didn't."

Alana sighed. "No, I didn't. I'd love to adopt her, but she'll need another home when I leave in the fall."

"Sorry, Lanie." She shook her head. "Ben isn't crazy about cats."

Disappointed but not defeated—yet. "That's okay. I have a couple more ideas." She pulled her car key from her jeans pocket.

"Have you thought about asking Kate?"

"She's next. I have to get these flowers in the ground. I'll see you later."

CHAPTER TWENTY-FOUR

The flower beds looked great, free of weeds and filled with flowers. The mulch gave the new annuals a finished look.

Alana took some pictures on her cell phone and sent them to Mama, who texted back.

Beautiful! Thank you.

Tired but content, Alana ate supper. After showering and dressing in her pajamas, she grabbed her phone and cuddled on the sofa.

She called Kate first, so she'd have more time to talk to Mark.

Kate said yes to her supper invitation and no to the kitten. They had plans to travel for their anniversary in the fall.

One more to go.

Her phone rang. Mark's name appeared on the screen.

"Hi, Mark." She switched to speaker phone. A cat on her lap while talking would be nice.

"Hi, Lanie." She loved hearing him use her nickname. "How was your day?"

"Busy. I planted Mama's flower beds." And she had the aches to prove it. "How about yours?"

"Long and difficult." He sounded discouraged.

"What happened?"

"I dropped a large bag of screws and had to pick them up. Have you ever had to pick up five pounds of screws?"

He definitely needed a hug. "No, I can't say I have, but I did pick up a dish of straight pins I dropped once."

"I also cut a couple of boards the wrong length. They were only a fraction of an inch off, but they couldn't be used."

It was the same with sewing, crafts, or cooking. A small mistake could ruin a project.

He sighed. "Then there was Carter."

"Who's Carter?" Should she know Carter?

"Dennis Eastman's son."

"Oh." She'd never met him. "What happened?"

"Let's just say he's a difficult person to like."

"What did he do?" She leaned against the throw pillows.

"It's his attitude more than anything. Whenever he comes in, it sets us behind in our work because he argues with his mother, and Dennis has to leave what we're doing and deal with him. When Carter leaves, it's like Dennis and Grace are the wounded left on the battlefield. If he only understood how blessed he is to have parents who love him."

"I'm sorry." Alana's heart hurt for Mark, who didn't have his parents and felt the loss even as an adult. She'd pray for Mark and the Eastmans.

Mark sighed. "I'd rather talk about us." Something beeped. "I wish I could see you tonight, but I got home from work only a few minutes ago. My TV dinner is in the microwave."

"A TV dinner. Do you have them often?" She hoped not.

"Only when I'm too tired to fix a meal, or Kate doesn't offer leftovers."

Tomorrow night, he wouldn't have a TV dinner if she had her way. "Mark, would you like to come over for supper tomorrow night?"

"At your house?"

"Yes. I've invited Ellie and Ben. Jack and Kate are coming too."

"You know I never pass up an invitation for a home cooked meal."

"So, I've heard." She giggled. That must mean yes.

"May I bring something?"

"Just yourself. Well, there is something else." It was only fair to warn him.

"What's that?" His microwave beeped again.

"Ellie and I want to work out a schedule for me to take care of Ian, and we thought … I thought you guys might like something to do." Although he might prefer to relax after working all day. She put her arm around her knees and squeezed. "Will you … ? I mean, I'd like to plant a vegetable garden, and I need someone to till the ground for me. My father's tiller is in the shed."

"I'll be glad to do it for you."

"Thank you." She might as well make her other request. "Do you know the Woods family who live down the street from my parents' house?"

"I've met them. They visited church a few times. Why?"

"Their little girl, Carolyn, came into my yard this morning and asked me if I wanted a kitten. Oh, Mark, it's the cutest thing, gray with white paws."

"Did you get a kitten?"

"No. Not yet anyway. I'd love to adopt Mittens. She'd be great company for me. But I won't do it unless I can find someone to take her when I leave."

Was she crazy to expect he would take in a kitten? Mittens would become a full-grown cat one day.

He didn't respond right away, so she prepared to be disappointed again.

"Alana, are you asking me if I'll take your kitten after you leave?"

"Well?" She held her breath.

"Ouch! That's hot! I'll do it."

She had to breathe. "What?"

"I burned my fingers. I'll be glad to take Mittens when you leave."

"You will?"

"I've thought about getting a cat or a dog for company. I think a cat will work better in my upstairs apartment. There's less chance a cat will disturb Jack's customers, and keeping a cat will be easier for me."

"She's not quite ready to leave her mother, so I'll have a few days to get ready for her. Thank you, thank you, Mark." She wanted to hug him and do a happy dance.

"You're welcome. We'll be doing each other a favor. While you're away, I'll think of you when I take care of Mittens."

Her leaving was inevitable, but she didn't want to dwell on it.

A few seconds passed, and they said nothing.

"I'm sorry, Mark. Am I keeping you from your supper?"

"No, I'm eating it now. I'll try not to chew in your ear."

She laughed. "You must be a quiet chewer. I can't hear you."

"I enjoyed our time together last night." The alluring tone of his voice made her shiver.

She pulled a pillow into her arms and squeezed it. "So did I. Especially the chocolate chip cookie."

"I ... The chocolate chip cookie?"

Had she wounded his feelings, or was the hurt in his voice a put on? She giggled. "The cookie was good, but being with you made it special." In all seriousness, she couldn't deny the fullness of her heart when Mark was around. "Thank you for not letting Nicholas's unexpected visit stand in the way of our date."

"It wasn't your fault he showed up. Too bad he didn't accept your invitation to go to church. He missed out on an excellent chocolate chip cookie."

"Nicholas has a lot of head knowledge about the Bible and Christian beliefs, but he refuses to allow his heart to know."

"If he had come, I might have been able to talk to him. On the other hand, I couldn't have talked to you about us. It was only fair to let you know about seminary and becoming a pastor."

"You have to go where God leads you." She wanted to be the person Mark thought her to be.

"Oh, Lanie, have you ever been up in a hot-air balloon?"

Where did that question come from? "No, although I've watched them and wondered how it would feel to be in one."

"I'd like to try it sometime. Will you go with me?"

Not much different than flying in an airplane, right? "I'd like that."

"Will you go out with me Saturday night?"

"In a hot-air balloon?" Did hot-air balloons fly at night?

"No, no. Out to dinner." He chuckled.

She couldn't hold back a giggle. "I'd love to have dinner with you."

"Good. If it's all right with you, I'll pick you up at 5:30."

"I'll be ready. Tomorrow night, we'll eat at six."

"I'll be there."

HER OTHER GUESTS had already left when Mark joined Alana in the backyard after changing out of his work boots and washing his hands. "I enjoyed tonight, and dinner was great! Thank you for inviting me."

Her fingers entwined comfortably with his as they strolled around the yard. "Thank you for tilling the ground. I probably could have done it, but Daddy's tiller is hard for me to handle. I can hardly wait to plant the seeds and see them grow."

"Ben and Jack were a great help, commenting on the crooked furrows and telling me how to handle the tiller." They stopped to view the tilled ground. "Do you need help with planting?"

She already had the garden planned, but his offer was tempting. "I think I can do it myself tomorrow. You have work."

"All right." With gentle fingers, he turned her face toward his. "Promise me you won't overdo."

Her eyes met his, and she could hardly draw air into her lungs. "I know my limits. I learned my lesson last weekend."

He dropped his hand and faced her. "Did you get the daycare schedule worked out with Ellie?"

"Yes, we're all set. I'm going to love my time with Ian, and Ellie will be able to concentrate on work." She loved the idea of practicing mothering skills.

"I'll go now since we both have a busy day tomorrow." He drew her into his arms. "I'll pick you up at 5:30 for dinner."

She tipped her head up. "I won't forget."

He lowered his gaze to her mouth and leaned toward her. Her eyes closed as his lips touched hers, and a thrill passed to her toes. She put her arms around his neck, and he pulled her closer. He deepened the kiss, and she responded, her heart throbbing. Too soon, the kiss ended.

For a moment, she rested her cheek against his firm chest, catching her breath. His heart raced in time with hers.

"I've wanted to do that." His voice rumbled in her ear.

"Me too."

When he stepped back, she reluctantly released him.

He brushed a curl from her forehead. "I'd better go."

"I know." Her lips still tingled, and she missed the warmth and comfort of his arms.

Her hand clasped tightly in his, she walked him to the front of the house and watched him amble away. He turned once and waved.

Should she feel guilty her work with the IAS didn't appeal as much to her?

CHAPTER TWENTY-FIVE

lana dressed in jeans, a cotton knit top with red and blue stripes, and ankle hiking boots. Mark had bought tickets for the Hot-Air Balloon Festival in Sayre's Point for today, the second Saturday in June. He told her natural fabrics were safer to wear, and they needed sturdy footwear in case the balloon landed in mud.

Nervous jitters struck her stomach when she thought about going up in a basket attached to a large balloon. She could have said no, but with Mark's long hours at work and his online classes, plus the time Pastor Clary mentored him in pastoral responsibilities, they had little time together. He looked forward to going, and she'd be safe with him.

Slipping her sunglasses on top of her head, she laid her red, snap-front sweatshirt on the table and tucked her camera into her bag.

Mittens curled herself around Alana's ankles. Alana lifted the kitten and laid her cheek against the soft fur.

"Kate promised to check on you at noon. You have food in your dish and water. You should be fine for the day." This was the first time Mittens would be alone for a whole day.

When Mark knocked at the door, Mittens scooted away. She had many hiding places.

Mark stepped inside, pulled her forward, and gave her a gentle kiss on her lips. When he gathered her to his chest, she listened to his heartbeat and breathed in his familiar scent, secure in his arms.

"I've missed you. I'm looking forward to spending today with you." He looked down at her with mesmerizing blue eyes. He kissed her again, leaving her breathless. "Are you ready?" He released her and stepped back, his hands remaining on her arms.

"Of course. Let me get my things." She took a moment to steady herself and catch her breath.

Despite her sweatshirt, Alana shivered in the cool morning air. The sky turned a lighter gray as Mark merged his car with the traffic on the highway.

"I checked the website this morning. So far, conditions look good for the balloons to go up today."

"I'm glad. I know how much you're looking forward to a balloon ride." She'd go for Mark's sake.

"I am. But if you don't want to go, we don't have to." Mark glanced at her.

She wouldn't back down now. "I want to do this, Mark. I'll be fine." *Like flying in a plane, right?*

"If you're sure."

"I am. You'll be with me." Her words brought a smile to his face.

He passed a beige van and pulled back into the right lane. "So, the doctor gave you a good report at yesterday's appointment."

"Yes. I don't have the results of the blood tests yet, but he was pleased I'd gained weight and said he thought I'd be ready to go back in October." She didn't want to think of that right now. "How's work?"

"Good. We're installing kitchen cabinets in a mansion. I think it must have twenty rooms. It's huge and elaborate."

"I don't think I'd like having to clean a house that big." She could only imagine what it would be like to live in the home Mark described.

"The people can afford a housekeeper."

The eastern horizon glowed with the impending sunrise.

"No more problems with Carter Eastman?" Alana had been praying over the situation.

Mark clenched his jaw.

Why did she bring up Carter? *Foolish tongue.*

"No, he hasn't been around much, and Dennis said he hasn't found a job yet."

"How are you doing with your class?" This was something he liked talking about. Once he'd received his acceptance from the seminary, Mark had signed up to take a summer course.

"It's intensive because it's a six-week class instead of the usual sixteen. I had to finish a paper and submit it last night. I'm also getting credit for my mentorship with Pastor Clary. There's so much to learn."

He needed a day to relax and enjoy himself.

At the park where the annual festival took place, Alana couldn't count the number of colorful patchwork balloons tethered. Some lay flat, and others had been filled and stood ready for flight. A soft breeze blew against her face. The sky turned from gray to blue as the sun peeked over the horizon.

"This is amazing! Kate would love it. Imagine the paintings she could create." She pulled her camera from her bag and snapped some pictures as they followed another couple to the entrance gate.

"I invited them to come, but Jack has to work today, and Kate has a painting she must finish. Besides, I like just the two of us being here."

She agreed. She'd treasure every moment. Today was a day

to create memories for the two of them, memories Mark could carry with him when he was lonely for her, when he faced a challenge with an assignment, work, or Carter Eastman.

A few balloons floated overhead, the occupants waving and shouting from the baskets.

Alana waved back. "It looks like fun."

Placing his arm around her shoulders, he whispered in her ear, "Are you ready to fly away with me?" His breath tickled her ear, and she shivered.

He grinned when she softly sang the first line of the gospel song "I'll Fly Away."

She eyed the field of balloons across the way and the lake beyond them. "Can we wait a little while before going up?"

"Not too long. We have to go before the air gets hot." He grasped her hand and pulled it through his arm. She trembled. "Are you afraid? We don't have to do this."

"I'm a little nervous, but I want to go up. You're looking forward to it, and I agreed to come with you."

"Are you sure? I want both of us to enjoy this."

"I'm sure." She couldn't back out now.

"I'm a little nervous too. But it's been on my bucket list for a long time." He squeezed her hand. "Which balloon shall we choose?"

It was hard to choose. "I like the one over there, with the red, yellow, and blue panels."

As they listened to the pilot's explanation of the balloon and their flight, Mark glanced at the woman beside him. She leaned toward him. "This is interesting."

He agreed. When the demonstration finished, he faced her. "What do you think?"

"I guess he has to know what he's doing. I'm ready to go up."

Mark helped Alana climb into the basket, called the gondola, and then he followed. A man with a preteen boy and girl also got in. Mark grinned with excitement as the pilot released a valve and a flame whooshed toward the balloon, called the envelope, filling it with hot air. An assistant on the ground released the ropes fastened to the gondola, and Mark's stomach took a nose-dive as the balloon rose in the air.

"Huh!" Alana's grasp on his hand tightened. He squeezed back, and she smiled at him, her eyes big. "I love this."

The stress created by his busy schedule and recent run-in with Carter Eastman peeled away, and his heart sang because of the woman beside him.

They rose higher and broke into full sunlight, and the balloon changed directions. People and vehicles became miniatures below them, and the wind took them across the lake.

Mark's fingers had gone to sleep by the time Alana relaxed her grip, and he flexed them when she let go. He missed the warmth of her hand in his, though.

Peering over the edge of the gondola, she said, "Look, Mark!" She lifted her camera and snapped photo after photo.

Mark joined her and looked down on a panorama of tree-covered hills and green fields. "This is amazing!"

They floated over tiny cars, people, and buildings. Black and white cows grazed on green pastureland, a large white barn sat nearby, and some kids in the farmhouse yard waved and jumped up and down. The balloon's shadow followed them on the ground below.

What an exhilarating experience!

"We'll be in the air for about an hour. We'll land on a field where someone will be waiting with a van to bring us back to the park," the pilot said.

"Why don't we fly back in the balloon?" The question came from the boy, who looked to be about ten.

"The balloon can only go in the direction of the wind. So, after landing, we have to pack up our equipment and bring it back."

Mark chatted with the pilot and the other man while Alana took pictures. She turned and aimed her camera in Mark's direction. Her cheeks glowed, her eyes sparkled, and the weight she'd gained back enhanced the curves in her face and body. She wore red well and often, probably her favorite color. He tucked that away as an important bit of information for the future.

"Okay, everyone, we're going down. Hold on to a support so you won't be thrown if we have a bumpy landing." The pilot released air through a vent in the top of the envelope, and the balloon began its slow descent.

Mark leaned against Alana and placed his hand above hers. The heat from her body seeped into his, and he bent his head to inhale the scent of her hair.

When they returned to the festival grounds, Mark clasped Alana's hand as they walked. A musician sang country tunes from the entertainment tent. The balloon ride had been all he expected and even more exciting. *Magical* Alana called it, and he agreed, made more so by her presence and joy.

They strolled among the booths and tents, stopping to watch two young women paint children's faces and a man tying balloons into dogs, swords, and other things requested by the children clustered around him. Families were everywhere, parents, children, grandparents, and he loved being here with them and sharing this experience with Alana.

He rested his head against hers. "After Blythe died and I lost my job, my life bottomed out. You've made me feel alive again, Lanie."

"Oh, Mark." Looping her arm through his, she leaned her

head against his shoulder. "And this is the best I've felt in a long time. I think because I'm with you."

Their fingers entwined, they meandered through the craft booths, where crafters displayed their creations—everything from jewelry, to paintings, to bird houses, to clothes, and toys.

Mark searched for a perfect gift for Alana, something she could take with her wherever she went. Something that would remind her of their time together today and would fit in her suitcase.

They walked through a tent with stuffed animals and dolls that waited for the arms of a child. Alana turned to him with a stuffed white lamb in her hands. "Which of these do you think Ian will like the best? This lamb, the blue dragon, or the brown puppy?"

"You're asking me to help you decide?" He'd been looking at the bears, but she didn't say anything about a bear. He still had Blythe's stuffed animals and dolls packed away in the attic at the cottage. He'd chosen many of them for her, and she'd loved every one of them. "The lamb is cute, but it's white and will get dirty fast."

She nodded and set the lamb down.

"The dragon is a fierce-looking fellow. I think Ian would like the teeth and the long tail. He could probably grab the tail."

She picked up the dragon, growled, and thrust it at Mark. He took the dragon from her with a smile and returned it to the display. He enjoyed her playfulness.

"Now, the puppy. Little boys like puppies." He picked one up. "This one has floppy ears and a long tail. It's soft and cuddly, and he'll be able to grab it easily."

Taking the puppy from him, she flipped its ears and wiggled its tail. "I think you're right. Ian will like the puppy. How did you become so wise?" Her eyes sparkled when she tipped her head and smiled at him.

"I was a boy once, and a father." A stab of pain shot through his chest, and his eyes stung. Memories sometimes brought on pain and tears at unexpected times.

She stepped closer. "Are you all right?"

He pressed his lips together and nodded. "I miss Blythe."

Her eyes filled with compassion, and she grasped his hand. "I'm going to pay for this." She let go of his hand and took out her wallet.

From the stuffed animal display, he lifted a pink bear that looked like the bear Blythe had slept with each night. The bear he bought her when she was born.

Alana turned back to Mark with a bag in her hand.

"Are you ready to go on?" Mark set the bear down and took the bag from her.

He spent so much time watching her, he often forgot to look at the items for sale.

Was he falling for her too fast? Although only five years stood between them, he sometimes felt older. He'd been married, had a child, lost a job he loved. He'd be thirty on his next birthday. Yet, being with Alana rejuvenated him.

He finally found it, a chain with a hot-air balloon pendant, a memento of their time here together. While she searched through racks of handmade children's clothing, he purchased it and tucked the small box into his pants pocket to give to her at the right moment.

It was a small gift, but if he had his way, he'd have many opportunities in the future to give her bigger ones.

CHAPTER TWENTY-SIX

On Wednesday morning, Alana slipped the chain over her head, and the pendant settled against her T-shirt. The small hot-air balloon replica reminded her of all the wonderful moments with Mark on Saturday. And his kiss as he left her at her door that night.

A little doubt niggled in the back of her brain, and, like a balloon descending from the sky, she slowly came down from the cloud she'd been on.

Would Mark change his mind when she had to leave to finish her contract with the IAS? And what if she didn't meet his expectations? Could she fulfill the responsibilities of a pastor's wife?

Lord, I'm trying to figure this out. How do I get past my doubts? Please increase my faith and trust.

She lifted Mittens from her bed and carried her into the kitchen. Setting out food and fresh water for the kitten, she then prepared breakfast for herself.

Ellie would arrive soon with Ian.

Alana had purchased a second-hand portable crib and a high chair for Ian, who now came on Wednesdays through Fridays from eight-thirty to five. Ben picked him up after work on those days, and he cared for his son Saturday mornings when Ellie worked. Ellie had Monday off, and on Tuesday she took Ian to work with her because it was a slower day at the shop. So far, the schedule had worked out well.

Alana treasured her time with Ian. It would be over too soon.

Tying a red bow around the stuffed puppy's neck, she set it on the sofa to give to Ian today. At almost five months, he loved playing with toys. He and Mittens had become friends, although Alana never left them unsupervised.

Mittens jumped on the sofa, a skill she'd recently learned, and sniffed the puppy. She sat and observed it, then tapped it with her paw, making Alana laugh.

In answer to Ellie's knock, Alana hurried to the door. Ian smiled as Alana unbuckled him from his carrier and lifted him into her arms. She kissed his cheek. When Alana laid him on the blanket she'd spread on the floor, he grabbed his feet and stuck his toes in his mouth.

"He's fascinated with his toes," Ellie said.

Alana chuckled.

Then he spotted Mittens peeking at him from the sofa, and he squealed and waved his arms and legs.

"See what I have for Ian." Alana handed the stuffed dog to Ellie. "I found him at the balloon festival, and Mark helped me choose him. Mark said a boy should have a puppy."

Ellie took the toy from Alana, squeezed it, and looked at its face. "He's adorable. Thank you. Let's see how Ian likes him."

Ellie held the puppy over Ian's face. He stared, then grabbed an ear. Ellie released it, and it fell on his chest.

"He's content, so I'll go now. You know where I am if there's a problem. Bye, Ian." She bent over and kissed him.

When Alana sat on the floor beside Ian, Mittens stood on the edge of the sofa cushion and peered down at them. "It's still a little daunting for you to jump down, isn't it, Mittens?" She lifted the kitten and cuddled her.

Ian stuffed the puppy's floppy ear into his mouth, then examined its face and cooed. The purring kitten watched him from Alana's arms.

If she had children, she'd like four, girls and boys. Mark liked children and said he and Rachael had wanted more.

"I suppose we have to find a name for your puppy, Ian." When he heard his name, her nephew smiled at her. "We can't just call him *Puppy.* Well, we could, but it wouldn't be very original. I wish I had asked Mark."

Ian let the toy drop to his side and twisted his body. His hand touched Alana's ankle. She held Mittens close to him and guided the baby's hand to touch the soft fur. Mittens continued to purr. Alana hoped soon she could give them more freedom around each other.

"What do you think of the name *Charlie*?" She picked up the puppy and shook it so its ears flapped. Mittens grabbed for an ear but missed it. "I think he looks like a Charlie, don't you?" Ian laughed. "Okay, Charlie it is."

She took photos of Ian with Charlie and Mittens—memories to take with her and for her parents because they weren't here to watch him grow day by day. Of course, she messaged the pictures to Ellie.

The bright sunshine invited Alana outdoors for a walk. Strapping Ian into the stroller Ellie had left by her door, she pushed him along the side of the street and waved to Carolyn and her brothers playing in their yard.

Turning the corner, she pushed the stroller up on the sidewalk on Cedar Street, where the large homes had been built in the early part of the 20th century, with big front porches and fenced-in yards. She and Ellie had called them mansions and talked about how many rooms they had and how long it would take to clean them. The owners entrusted the care of their manicured lawns to professionals.

Burkley Maines's mother lived on this street. The wealthy Mrs. Maines had always been less than cordial to the Somers family and to others of moderate income. Mr. Maines had driven a red Corvette, and his work as a bank executive in a neighboring town gave him an excuse not to attend school concerts and sports events, even when Burkley participated.

Alana hadn't promised Burkley she'd visit his mother, but it bothered her she hadn't. She allowed her prejudice to stand in the way of showing compassion for a lonely widow.

A white-haired woman sat alone on the porch of the Maines's home. Mrs. Maines was the same age as Mama but looked ten years older.

Alana's conscience nudged her. Stepping out of her comfort zone, she stopped in front of the house. "Hello, Mrs. Maines." She smiled and waved at the woman on the porch.

Mrs. Maines responded with a frown.

She hasn't changed.

"Your baby?"

"N-no, he's my sister's baby." The question brought heat to her face. "His name is Ian."

Mrs. Maines leaned forward. "You're one of the Somers girls, aren't you?"

"Yes, I'm Alana Somers." *She recognizes me?*

"I heard your grandmother has dementia. How is she?"

Her jaw nearly dropped. Mrs. Maines knew about Grammy?

"Thank you for asking, Mrs. Maines. My grandmother has good days and bad days." Mama told her Grammy's memory was worse. And she hadn't taken the time to visit her again.

"Poor woman. I've known her for a long time."

Does she really care? "I saw Burkley in church on Mother's Day, and he said you've been ill. I've prayed for you." Mrs.

Maines would probably be happy to know people cared about her.

"Well, my son had no business revealing my personal issues to anyone."

Alana bit her lip to keep herself from a sarcastic reply. Maybe Mrs. Maines didn't know how to accept concern or help from other people.

Ian fussed. Alana leaned around the stroller and peered at him. He grinned at her, but she had her excuse to move on.

She pushed the stroller. "Have a nice day, Mrs. Maines."

To Alana's surprise, Mrs. Maines lifted her hand and waved.

Farther along the street, on the other side, a young man with his hands in his pockets caught Alana's attention, although he didn't seem familiar. He paused in front of each house as though he admired the older homes as much as she did. Yet, with his brush-cut hair and ripped jeans, she thought he'd prefer modern home architecture. He took a small notebook from his shirt pocket and wrote in it.

She kept walking, not paying much attention when he crossed the street, until he stood in front of her, blocking the sidewalk.

"Excuse me," she said. When he didn't move, a slice of fear cut through her. "Please let me by."

"Well, well, we meet again." His patronizing tone disturbed her.

"I don't believe I've ever met you before." She grasped the stroller handle harder, trying to control the tremor in her hands.

"I saw you in church. You sang and played the piano. Remember, on Mother's Day?"

She shook her head. "You may have been there, but I don't know who you are."

He smirked. "I'm disappointed that Mark Chambers didn't tell you. If I had known then you were buddies, I'd have had him introduce us."

Fear crept down her back. *He knows Mark?* Recognition dawned. "You're Carter Eastman." She had seen him when Mark seated the family.

"One and the same. This your kid?"

She didn't like his tone. "What do you want?" All women on her IAS team had been taught self-defense. Would she have to use it for the first time now?

"I just want to be friends." He stepped closer.

She pulled herself to her full height, a couple inches shorter than him. "The feeling is not reciprocal. Please let me by."

He grabbed the side of the stroller.

"Get your hands off!" No way would she let him hurt Ian.

An approaching voice cut into their confrontation. "Is there a problem? Do I need to call the police?"

Mrs. Maines.

Carter spun on his heel and hurried away. Alana slumped against the handle of the stroller, her legs like jelly, her body trembling, and her hands shaking.

"Are you all right?"

Alana looked over her shoulder. The older woman's face creased with concern.

"Thank you, Mrs. Maines. I'm fine, just shaken. He didn't hurt me." She checked Ian, who'd fallen asleep. She wanted to hold him but didn't want to awaken him.

"I've seen that young man around here before. He doesn't live on Cedar Street, and I don't know who he is."

"His name is Carter Eastman. His father owns Eastman's Cabinetry. I've never met him until now, except by reputation." Mark would be furious if he learned about Carter's actions. She wouldn't tell him. "Perhaps you should call the police the next time he comes around, at least so they can check up on him."

"I may do that. So long as you and the little one are all right, I'll go back to my house."

Alana laid her hand on the older woman's arm. "Thank you

for intervening, Mrs. Maines. I hope he doesn't cause any trouble for you."

"He won't. Please stop by again some time." Mrs. Maines walked with a cane, but her step indicated purpose as she returned to her yard. She waved before entering through her gate.

Mrs. Maines invited her back? Under all that crustiness, there must be a soft heart.

Not wanting to meet Carter again, Alana retraced her steps and returned home. After laying Ian in the portable crib in her bedroom to finish his nap, she dropped onto the sofa in the living room. Mittens jumped into her lap.

What would Carter have done to her or Ian if Mrs. Maines hadn't interrupted him? She cuddled Mittens against her chest, the kitten's purr comforting.

"Heavenly Father, thank You for Mrs. Maines's intervention and your protection. Please forgive my judgmental attitude toward a person I don't really know."

CHAPTER TWENTY-SEVEN

Mark drove to the Summit Hills Seminary after the Fourth of July, where he met with his faculty advisor, discussed his goals, chose his courses for the fall semester, and laid out a plan for the course credits he'd have to earn to graduate, confident he'd followed God's will for his future. He stopped at the business office and paid tuition for the fall semester.

He wanted to call and share his excitement with Alana and tell her everything that happened, but she'd be busy with Ian now. She loved caring for her nephew and would be a wonderful mother. He'd see her in a few hours and talk to her in person.

To give himself time to reflect and pray, he turned off his phone for the drive home.

"Heavenly Father, Alana said she wouldn't come between Your call to the ministry and me, but she didn't say she'd be willing to commit herself to life in the ministry. I thought she'd be excited. You know I love her, and I believe we belong together. Make her willing, Lord, but only if it's Your will."

Something wasn't right, but he didn't know what.

He checked for calls and messages when he stopped at the

first rest stop and again when he stopped for gas. By his third and last stop, Alana had called him three times. Standing outside his car, he called her back.

"Mark, I'm so glad you called."

Was she crying? "What's wrong, Lanie?"

"Oh, Mark, Grammy is missing!" She sobbed.

"Missing?" His heart clenched for Alana and her grandmother.

Alana sniffled. "Daddy said Mama missed her a couple of hours ago." Her voice broke. "She somehow figured out how to unlock the door. No one in her neighborhood has seen her."

"Where are you?"

"I'm home. I'm getting ready to go to Kellersville."

"Are you driving? Is anyone going with you?" In her state of mind, driving herself would be dangerous.

"Ellie and Ben won't be able to go until tomorrow morning. I don't want to wait for them. I have to go. Grammy is …"

She didn't complete her thought, but with Grammy's mind and body diminished, Alana's grandmother could die.

He headed for the restroom. "Lanie, listen. You're upset and shouldn't be driving alone. I'm about an hour away. Will you wait for me?"

"You'll go with me?"

"I'll drive you. You shouldn't go alone."

"Oh, okay. I'll wait. Thank you, Mark." Relief filled her voice.

"Have you called Pastor Clary?"

"Y-yes. He started the church prayer chain. Mrs. Clary came over and prayed with me."

"Good. Hold on, sweetheart." The term of endearment slipped out. "I'll be there soon."

"I'll wait for you."

He ended the call and silently prayed for Grammy and the granddaughter and family who loved her.

DID he know he called her sweetheart? Alana's heart skipped a beat.

Hearing Mark's voice and knowing he was on his way comforted her. He'd become important to her. If she let her insecurities stand in her way and chose to break up with him, would she be alone all her life with no one to lean on?

Ellie had already picked up Ian, and the sisters had cried and prayed together. Alana's packed suitcase sat by the door.

With Mittens on her lap, she sat on the sofa, stroking the kitten's soft fur. Mittens purred, but her eyes followed Alana's every move as though she sensed Alana's stress.

"Lucinda said she would feed you and check on you three times a day. I know Carolyn will help." How long she'd be gone, she didn't know. But at least Mittens would have good care.

She called her father. "Hi, Daddy. Mark's driving me to Kellersville."

"I'm glad you don't have to come by yourself. Mark's a good man, and I know he'll take care of you." His voice was thick with tears. He didn't cry often, but he wasn't afraid to cry.

Daddy's trust in Mark warmed her heart. "I guess you haven't found Grammy yet."

"No, we don't know where she could have gone. She's lived here a long time, and she knows her way around, or she used to." His voice broke. "We don't know how her mind is working, or if it's working enough for her to be safe."

Alana's chest tightened. "I'm sorry, Daddy." Where had she gone? "How's Mama?" Alana wandered from room to room as she talked, unable to sit still.

"She's distraught and feels responsible. She'll be glad to have her girls here—we both will, although I'm sorry it has to be for this reason."

If only she and Ellie had visited Kellersville earlier this

summer with Ian as Alana had hoped. "Ellie and Ben will leave here as early in the morning as they can get out. Mark and I should be there before nightfall."

"The neighbors here are out looking, and the police department has sent out an official alert. Everyone is being kind and helpful."

"Pastor Clary started the church prayer chain for her. Do you think she's okay?"

"Oh, Lanie, I don't know." His voice trembled. "All I know is, she's in God's hands."

Alana breathed deeply and blinked back tears. "Please give my love to Mama and tell her we're all praying. I'll see you soon."

"All right. Love you."

"Love you back. Bye, Daddy." She wiped away a few more tears.

After checking the house upstairs, she made sure she had everything she needed for her trip and lay back on the sofa to rest. As limp as a wet dishrag from her anxiety and tears, she needed to recoup before Mark arrived.

Her phone rang. Mark.

"I'm at my apartment. How are you doing?"

"I'm hoping and praying for the best."

"I'll be over in a few minutes."

"Thanks. I'm ready."

Too agitated to wait for him to knock at her door, she stood outside and met him in the driveway with her suitcase when he arrived.

"Mark." She set down her suitcase and melted into his arms, soaking in his strength and comfort. She didn't cry. She'd cried enough to drain her tear ducts for a while.

"Has there been any news?" His voice rumbled in her ear.

Lifting her head, she gazed into his eyes filled with tenderness and concern. "No, they haven't found her yet. I talked to my father a little bit ago. Mama is very upset, and I know Daddy is worried. Isn't it strange we've all prayed and know God is taking care of her, but we're still worried?"

"It's our human nature. It's hard to let go of something that's out of our control, to let God take care of the situation, even though we believe He's capable. Our trials test our faith. Our head and heart need to connect." She absorbed his words.

After praying, Mark released her and placed her suitcase in the trunk. He opened the car door for her before getting into the driver's seat.

"I don't want her to die, Mark." There, she said something she couldn't say to Ellie or Daddy. She believed she'd see Grammy in heaven, but she couldn't imagine life on earth without her.

He grasped her hand and leaned his forehead against hers. "I know. It's hard to say goodbye to those we love, even if we know we'll see them again one day."

From their emails and conversations, Mark's experience with grief certainly had been hard. After kissing the back of her hand, Mark released it and started the car. "Your grandmother has lived a full life." He backed out of the driveway.

She slid her right hand over her left, the touch of his lips leaving a lasting tingle. "It's heartbreaking to watch her now. She's so feeble, her body's so thin, her eyes so empty when she retreats into who knows where. I know if she dies, she'll be whole again, and she'll be with the Lord and my grandfather." She took a deep breath. "Thank you for listening. I had to talk to someone."

"I'm here for you and for your family."

Thank God, he was. She rested her head against the back of the seat. He set the radio on low volume to a Christian station, and she tried to relax.

She lifted her head. "Did your visit to the seminary go well?"

"Very well. I'm all set for my fall classes." He described

what he did and who he met. "I feel more confident I'm following God's will."

"I'm glad for you." If only she knew where God wanted her.

"How about you? Have you chosen a nursing school?"

She shook her head. "No, I've been searching online, but I haven't made a choice yet." In fact, she'd been procrastinating, questioning whether nursing was God's idea or hers. Nurses were essential in caring for the body, mind, and spirit of suffering people, but was it the best way for her to make her life count?

Music helped broken people like her grandmother. In the refugee camps, she witnessed how music lifted the spirits of suffering people. And music conveyed the message of hope in Jesus in a beautiful way. Wouldn't it be wrong to set aside the talent God had gifted to her?

"I have time before I have to choose." *Prayer was definitely needed.*

Mark nodded and glanced at her. "That's true."

He laid his hand over hers, and she turned hers, intertwining her fingers with his. She couldn't deny her greatest desire was to be Mark's wife and have children with him. She was glad for his certainty in his calling, yet still uncertain how she fit in his future. "Oh, doesn't your other summer course begin on Monday?" She laid her hand on his arm.

"Don't worry. I plan to go back on Sunday afternoon, since Dennis is expecting me to work on Monday. But I have my laptop with me should I need it in an emergency."

Alana shivered, thinking what that emergency might be.

"Ellie and Ben will be coming tomorrow, so I won't be stranded. Hopefully we'll find Grammy, and she'll be all right." She could hope and pray. The highway stretched before them in the shimmering light of the late afternoon sun.

"Did you ask Kate to take care of Mittens?"

He hadn't met her kitten yet.

"No, Kate's parents are coming this weekend. I asked Lucinda Woods."

"Mittens is good company for you."

"Yes, she is. I can't imagine life without her. I'll have to make sure the two of you spend quality time together before I leave." Still three months away.

"That will be fun so long as you're there too." Mark's gaze sent warmth through her.

White clouds skimmed along the surface of the sky. The trees and fields wore their summer greens. She loved days like this.

Had Grammy looked out her window at the beautiful day and decided to take a walk? She loved Psalm 19:1, *The heavens declare the glory of God; and the firmament shows his handiwork.* But where would she go?

CHAPTER TWENTY-EIGHT

"Smell that, Mark?" Alana inhaled as they walked up to the door. "Mama's made her vegetable beef soup."

Before Mark could respond or she could touch the knob, Mama threw open the door. "I'm so glad you're here, Lanie."

Alana and Mark stepped inside.

The lines on Mama's face aged her. Her body trembled, and she sagged into Alana's arms. With Mama's quiet, confident demeanor shattered, Alana had to be the strong one this time.

Mark set their suitcases down and waited beside her.

"We came as soon as we could."

Mama stepped back and wiped her eyes. "I know. And your father should be back soon from going to talk to the policeman in charge. Everyone is trying to help. Grammy is out there … and I feel responsible."

"Oh, Mama, you're a good caregiver. We have to believe God is taking care of her." She met Mark's gaze. They'd talked about this.

Mama nodded. Noticing Mark for the first time, she pulled him into a hug. "Oh, Mark. I'm sorry. I didn't mean to ignore you. Thank you for bringing Alana. I'd have worried more if she tried to drive alone."

"I'm glad to help."

Alana inched sideways and clasped his hand, absorbing confidence from his touch.

He squeezed her hand. "As I told Alana, I'm here for you, to help in any way I can."

"We're glad you're both here." Her mother led the way into the living room. "I hope you won't mind sleeping on the sofa tonight."

"Not at all."

"There's soup if you're hungry."

Mama's words aroused Alana's hunger. Mark probably needed to eat too. "Let me put my suitcase in my room. Mark, the bathroom is this way if you need it."

They returned to the kitchen, and Alana filled two bowls with soup. "Are you eating, Mama?"

"No, I had some earlier. I left this for you."

Mark clasped her hand as he thanked God for their safe trip and for the food. He included a plea for Grammy's safety.

Alana's mouth watered. She blew on a spoonful of soup and placed it in her mouth. "Mmm."

When Mark tasted the soup, pleasure crossed his face. "Your soup is delicious, Mrs. Somers." He knew the right words to make her mother feel better.

Mama stopped pacing from window to window. "Thank you. I had to do something today. To me, homemade soup is a comfort food. I wanted something nutritious that I could feed anyone who came without much fuss."

"I think the IAS will have to hire you to make your soup for the refugees in camp, Mama." Her mother smiled. Good. Alana had distracted her from sad thoughts for a moment.

Daddy came in through the back door. Mama looked at him, and he shook his head. She stepped into his arms, and they stood locked in an embrace for several minutes, as though gathering strength from each other to go on.

Alana glanced at Mark without speaking. Her parents had forgotten them, but that was all right. They needed their time together. She and Mark finished eating.

Daddy raised his head. "Lanie, Mark, you're here." He stepped away from Mama. "It's so good to have you."

Daddy's red-rimmed eyes broke her heart. He sobbed once when her arms went around him. "We're going to help you find her, Daddy."

He looked in her eyes. "I know, Lanie." Turning, he gave Mark a quick, hard hug. "Thank you for coming, and thank you for taking care of my girl."

"It's my pleasure, Mr. Somers."

Alana put their dishes in the dishwasher and wiped off the table. Then she and Mark joined her parents in the living room.

"The police chief showed me the areas that have been searched. A few people are still looking, but most have stopped for today because it will be dark soon. More will go out again at first light. They have a search and rescue team with dogs ready to join the search tomorrow."

Alana shivered at the thought of Grammy being out all night, alone and in the dark.

"Mr. Somers, I'd like to pray with all of you. May I?" Mark's unsurprising offer to pray comforted Alana.

"We can use all the prayer we can get," Daddy said. He and Mama bowed their heads.

Alana clung to Mark's hand as he prayed.

"Our heavenly Father, we come to You in prayer on behalf of Mrs. Somers. She's still out there, but we know You are with her. She belongs to You. Be her protector, her shelter, her shield. I pray she will remember You and sense You are there beside her.

"Thank you for the people who have joined the search.

Please give them safety and success. We ask that, by tomorrow morning, she will be found.

"I pray also for the Somers family as they wait. Give them the faith and confidence in You to believe You will do what's best for her. Give these people rest and peace that only comes from You. In Jesus's name, amen."

Peace settled over and within Alana. Her hand lay clasped in Mark's as they sat on the loveseat. On the sofa, Daddy's arm rested around Mama's shoulders as she rested her head against his chest.

Mark squeezed her hand. When she looked up at him, a memory surfaced.

She jumped up. "I know where Grammy is!"

Everyone stared at her.

"Grammy and I used to go somewhere she called her secret place, where she went to pray and think through problems. She told me that I was the only one beside Grampy who knew about it."

Daddy spoke first. "Where is it?"

"It will be easier for me to show you than to tell you. Mark, will you go with me?"

He stood beside her.

"Don't you think you'd better wait until morning?" Mama leaned forward.

"If we can find her tonight, won't that be better? It's not cold, but she's out there alone, and we want her safe." She shivered again.

"Mark?" Her father looked thoughtful.

Daddy wanted to protect her. Her family didn't know about the dangers she experienced in her work from both animal and human predators. They'd had good security, however.

Licking her lips, she bounced on her toes, waiting for Mark's reply. She wanted her father's permission, even though she was of age to make her own decision. He didn't need someone else to worry about. And she wouldn't go alone at night.

"We can try, Mr. Somers. I'll go with Alana, but we'll need a strong flashlight."

Yes! She could hardly stand still.

"All right. I have one." He went into the kitchen and returned with a large lantern. "I'll go with you."

"No, Daddy, you stay here with Mama." She laid her hand on his arm. "You've been searching all afternoon, and Mama needs you here with her. If we find Grammy, we'll call you right away. I promise we won't do anything dangerous."

He nodded and handed the lantern to Mark.

She hugged each parent. Mark followed her out the door. They had to find her.

Floral scents filled the warm night air, and the Milky Way spread across the sky, making it the kind of night Grammy loved.

Mark stopped her and grasped her arms as they came to the end of the sidewalk that met the driveway. "Are you sure about this, Alana?"

"Yes, I'm not being reckless, Mark. Her secret place isn't far, within walking distance, and it's really not hard to find. You just have to know where it is." And she did.

"Are we walking, or do you want me to drive?"

"If you drive, we'll have the car with us to bring her home." If they found her in time.

"I think that's wise." He kissed her forehead before releasing her.

They got into the car, and he backed out of the driveway. "Did you and your grandmother go to her secret place often?"

"Turn here." She remembered the directions clearly. "Ellie and I spent part of every summer with my grandparents as long as I can remember. When we got older, Ellie and I came at different times. It was exciting for me to share a secret with

Grammy. I felt so special. I never told anyone." She laughed. "I wonder if Grammy did the same thing with Ellie."

"My grandparents all passed away before I knew them. I may have met them, but I don't remember them."

"I'm so sorry." She laid her hand on his arm. "I guess I'm talking too much about mine."

"No, I like hearing stories about your grandparents. Families are important. I always wished Rachael's parents had taken more interest in Blythe, especially after Rachael died." He took a deep breath. "They didn't want anything to do with our Christian faith. I haven't heard from them since I called and told them about Blythe." Mark carried sadness she never knew about. His Adam's apple bobbed as he swallowed. "They didn't come to her memorial service, claiming they were unable to come. And that was that."

"I didn't know." She rubbed his arm.

He laid his hand over hers. "Jack knows, but I haven't told anyone else. I sent them a Christmas card and enclosed a picture of Blythe. I never had much connection with them and none now." He returned his hand to the steering wheel.

"I'm sorry," she whispered.

In the dusky light after sunset, adults sat on front porches as children played in the yards. People walked their dogs. Everything looked peaceful, but Alana's heart ached for her grandmother. *Please, God, let her be there.*

"Stop!" She remembered this place even at night. A streetlight shone on an old mill turned into a museum. "There's a trail back there, through the woods. We shouldn't have trouble seeing it with the lantern. It goes up to a small waterfall. Grammy and I climbed up on a big rock to sit and sing and talk."

Mark locked the car doors and pocketed the key. He turned on the lantern and looked around. "Do you think she's up there? I can't imagine how she could find her way through the woods."

"They looked for her in all the obvious places this afternoon.

Her thinking process is mixed up. But she loved the spot and went there often. I have a feeling she's there. I have to try."

His arm came around her. "Lead the way, Lanie. You may be right. It's worth trying. We'll do this together and trust that God is leading us to her."

The lantern formed a bright halo around them. They met no wild animals, although rustling in the bushes along the way made her heart thud.

"Listen!" She paused, and Mark stopped beside her. "It sounds like someone singing."

"I hear it. Let's go." Mark held the lantern to light the way and held tightly to her hand.

The sound of running water met her ears. "The waterfall. I didn't know if it would be running."

They broke through the trees. The lantern light revealed a small form on top of a large rock. A broken voice sang, "Great is Thy faithfulness …"

"Grammy's favorite hymn!" Alana stopped and called out, not too loud, "Grammy, I found you."

The singing stopped. "Is that you, Alana? I've been waiting for you to come."

Alana looked at Mark. "I'm here, Grammy. It's time to go home."

"Come up here for a minute. I want you to see something."

She scrambled up the rock as Mark held the lantern so she could see. The rock wasn't as big as it used to be and seemed easier to climb. How her frail grandmother climbed up by herself, however, she didn't know.

Sitting beside the old woman, she took her hand. "I'm here, Grammy. I'm sorry it took me so long to get here."

"I know, Lanie. You sometimes have other things to do. But I'm glad you're here."

Alana turned her head. Mark stood beside the rock. His eyes met hers in the lantern light. "Mark, will you call my father, and let him know we found her? Here's my phone." He took it and did as she asked.

She put her arm around Grammy. "I love being here with you." Her throat hurt and her eyes stung. Now was not the time to cry. There would be plenty of time for that later.

"God is so good, Lanie. He made this beautiful place. It's my special place. I've been here praying and singing. Sing with me."

Alana joined her in singing "Great Is Thy Faithfulness." Alana closed her eyes, sensing the presence of God.

"Hear them, Lanie—do you hear the angels singing?"

Alana's breath caught and tears dripped down her cheeks. She rubbed her grandmother's arm. "Grammy, it's time to go home. Your son is worried about you because you've been gone so long. You don't want him to worry, do you?"

When her grandmother looked at her, the dim light obscured the expression in her eyes. "Yes, it's time."

Grammy tried to push herself up but failed. Mark stepped forward and handed the lantern and phone to Alana.

"Why, Noah, it's so nice you came here with my grand-daughter. It's our secret place, you know."

It didn't matter that she called Mark by his father's name. "Yes, Mrs. Somers, Alana told me. Let me help you down. Can you slide over here a little bit so I can reach you?"

Alana helped her move her legs, so they hung over the rock. Mark put his arms on either side of her. Alana slid off the rock and stood ready to help if needed.

The old woman slid into his arms, and he set her on the ground. "She's light as a feather, Lanie," he whispered. He continued to support her with one hand under her arm and his other arm around her back. "Your dad said to call 911. You can tell them how to get here. He wants her to be checked out at the hospital. Your parents will meet us there."

She made the call, then stepped to Grammy's other side. Alana clasped Grammy's hand with her arm under Grammy's while holding the lantern with her free hand. They made slow progress along the trail and arrived back at the museum building as the ambulance pulled in. Alana had asked the 911 operator to tell the ambulance driver to keep the flashing lights and siren off because they might frighten her grandmother.

The EMT helped Grammy lie on the gurney and covered her with a light blanket. Grammy remained still with her eyes closed as the EMT examined her. Alana let out a breath, thankful for the comfort of Mark's arm around her.

"She has dementia and wandered away from her home this afternoon," Alana told the EMT.

"Ah, yes, Mrs. Somers. I heard the call come over the radio. I thought they'd stopped looking until morning."

"I'm her granddaughter. She used to bring me here." Her voice shook, and she shivered. "When I remembered this place, I couldn't wait until morning."

"We'll get her to the hospital. Are you responsible for her care?"

"No, my parents will meet us at the hospital."

"She's all right for the moment. You can follow us."

Mama and Daddy met them at the emergency room door when they arrived.

CHAPTER TWENTY-NINE

fter the doctor verified that Grammy wasn't hurt and said there was nothing more to be done for her at the hospital, Mama put Grammy to bed at home, and they sat together in the living room, Mark and Alana on the loveseat facing her parents on the sofa. Her mother set the baby monitor, which emitted Grammy's soft snores, on the coffee table.

Daddy looked at Mama. She nodded. He licked his lips. "We're making arrangements for home hospice care."

Alana's stomach knotted. "How long?" She wasn't ready for her grandmother to die.

Mark squeezed her hand. He understood.

"It could happen any time. She does little for herself now, and your mother needs help with her."

Mama put her arms around Daddy.

"You should have told me. I could have come more often." She'd been so wrapped up in her own life, she'd neglected her family.

Mama shook her head. "That's all right, honey. We've had help. You've been stepping in for me by helping Ellie with Ian. And you're here now."

"When I said it was time to go home, she agreed. Do you think she meant heaven?"

"We may never know for sure, Lanie." Daddy shrugged. "Her health and memory have been failing for a long time. She's ready to go."

"What a wonderful legacy she will leave." Mark's words eased her sadness.

"Yes. And for now, she's home and safe in bed." Daddy stood and pulled Mama up. "We've had a long day, and tomorrow will be busy. I suggest we all get some sleep."

In the hallway linen closet, Alana found sheets, a blanket, and a pillow for Mark. She began to unfold a sheet when he laid his hand on her arm. "I'll make up the sofa. You need to get some rest."

"I am tired." She dropped the sheet and yawned. "It's been a stressful day. I'm so glad you came with me, and that you helped me find my grandmother."

"It's not a problem." He rested his hands on her shoulders. "I know this is a hard time for you. It's a privilege for me to be allowed to join your family in this."

"My parents like you, Mark. They're happy to have you here. Perhaps there's a reason God is allowing us this time together."

He drew her to him with an intensity in his blue eyes that sent a chill down her spine. She closed her eyes as their lips met in a tender and comforting kiss. He released her when she pushed gently against his chest before the kiss became too intense.

"Good night, Lanie." He kissed her forehead.

"Good night, Mark."

TWO WEEKS LATER, Mark attended the memorial service for Alana's grandmother. Friends and relatives packed the church in

Kellersville. Many people shared stories about her, some made everyone laugh, some brought everyone to tears, including Mark.

As in Mark's time of bereavement, such an outpouring of love brought comfort and strength to the grieving family. These people mingled so much joy with their sorrow. Laughter brought healing to the heart.

After a dinner for the family and friends in the church fellowship hall, a small group of family members gathered at Mrs. Somers's house. Mark couldn't remember the names of all Alana's relatives he'd met today, but there'd be plenty of time in the future to learn them.

Alana motioned to him, and he followed her into the kitchen. She sighed and sat at the table. He took a seat beside her and clasped her hand.

"I'm tired." She covered a yawn.

"It has been a busy day for you and your family. Grief drains a person's reservoir of energy." He rubbed his thumb across the back of her hand.

"It's strange here without Grammy. It feels empty, even with a house full of people. Her belongings are still here, but her presence is gone. Does that make sense?"

Mark squeezed her hand. "I believe I know what you mean. It's different than when she'd go out for a while and you expected her to come back. She's left the Earth now."

"I'm so glad I could be here for her last days, even though she spent a lot of time sleeping in her room while we took turns sitting with her. I'm so grateful for the time Daddy carried her out, and I played the piano for her." Alana licked her lips.

"I'm sure she enjoyed that."

"And when she passed, it was a beautiful moment. Mama and Daddy, my aunt and uncle, and I were all there. She opened her eyes and reached out, and then we knew she was gone. She's up there singing in the heavenly choir." She ended with a sob.

He listened to her, his heart full. With his thumb, he gently wiped a tear from her cheeks.

"Maybe she, Blythe, and Rachael are singing together." His comment brought a smile to her lips.

"I miss her, but I'm glad she doesn't have to suffer anymore and that my parents don't have to continue giving up so much of themselves to keep her at home, even though they loved caring for her." She got up and pulled a tissue from the box on the counter.

"Do you feel up to taking a walk?" He held out his hand.

She grasped it. "I do. Let me tell my parents and say goodbye to any of my relatives who will leave soon."

Alana hugged her relatives, and Mark shook their hands. He and Alana left the house by the front door and headed down the street as everyone except her parents and the Jakobs drove away.

He intertwined his fingers with Alana's, and they strolled hand in hand along the street and turned the corner toward the school. "You and Ellie sang so beautifully at the service. I know it touched and comforted many hearts to hear your grandmother's favorite hymn."

"Thank you."

"I also loved how you sang it with her that night at the waterfall. Is it too far for us to walk there now? I'd like to see it in the daytime." A perfect place to talk in private.

"It's about fifteen minutes from here. I'd like to see it again too. Now that Grammy's gone, I won't have a reason to return to Kellersville."

"Let's do it then. There's plenty of daylight left."

Now that they had a destination, they quickened their steps. In a few minutes, they crossed the schoolyard and entered another residential neighborhood. Kids screamed from backyard swimming pools, people tended gardens, and the scent of barbequed meat made Mark's mouth water.

The sun filtered through the trees along the trail. The sound of the waterfall reached his ears before it came into view. Alana didn't speak. He remained quiet as well, giving her time to process her thoughts and memories and giving him a chance to pray about what he would say.

She scrambled up on the rock without his assistance. He followed and settled beside her.

"I can see why your grandmother loved this place."

The water shushed as it fell over the rocky ledge. A cardinal called, echoed by another across the way, and a robin sang. The leaves on the trees trembled in the light breeze.

Alana rested her head on his shoulder. "I was scared that night, Mark, so afraid we'd find her unconscious or dead. Thank you for going with me."

"You stayed calm, and this place came to your mind right after we prayed, which I'm sure was no coincidence." *A God thing.*

"And we found her together. I don't know how she ever made it this far alone and without anyone seeing her." Her voice trembled. "But she remembered the way, and God was with her."

He put his arm around her. "She seemed to be present, yet somewhere else at the same time."

They sat without speaking for a few minutes, and Mark absorbed the peace surrounding him. Alana's faith and compassion drew him to her, and an acute awareness of Alana's softness and scent filled him with hope and desire.

"Lanie?"

"Yes."

He licked his lips. "I'm excited about becoming a pastor. I know there will be bumps along the way, but I'm as sure as I can be that I'm headed in the right direction."

She gazed up at him. "I know you are, Mark."

Her confidence gave him courage. "I want you with me, as my wife."

She pulled away from him, wrapped her arms around her

legs, and rested her chin on her knees, saying nothing. His side grew cold where her body had leaned against him. His stomach bubbled.

The minutes before she spoke crept by like hours. "I love God, and I love God's people. Church has been a big part of my life as long as I can remember. But it scares me to even consider being a pastor's wife."

"Why?" He had to know.

She rocked back and forth. "I'm afraid I'll fail."

"You're a woman of compassion and courage. You've faced disasters in your work among refugees in Third World countries. God has gifted you in many ways." How could he convince her?

"I'm not a leader, Mark, not like you. Not like Mrs. Clary."

Is this what has been bothering her? He laid his hand against her back. She inhaled sharply but didn't pull away. "Leadership in a church is an awesome responsibility," he agreed.

She turned her head and studied him.

"I'm a fallible human being. When I think that my lack of knowledge, mistakes, or sins as a spiritual leader could influence another person's decision to accept or reject Christ, I'm fearful of failing too. That's why I need God's Word, prayer, and the Holy Spirit. I'm not in this alone."

He removed his hand and rested it on the stone. He longed to trace her profile with his finger and touch the softness of her cheek, but she had to think this through without distraction. With or without her, he'd obey God's call into ministry, but he'd envisioned her by his side.

She turned her body and faced him, setting up a barrier by crisscrossing her legs in front of her. "My path is not as well-defined as yours. I still have my commitment to the IAS, and after that, probably nursing school or something else."

"And …?"

"I can't talk in front of groups of people. When I'm asked about pain and suffering and death, I don't have answers. I misjudge people and jump to conclusions about them. Not one of my IAS coworkers has become a Christian because of me." She stared at the waterfall.

"Your fears and doubts can be overcome with God's help." *If she'll let Him.*

She leaned her forehead on her knees. "You need someone who won't hold you back."

"Alana." He touched her arm.

She jumped and raised her head, but avoided his gaze.

"Please, forgive me." He removed his hand. "It was thoughtless of me to bring this up now. It's not a good time because you're grieving."

"I forgive you." She inhaled and exhaled slowly. "I don't want to argue with you."

"Thank you," he whispered. His heart ached. A cloud of uncertainty hung between them.

Had he misread the signs, or was it her grief speaking? She'd encouraged him to follow God's leading. Would he be continuing on his way without her?

She didn't look at him, didn't touch him. He longed to hold her and make it right between them, but the stiffness in her body created a wall between them.

She turned away. "We'd better go back now, or my parents will worry."

No, they won't worry. I'm with you, and you have your cell phone. He didn't contradict her out loud. "Do you think they'll send Ellie and Ben out looking for us?"

Alana frowned. "I hope not." She shrugged. "But you never know."

She didn't smile at his attempted humor.

He slid off the rock and turned to catch her. She landed beside him without his help.

~

ALANA HELD Mark's hand on the way back, hating the tension that lay between them. He didn't talk, and neither did she. She pressed her lips together and suppressed the threatening tears. She'd cry in private.

The past two weeks had created a tighter bond between them, a greater knowledge and understanding of one another. He'd gone out of his way to support her and her family at a time of crisis and loss.

Instead of asking him to wait for an answer, or saying she'd pray about it, she blurted out the fears that had been brewing in her mind since he first told her. Did she really want to come between Mark and God, make him choose? No, she didn't. She loved him and didn't want to lose him, but her fears were real. How could she be so messed up?

Help, Lord.

"I have to leave when we get back to your grandmother's house." He'd come to Kellersville this morning to be with her for the memorial service.

"I know. But, Mark—"

"Let's leave it for now, Alana." His clipped tone shut down her protest.

She'd hurt him. "All right." Her heart dropped. It wasn't all right.

Soon after they returned to the house, Mark said goodbye to her parents and Ellie's family and drove away. Alana let her family believe grief for Grammy alone caused her depressed spirits.

CHAPTER THIRTY

lana slept in on Saturday, after returning to Millvale late Friday night. Mark was busy all day on Saturday with work, a meeting with the pastor, and catching up on his coursework. They briefly texted one another, but she didn't see him.

When they sat together in church on Sunday, neither she nor Mark spoke about what happened between them on Friday. A home visitation with Pastor Clary and an emergency meeting with the deacon board filled Mark's afternoon. He kept yawning during the evening service and excused himself from their usual tea and chocolate chip cookies at the diner afterward. He stayed busy during the next week with work and ministry. She didn't see him for several days.

Finally, on Thursday, Alana waited for Mark on a park bench along the River Walk. They often walked here on Thursdays when he finished work early enough. The intense heat of the summer day had cooled somewhat, and a slight breeze blew across the river.

Would he come to the park this evening?

Could the damage she'd done to their relationship be repaired? She could only try.

When he appeared in the distance, she trembled and curled her fingers around the edge of the bench so she wouldn't jump up and run to him.

Mark, I'm sorry, I didn't mean what I said. No, that wasn't right. *Mark, I'm sorry I hurt your feelings.* She was sorry, but that's not what she wanted to say. *Mark, I don't want to lose you.*

"Hello, Alana." He stood in front of her, still in his work clothes, handsome as ever. "I thought you might be here."

His beloved voice drew her eyes to his face. "Mark, I ..." Anything she planned to say escaped her mind. She sank into his sapphire gaze. Instead of condemnation, his eyes expressed tenderness and concern.

He dropped beside her and gripped her hand. "Lanie, I'm so sorry."

"What? Why?" She'd been the one to offend.

"I was thoughtless. In my excitement for myself, I sprang something you weren't ready for. Please forgive me." His thumb rubbed the back of her hand, sending a tingle up her arm.

She'd already forgiven him. "I forgive you," she said. The knots in her stomach loosened.

"Thank you." The lines on his forehead relaxed.

She lowered her eyes to their joined hands. "I want to explain why I reacted as I did." If she pulled her hand from his, she could think better. Yet, his warm grasp encouraged her.

"You don't have to. It was bad timing on my part."

"Yes, I do." She had to get this off her conscience. She withdrew her hand from his.

"I'm listening." He sat back.

Folding her hands in her lap, she glanced at him and looked away.

"My sister is a leader, but I'm not. I've never liked getting up in front of people. I'd rather help in the background."

He nodded.

"I met with Mrs. Clary yesterday. She told me to pray about

my fears and talk to you. She reminded me all Christians are sinners and imperfect. And she told me about some of her experiences as a pastor's wife."

Mark leaned forward and rested his arms on his legs. "Pastor said they've made their share of mistakes in their years of ministry."

"We talked about personalities and gifts, and how God made each of us and uses us in different ways. I'm not surprised God called you, but I don't know how I will fit in." She met his gaze. "My greatest fear is that my failures will hold you back."

"When I look at you, I see your strengths, not your weaknesses." He leaned toward her and took her hand. "I'm not perfect either. I'll succeed in ministry only with God's help." He squeezed her hand, his grasp warm and confident. "We'll take this slowly, and I'll wait until you're ready."

She nodded, wanting to believe. Her schoolgirl's dream had become reality, and Mark offered her a lifetime with him. What if she couldn't overcome her self-doubt and fear? What if Mark couldn't wait for her as long as she needed? What if God had other plans?

Two sweaty joggers passed along the walk, pulling her eyes from Mark's face. A family of bicyclists followed on their way to the beach. A couple walked by with a dog on a leash.

She had a favor to ask of Mark, but would he do it? With what had transpired between them, did she have the right to ask?

Alana clasped her hands in her lap. "Ellie and I have to go back to Kellersville to help clean out my grandmother's house this weekend. Will you take care of Mittens for me?"

She held her breath. If he refused, she'd ask Lucinda. But she wanted him to meet Mittens.

He didn't hesitate. "I will. Mittens and I can become acquainted before ..."

Before I leave. She didn't want to say those words either.

"Thank you." She breathed again.

While she completed her work with the IAS, would Mark wait, or would he change his mind?

What had Mark said? With God's help, she would have to find a way to overcome her fear.

LOVE AT FIRST PURR. Playful, curious, and cuddly, Mittens made herself at home in Mark's apartment.

On Friday after work, he sat in his recliner with his computer doing some online research for an assignment. Mittens sat on the floor beside his chair and looked up at him. Her blue-green eyes blinked, and she tilted her head. "Mew."

Mark chuckled. "All right, little one. I guess there's room up here for you." He scooped her up and set her beside him. Immediately, she curled up.

"Ouch!" He grimaced and pulled her claws from his pant leg. She curled up in a different position. He stroked her soft fur. He could easily get used to having the kitten around all the time. However, he'd rather have Alana.

Having Mittens there made Mark long even more for Alana's presence as his wife.

After Alana's response to his declaration last Friday, would that ever happen? Even after their talk in the park, he couldn't be sure.

Finishing his research, he made an outline, then turned off his computer. Mittens followed him into the kitchen, where he got a drink of water. When he returned to the living room, he called Alana. Mittens jumped into the chair and helped herself to his lap.

"Hello, Alana … Mittens is fine, making herself at home. Have you made progress with your grandmother's house?"

That night, Alana appeared in his dreams, leaving only an impression of her presence in his memory. He awoke with a light, warm weight pressed against his back. He turned over carefully. Mittens looked up at him and blinked.

"You know, kitty, I might have to convince Alana to let me keep you."

When he returned from his morning run, Mittens waited for him just inside the door. After he showered and dressed, Mitten's gaze followed his hand as he ate breakfast. He laughed. She stared at him, then washed herself.

After texting a morning message to Alana, he scooped the kitten up. "I haven't seen much of my brother lately. Let's go see Jack." Did everyone who owned a cat talk to it?

After closing and locking his door, he climbed down the stairs. He stopped at the bottom.

A tingling sensation ran across his neck. "Is someone there?" No response. Mittens pricked her ears and stared at the bushes beside the parking lot. Mark walked over, certain this time to find someone. A stalker? Someone targeting Jack's business?

A bird twittered and flew out from the branches. Mark gasped and laughed at himself.

Inside the store, he set Mittens on the counter and introduced her to Jack and his employees. Mark wiggled his fingers at the kitten, and Mittens pounced. She rubbed her face against his hand, then she rolled over and caught it between her front paws. Mark couldn't stop the grin that spread across his face.

"You seem smitten." Jack took his turn, stroking her back.

"I'm not sure I'll give her back when this weekend is over."

"Alana may take exception to that."

"We'll work something out." He lifted Mittens from the counter and headed for the door. "I don't have to work today, but I have a book to read for my course, and I know you have work to do. Say hi to Kate for me." He debated whether he should invite himself to Jack and Kate's for supper.

"Speaking of Kate."

Mark turned back.

Jack stepped up to him. "She mentioned you haven't been over for a while. She's making spaghetti and meatballs tonight. The scent of her homemade sauce made the house smell heavenly this morning. She said to invite you over if you want to come."

"I'll be there." Only having Alana to go with him would be better.

❧

THE SUNSET PAINTED a rosy glow along the western horizon. Mark pulled into the parking lot at home, the dish of leftovers sending out a delicious aroma. The evening with Jack and Kate had been a relaxing way to end a busy week. Only Alana's absence kept him from calling the evening perfect.

He pressed the button on the key fob to lock the car door and headed for the stairs. All remained quiet, except for a robin's cheery evening song, a dog's bark, and the yelling of some children at play.

Mittens greeted him at the door, meowing and rubbing against his leg. He set his food in the refrigerator and picked her up.

"It's time to call Alana, kitty. She'll be home tomorrow." He longed to see her.

A thread of unease still hung over him. Even if she overcame her fears, she might decide the life he'd chosen wasn't for her.

By the time he finished his call, the dim light from above the kitchen sink shined through the doorway, leaving the room otherwise dark. Alana's family had completed their task, and she and her sister would return to Millvale in time for church tomorrow evening. He could hardly wait.

He stood by the living room window, looking out over Main Street. A few vehicles passed by.

He started to pull the shade down, when three figures

stopped in front of the building. In the streetlight, they looked like young men, and they stood close together, as though sharing a secret. They gestured with their hands and pointed at Jack's store.

When they turned to face the building, Mark stepped to the side of the window, so they wouldn't see him. Were they up to something? One of them turned his head.

"What is Carter Eastman doing in Millvale, on the street in front of JC Computers, at ten o'clock at night?"

Probably no good.

The three walked away five minutes later. Mark checked from different angles to see where they'd gone. He looked out his other windows and detected no movement nearby. Relieved, he pulled down the shades. He didn't want trouble with his boss's son.

Every attempt Mark made to be cordial, Carter took as an invitation to insult him. Was he jealous because Mark worked for Eastman's Cabinetry, or was there something more going on—a spiritual battle within the young man that manifested itself in anger and disrespect? Mark saw in their faces that Dennis and Grace both carried wounds from their son's rebellion. He prayed for all three, but he didn't know how to help them except to pray.

CHAPTER THIRTY-ONE

"*H*e's asleep, Ellie." The mirror behind Ian reflected the peaceful face of Alana's nephew in his car seat.

"I think he'll sleep the rest of the way. He's had a busy weekend." Ellie looked in the rearview mirror and then at the side mirror as a minivan passed.

Alana straightened and faced forward. The weekend had been bittersweet, and they were returning to Millvale.

She and Ellie, along with their aunt and uncle and some cousins, had finished sorting through Grammy's personal belongings. Each of them chose a few items to keep. Alana picked some of her favorite music books and sheet music as well as a necklace and earring set and some photos.

Alana took a deep breath and released it as she leaned back in her seat. "Ben will probably be glad to have you and Ian back."

"Yes, and we'll be glad to see him and be back home. He's kept busy and had a good time with Jack and Kate and Mark at the diner after the morning worship service."

"Mark texted they'd eaten there."

"I know I can be nosey, so I've tried not to pry, especially since I said what I did about Mark at our dinner on Mother's Day." Ellie glanced at her with the same teasing twinkle Daddy often had.

"That was embarrassing." But she could laugh about it now.

"You and Mark seemed to be getting along well. But recently, I've noticed some tension between you. Is everything all right?" Ellie gave her a concerned sister look.

Ellie didn't have to know what happened after Grammy's memorial service. It was between Mark and her and God.

She took a deep breath. "Mark and I still have some things to work out." She frowned. "Don't begin planning our wedding yet."

Ellie laughed. "You just want to spoil my fun. Whenever you're ready, I'm here to help. You know I'll at least do your flowers."

"Thank you." Would she ever be ready?

Ellie parked her van in the church parking lot ten minutes before church time. Ben, waiting on the steps, hurried to meet them. Ellie got out and embraced her husband.

Would Mark one day meet her and embrace her like that?

Alana unbuckled Ian from his car seat. He gave her a sleepy smile, and she kissed his cheek before his daddy claimed him.

Hanging her purse strap over her shoulder and retrieving her Bible from the back seat, she walked into the church. Mark stood in the aisle talking with Mrs. Matthews. He looked over his shoulder at Alana, and his eyes lit up. Her breath caught, and her heart beat double time. How she'd missed him.

Mrs. Matthews looked from him to her, smiled, and patted his hand before joining her husband where he sat in a pew.

Butterflies took over as Mark walked toward her, lips curving into a wonderful smile. The clasp of his hand sent warmth through her.

"It's good to have you home." The welcome in his eyes drew her into their blue depths. "How did it go?"

"We finished. My parents will return to Millvale by Friday." She followed him to a pew. "Did you have any problems with Mittens?"

"Not a bit."

The prelude music indicated the service was about to begin. She slid into the pew, and he sat beside her. The rest of their catching up would have to wait until after the service.

Mark took notes during Pastor Clary's sermon. Alana listened as she followed along in her Bible, but it was difficult to not be distracted by the man beside her.

A sudden stir in the auditorium caught her attention. An usher whispered something in Jack Chambers's ear. He stood and looked at Mark, tilting his head toward the back, his face grim and pale.

"I'll be back. Something's up," he whispered in her ear.

Mark went out with his brother. Alana looked over at Kate, who shrugged. She faced forward and attempted to listen as the pastor spoke.

Although still speaking, Pastor Clary had his eyes on the doorway through which the two men disappeared. Members of the congregation kept peering over their shoulders. The usher approached the pastor, who paused his sermon to listen. He nodded, and the usher returned to the back of the church.

Clearing his throat, the pastor looked over the congregation. "Jack Chambers received word that someone attempted to break-in to his store. We don't have any more details. I think we should pray before we go on with the service."

Kate gasped. Alana could hardly sit still as she waited for the pastor to finish his prayer. She didn't know whether she should stay put or go to Mark. As soon as the prayer ended, Kate rushed out, and Alana followed.

"Jack texted me to wait here." Kate folded her arms around her abdomen. "But he may need my help."

Alana pulled her trembling friend into a hug. "Jack knows you're safe at church. The police are most likely there. Why don't we wait here until the service is over? If the men aren't back by then, we can go."

Kate's gaze dropped to the ground. "I don't know if Jack took his van. I don't have a key for Mark's car."

"The van is still in the parking lot. Over there." Alana pointed. "They must have taken Mark's car."

"The thieves probably didn't account for Jack's excellent security system. He had one installed in the apartment as well." Kate still trembled as they went back inside.

When Alana returned to her seat in the pew with Kate beside her, the pastor gave them an almost imperceptible nod. Alana's brain didn't absorb the words or meaning of the sermon. She and Kate hurried out to the van before the final song ended.

Police cruiser lights flashed in front of JC Computers. Spectators crowded the sidewalk, and a couple of news vans lined the curb. After Kate parked down the street, Alana ran with her to the scene. Lights shined from the store windows and in the apartment upstairs.

Kate pulled her through the spectators and approached the police officer on crowd control. "I'm Kate Chambers, Jack's wife. Can you tell me anything?"

"Just a moment, ma'am. I'll see if I can find someone." The officer spoke to another, who stood by the door. He went in, and moments later, Jack came out. A news reporter must have spotted him because a camera flashed.

Kate threw her arms around Jack. He held her close and said, "The alarm system evidently scared them away. They broke in the back door and the apartment, but there's nothing missing from either place."

"Where's Mark?" Alana looked up at the lighted apartment windows.

"He's upstairs talking to the investigator. Some people across the street witnessed the break-in and gave descriptions of the perpetrators. The police will probably take another hour here, and Mark and I will speak to the media." The crowd-control officer was talking to a TV reporter from a local station.

Mark descended the stairs, and his sober look transformed into a smile when he saw Alana. She met him in the parking lot.

"Are you all right, Mark?" She rested her hand on his arm. He appeared calm.

"I'm fine. Nothing was stolen or broken." He turned so his arm lay around her shoulders, and she snuggled against him.

"Jack said there were witnesses who gave descriptions of the would-be thieves." They had to be held accountable.

"I think it's only a matter of time before they're found. They fit the description of three young guys I saw out front last night." He held out a small body. "Here's someone I think will be glad to see you."

"Mittens!" Mittens stared at her with wide eyes, her little body trembling. "Poor kitty." Refugee children often wore the same look of terror. No purr vibrated from Mittens's throat as Alana held her to her chest.

"I found her under my bed, and it took me a while to coax her out. The noise from the alarms must have terrified her." He scratched the kitten's head. "Let's go see Jack and Kate."

Jack and Kate faced each other in front of the store. Kate's tense posture and Jack's hand gestures indicated a disagreement.

"I told Kate she should go home." Jack's lips were set in a straight line. "We'll be finished here soon."

"If I have the van, how will you get home?" Alana frowned. Kate only wanted to be with the man she loved in his time of crisis.

"I'm sure my brother will take me."

Mark nodded.

"Kate, why don't you come to my house?" Alana looped her arm through Kate's. "I'm sure the guys are hungry. I know I am. We can have something ready for them to eat when they come."

Jack shot her a look of appreciation.

"All right." Kate relaxed. "I guess I can't help here." She gave Jack a quick kiss.

Mittens settled into the crook of Alana's arm, and a contented purr poured from her throat.

Mark squeezed Alana's shoulder. "We'll all need some time to unwind after this, although I think Mittens has already relaxed. I'll bring her things when we come over."

When Mark kissed the top of Alana's head, a tremor passed through her. "Thank you, Mark. We'll see you in a little while."

MARK HESITATED to name Carter Eastman as one of the would-be robbers. However, the witnesses' descriptions fit him, and he'd seen Carter in front of the store late last night. Also, Carter had been angry when Jack turned him down for employment at JC Computers.

How could he face his employer if he identified Carter by name?

Because Carter always gave Mark a hard time, Dennis might think Mark was out to get his son. Yet Dennis was a fair and reasonable man. They'd worked together long enough that Dennis trusted Mark and his work.

If Mark turned Carter in, would Dennis ever trust him again as a friend and as an employee?

"God, help me do what I have to do," he whispered as Alana and Kate got into Jack's van and drove away.

"Mark!" Jack waved him over. The police investigator stood in front of a microphone where he gave a statement and answered a few questions from the media. Jack and Mark then gave statements. Once the interview ended, the crowd drifted away, and the media vans drove off.

Jack went into JC Computers to turn off the lights and lock up, while Mark remained to talk to the police. Before Mark left, he collected Mittens's supplies from his apartment, reset the alarm, and locked his door. He met Jack at his car in the parking lot.

Mark buckled his seatbelt and leaned back in the driver's seat. "Several times recently, I thought someone was watching me from the bushes. I never saw anyone, but I wonder if they were spying, searching for the best time to break in."

"They knew we're gone on Sunday nights, because the store is closed, and you're at church."

"Yes." He placed the key in the ignition and started the car. "I told the police I know one of the suspects."

Jack's head whipped in his direction. "You do?"

Mark nodded. "Carter Eastman."

"You're sure?"

"He was one of the men I saw in front of the store last night. And the description from the witnesses tonight fits Carter." He'd tried to reach Carter but failed.

"He was pretty angry after I refused to hire him. He came back one other time. I never imagined he'd do something so stupid." Jack shook his head.

Mark rubbed the back of his neck. "He's a troubled young man. His parents will be heart broken."

"Will this cause a problem between you and Dennis?" Jack buckled his seatbelt.

"I don't know. Dennis and his son are in a battle of wills, and he knows Carter doesn't like me. But he's still Dennis's son. If Dennis and Grace learn I identified Carter, I may be out of a job."

"That would be unfair."

"Maybe so. I hoped the police would apprehend Carter before I had to tell them I knew him. Carter needs help, and the sooner the police catch all three of them, the sooner this will be over. It's in God's hands now." He started the car. "I hope the girls have the food ready. I'm hungry."

He'd feel better once he was with Alana again.

CHAPTER THIRTY-TWO

"You're healthy and you've gained back your weight. When your blood test results come in, I'll probably clear you to go back to work."

Alana's heart dropped at Dr. Cole's words. "Go back to work? Already?"

She'd known the time might be less than six months, and she'd been feeling so well lately. She should have been prepared for this. But four months was too soon.

When she came home in April, she wanted to go back as soon as possible. Now? Well, now there was Mark.

Dr. Cole shrugged. "I don't see why not. I'm sure the IAS will appreciate having you back."

"Yes, I believe so."

The doctor typed something into his computer. "Will you be going back to the same place?"

"As far as I know, I will. Unless my team has moved on, or they reassign me."

"When your test report comes in, I'll let the IAS know you're ready to work again." He closed down his computer application. "Do you have any questions?"

"No, I can't think of any." *My brain is on hold.*

"Miss Somers, I wish you luck." He held out his hand. "Have a good life and stay healthy."

She shook his hand. "Thank you, Dr. Cole."

"You can pick up a summary of today's appointment at the desk." He went out the door, leaving it ajar.

Alana retrieved her appointment summary and turned to Kate in the waiting area.

"How did it go?" Kate stood and met her.

"Good." At least, the report about her health was good. She wouldn't tell Kate more until she had a chance to let Mark know she was leaving. Her heart sank.

❧

AFTER DROPPING Kate off at home, Alana drove by JC Computers to find Mark's car wasn't in the parking lot. He often worked late on Fridays if he and Dennis had a project to finish before the weekend.

Mittens met Alana at her door. "Oh, Mittens." She scooped the kitten up and kissed the top of her head. "I'm going to miss you."

With Mittens in her arms, she went upstairs to give Mama and Daddy a report. She told them the same thing she told Kate and would tell them the rest after sharing it with Mark.

Alana wrestled with her conscience. She had a job to return to and a contract to fulfill. Perhaps she'd become too accustomed to the comforts of home with family and friends around her.

❧

AFTER SUPPER at the diner on Saturday, Alana and Mark ambled along the River Walk, neither of them speaking. She didn't think her news alone troubled him. He told her his online class challenged him, but she suspected something else lay heavy on his mind. Since the break-in, he hinted at added stress at work.

She clung to his hand. When she returned to her job, she might lose him forever.

"When do you leave?" His question startled her out of her thoughts.

"Once the test results are in, IAS headquarters will be in touch with me. I expect no more than two weeks, maybe less." She looked past him at the river flowing nearby.

"I counted on you being here until October. My life in Millvale will be missing a piece without you, Lanie. You've filled the lonely places in my life." He pulled her hand to his chest.

"It's only for a little while." A lot could happen in the next few months.

"I know." He sighed. "The time will pass quickly, I hope."

"So do I." She'd stay busy.

They walked a little farther, the sounds of children playing on the playground, the flow of the river, and their soft footsteps filling the air.

"Mark, is something troubling you? I mean, something more than my news?"

"I don't want to burden you." He gave her a brief glance.

"Doesn't the Bible say we should share each other's burdens? You shared mine when I was ill and when Grammy died." She squeezed his hand. "Will you let me share yours?"

Mark's chest rose and fell with a deep breath. "I've enjoyed working with Dennis. He's a good teacher, and I've learned a lot of carpentry skills from him. I've enjoyed our discussions about God, faith, and the church."

His voice broke a little on his last sentence. He stopped talking and lowered his eyes.

She wanted him to talk out the hurt he held within. "But ..." she prompted.

"He's been different since Carter's arrest. As a man and as a father, I believe he feels responsible, thinks he's failed his son. He's absent-minded at work and makes mistakes. He often picks up a wrong tool, or he starts to fasten the hinges on a cabinet door backwards. He's had to cut new boards after measuring inaccurately. He uses strings of bad language, where before he only used one word occasionally."

His jaw clenched and released.

"Dennis said the police claim Carter's been selling drugs and using them. That gives him a motive for robbing Jack's store, to get money for drugs. One of the guys who broke in confessed to watching the store and my apartment, so they could find the best time to break in. I think Dennis is upset with me because I identified Carter."

Alana shivered, remembering her encounter with Carter and Mrs. Maines's intervention. She hadn't told Mark, and she wouldn't now.

She rested her free hand on his arm. "I'm so sorry, Mark. What can I do?"

He laid his hand over hers. "Will you pray with me, Lanie? Pray for healing in the Eastman family. Pray God will bring someone or something into their lives to give them hope and open their hearts to God's love and forgiveness."

"Of course." She pointed to a park bench located a short distance from the walk. With hands clasped, they sat side by side and prayed.

Her love for Mark was a melody reverberating in her heart. Strong, compassionate, with a desire to serve God, he'd drawn her to him and challenged her to share his life of dedication to and service for God.

Could she be who he needed? She had the months ahead, tested by a distance that might separate them, to discover the answer.

～

HOLDING A SINGLE RED SILK ROSE, Mark stood at Alana's door, waiting for her to answer his knock. He wore his brown suit with a red shirt because red was her favorite color.

He dreaded her leaving. He'd been left behind too many times in his life. *This time, Lord, please bring her back to me.*

She opened the door wearing the red dress she wore to church on Mother's Day.

His eyes locked with hers. "You look lovely." He handed her the rose.

"Thank you." She blushed.

He stepped in, pulled her into his arms, and kissed her. Her softness and sweet scent made his senses reel. He rested his chin on her head for a moment before letting her go.

"I gave you a silk rose tonight because you're going away. Otherwise, I'd have given you a bouquet of real red roses."

"Thank you, Mark." She laid the rose on a small table that held family photos. She recently added one of the two of them at the balloon festival. Gathering her purse and sweater, she joined him at the door. "I'm ready."

He'd made reservations at the restaurant beside Sayre's Point Lake. He chose Sayre's Point, because, that day at the balloon festival, he recognized her as a treasure. Like the virtuous wife in Proverbs 31, *her worth is far above rubies.* He wanted to be sure she understood he'd wait for her.

After seating them at a table by the window overlooking the lake, the waiter handed them menus. The lake rippled and reflected the lights along the walk between the restaurant and body of water. The soft lighting and cream and burgundy décor gave an air of elegance, yet families with children dined at some of the tables. In the peaceful atmosphere, with the woman he loved, Mark shed the tension from work that had held him in its grip during the past weeks.

"This is lovely." She opened her menu.

He smiled. "Yes, you are."

Her eyes, sparkling in the subdued lighting, met his over the top of her menu.

He admired her graceful, slender hands, the hands of a piano player, and the way her dark hair curled around her face. Her dress modestly accented her body curves, and the red color complimented her complexion.

After dinner, they walked arm in arm along the lake. "How about a moonlight boat ride on the lake?" He basked in the sweetness of her presence.

"We can do that? It sounds delightful."

"I made reservations. The dock is just ahead." He pointed.

They boarded a tour boat with other couples, and he led her to a padded bench along one side. He helped her put on her sweater as the cool breeze blew across the lake. When he placed his arm around her shoulders, she fit perfectly against his side. His heart raced.

"I'll remember this evening with you forever." She wove her fingers with his.

Resting his cheek against her hair, he said, "I want it to be memorable." Something to hold on to until she returned.

Moving slowly through the water, the boat's rocking soothed his nerves. The pilot steered around the contours of the lake. Trees and buildings along the shore stood faintly visible in the shadows.

"I didn't want to leave at first. I prayed I wouldn't have to go."

He leaned down to catch her softly spoken words.

"Now I'm ready."

Was he ready? "Will you miss me?"

She tipped her head up and lifted her hand to touch his cheek. "Of course, I will. There's no one else like you."

He rested his hand against hers. *Help me be worthy of her trust, Lord.*

After the hour-long boat ride, he took her home.

Alana gave Mittens one last hug before closing her into the cat carrier, then set a bag of cat supplies next to the carrier by the door. Mark would take Mittens with him tonight, leaving two less goodbyes for her in the morning before Ellie and Ben took her to the airport.

He kissed her, held her in his arms. How could he let her go?

"I love you, Lanie," he murmured against her hair.

"I know." She spoke from where her head rested against his chest.

He released her, disappointed she didn't say *I love you* back. He lifted the carrier and grasped the bag in his other hand.

After placing the carrier and the bag in the back seat, he turned for one more look at her. She blew him a kiss from her doorway.

CHAPTER THIRTY-THREE

"Welcome back, Miss Somers. You're looking well." Mr. Dickson, the head of the U.S. branch of the IAS, stood and shook her hand. He offered the chair in front of his desk for her to sit.

"Thank you." She sat, crossed her ankles, and folded her hands in her lap to keep them from trembling. She'd met Mr. Dickson several times while with the IAS. She liked his pleasant, business-like demeanor, but she always felt a little intimidated in his presence.

Returning to his chair, he folded his hands as he leaned on his desk. "The doctor has released you to go back to the field."

She nodded. "Yes, sir."

"You've been a valuable asset to our organization. I'm sorry you contracted malaria. It's one of the dangers of working in certain parts of the world." He lifted the top edge of a paper lying on his desk. "I see you have only a few more months on your contract. Will you be signing on for another five years?"

Alana had prepared an answer to this question. "I've appreciated my time with the IAS. It's a fine organization with a well-deserved reputation. I've benefited from the training and experience and met many great people. I've also gained a greater compassion for and understanding of people in other parts of the world." She took a breath.

"But …"He waited for her to say more.

"After my contract is up, I'm looking into possibly pursuing a career in nursing and, well, other things." Perhaps a lifetime with Mark.

He sat back. "It's difficult to see so much suffering and live under such harsh conditions. Many of our workers find other careers, and many get married. I'm not surprised by your decision, but I'll be sorry to see you go."

He shifted some papers on his desk. "I don't know if you're aware of it, but your team has been asked to leave by the country's leaders. They believe the crisis is over and the people can return to their homes."

"No, I didn't know." Busy taking care of Ian, preparing for her return, and spending time with Mark, she'd had little contact with her friends in the field.

"They're packing up, and they'll be leaving in the next day or two. After a brief home leave, they'll be reassigned."

"Where will I be going?"

He'd already stated her value, so he wouldn't fire her, would he? Perhaps the team would move to a more remote place with a different kind of danger. It wasn't likely he'd release her from the remainder of her contract so she could go home and begin the rest of her life now.

Mr. Dickson leaned forward and tapped his pen on his desk. "With the yearly turnover of staff, we always need to recruit more workers."

"Yes, I'm aware of that." He had her attention.

"I'm offering you the opportunity to remain in the U.S. for the remainder of your contract time, to represent the IAS as a recruiter."

"Me? A recruiter?" She swallowed. She'd have to stand in front of people and talk as she represented the organization.

"Your experience in the field is a key factor in this offer. You're already here at headquarters, your team is being reassigned, and you have less than a year left. The IAS will cover all travel expenses, and you'll receive your regular pay with time off for Christmas."

What do you want me to do, Lord?

Recruiting offered an opportunity for her to overcome her fear of public speaking. And she'd be home for Christmas.

Her decision made, peace settled over her. "I accept your offer, Mr. Dickson."

"I thought you might." He smiled. "We'll give you training for a week here at headquarters. The first part of your itinerary is already filled. You'll be working with another employee with field experience." He checked a paper on his desk. "Nicholas Ames."

"Nicholas?" She changed her position in the chair, her stomach tightening. "I worked with him in the field." She hadn't had any contact with Nicholas since the day he appeared on her doorstep. "He came home to take courses to update his medical license."

"A course in tropical medicine that he wants to take isn't available until January. He's helping us set up training classes for medical personnel who sign on with us."

Alana could work with Nicholas, remain friends, so long as he respected her boundaries.

Home for Christmas. Home meant family and Mark Chambers.

CHAPTER THIRTY-FOUR

After opening gifts and eating breakfast with her parents on Christmas morning, Alana helped Mama with dinner preparations. Ellie, Ben, and Ian had arrived mid-morning, soon followed by Mark. Mark's greeting last night before the Christmas Eve service had been warm and tender, and she'd clung to him. She'd missed him so much. In their few semi-private moments this morning, his embrace and kiss were a repeat of last night.

Now, Mama called for her help to set the table, and Mark was caught up in a discussion with her father and brother-in-law.

After finishing her task, Alana got down on the living room floor with Ian who was playing with his new wooden blocks. "Hey, Ian."

Her nephew grinned and held out two blocks to her.

"May I join you?" Mark lowered himself beside her, his shoulder brushing hers. She breathed in his clean, spicy scent, and his fervent gaze activated the butterflies in her stomach.

During four months on the road as an IAS recruiter, Alana's love grew with Mark's daily calls, texts, and emails. Although fear and doubt surfaced occasionally, she knew she belonged beside him in ministry. If he asked her to marry him, she had her answer ready.

He said he loved me and would wait, but is he willing to risk asking me again after my refusal?

He helped Ian stack blocks in his new wooden truck and push it around on the floor, making motor sounds. Ian laughed. Mark would be a good father.

Mark winked, sending shivers down her spine. Had he read her mind?

When the family sat down at the table for dinner, Alana's heart overflowed with joy and thanksgiving.

"Praise God from Whom all blessings flow …" she sang.

Everyone joined in. Then Daddy prayed.

Late in the afternoon, Ellie's family went home with dishes of leftovers and a box full of gifts. Mama and Daddy settled down in the living room to watch a Christmas movie.

"Shall we take a walk, Lanie?" Mark's invitation came with an extended hand and a look she couldn't resist. He had something on his mind, and she hoped she knew what it was.

"I'd love to." She'd had no time alone with Mark today and only one more day before returning to work.

She slipped her feet into her boots. Mark helped her with her red winter coat, a gift from her parents. She added her gloves, a hat, and the lovely red scarf Mark had given her.

"We won't be long," she called out as Mark opened the door.

"Have fun," Daddy's voice came back.

Alana shivered in the crisp air. Mark turned his coat collar up and pulled her against his side. The snow reflected the light from the streetlights and lawn decorations as they sauntered along.

"I'm blessed to be home this Christmas when I expected to be far away." She'd experienced homesickness at Christmas in the IAS camps.

"I'm glad you're here, and I love being with your family." He smiled. "They make me feel at home."

"Mama and Daddy have a gift for hospitality, and they love that you joined us."

"I'm thankful." He glanced at her. "I would have brought Mittens over to see you, but I thought the crowd of people might frighten her."

"Probably wise. I'll stop by to see her tomorrow." She didn't want Mittens to forget her. "Thank you for taking care of her for me."

"My pleasure."

The light wind blew some snow from a tree down on them. They laughed and brushed snow off each other. She nestled her hand in the crook of his arm, and they continued their stroll toward the park.

"Do you like recruiting with Nicholas?"

"He's been professional and a perfect gentleman." Strange. She hadn't expected Mark to bring up Nicholas.

"Good. Do you like recruiting?"

She shrugged. "I like meeting the people, and I'm learning to speak in front of groups. I'm traveling and promoting a good company. But I wouldn't choose it as a profession."

"Would you choose pastor's wife as a profession?"

Her heart beat faster. Did that mean what she thought it meant? Her gaze darted to his face, but she couldn't discern his expression in the dim light. Unable to speak, she nodded.

Although the park was closed for the night, Mark directed her to the large stone beside the entrance with room enough for them both to sit.

"Thanks for the books." He tucked his hands into his coat pockets. "They're on my 'want to read' list."

"Pastor Clary suggested them. He said he uses them often." She fingered her soft scarf, waiting.

"When I learned you'd be home for Christmas, I went out and bought this." He pulled a small red box from one pocket.

"Mark!" she breathed.

"Since you aren't working in the camp where jewelry might be a problem, I thought you could wear it now." He lowered himself to one knee. "Alana Somers, I love you. Will you marry me?"

When he opened the box, the diamond ring sparkled in the light at the park entrance.

"Oh, Mark, it's beautiful!" She looked from the diamond to the man holding it. "I love you. Yes, I'll marry you."

She removed the glove from her left hand. He returned to her side and slid the ring on her finger. His arms came around her, and he kissed her, his lips gentle and cold against hers. She closed her eyes as her arms encircled his neck, and their kiss deepened. She floated.

Breathlessly, they ended it.

Alana rested her forehead against Mark's. Pulling on her glove, she shivered when the wind blew.

"You're cold." He kissed her one more time, then held out his hand. "We'd better get you home. Your parents will be anxious to see your ring." He helped her up.

"They know?"

"I asked their permission. They know."

She looped her arm through his. "I want everyone to know." Her cold lips still tingled from his kisses. "I love you, Mark Chambers."

ACKNOWLEDGMENTS

Thank you, Linda Fulkerson and Scrivenings Press, for the privilege of having another novel published. Our community of authors is caring and encouraging. Also, I have gained much through the years from the faculty, staff, and writing friends at the Montrose Christian Writers' Conference.

ABOUT THE AUTHOR

A lifelong lover of books and reading, Beth E. Westcott's first Christian romance novel, *Meadow Song,* debuted in 2018, with Mantle Rock Publishing, and was republished by Scrivenings Press in 2020. *Heart's Desire* released in 2021, *A Heart's Journey* in 2022, and *Her Heart's Longing in 2023,* completing The Three Sisters series.

Lillenas Drama accepted some of her church holiday manuscripts for publication in their Christmas, Easter, and Thanksgiving *Program Builders.* Several devotions appeared in *Penned for the Heart,* and one in *The Secret Place.* Her short story "Sadie and the Princess" is included in *Heart-warming Horse Stories* on Amazon.

After graduating from Hartwick College in Oneonta, N.Y., she married Frank Westcott. They raised three children and now have five granddaughters and one grandson, who is in heaven. She enjoys reading, music, gardening, sewing, and photography.

First with Child Evangelism Fellowship and then in pastoral

ministry in several churches, Beth worked alongside Frank for 38 years. She taught Bible classes to children, teens, and women, and participated in church music ministry. A 4-H member for nine years, she became a 4-H leader when her children were in 4-H, and she home-schooled them for twelve years.

She now resides with her husband in Otego, New York.

Meadow Song—Book One of Love's Refrain

Artist Kate Greenway escapes her home town after the death of her finance. She finds a meadow to paint in, a young girl, and the girl's handsome uncle Jack Chambers, and begins to move forward in her life. When Kate's mother develops cancer, Kate has to return home to care for her. Jack cannot make a commitment. She tells Jack the Master Potter can create something new out of the broken pieces of their lives.

Get your copy here:

https://scrivenings.link/meadowsong

Heart's Desire

The Three Sisters—Book One

When Aubrey White and Jeremy Abbot meet again at her brother's wedding, neither of them is thinking about falling in love. Both focused on their education and careers, they are surprised by love, and they soon learn that falling in love doesn't follow a straight path to happily ever after.

The stress caused by busy schedules, misunderstandings, a broken promise, a sister's stubbornness, and a secret, threaten to uproot their plans for a future together.

Is God showing them that the desire of their hearts is not His plan for them?

Get your copy here:

https://scrivenings.link/heartsdesire

~

A Heart's Journey

The Three Sisters—Book Two

Haleigh Abbot returns to Greenlawn, her childhood home, seeking forgiveness and renewed friendships. Willie White hires her to work in his florist shop. Drawn to Willie by his kindness, strength, and faith, Haleigh refuses to allow their relationship to go beyond friendship. Although forgiven and accepted back into the Greenlawn community, shadows of fear and guilt from the past still cling to her. When a little boy and his dog under her care are hurt in a terrible accident, she goes into an emotional tailspin.

Haleigh has held a special place in Willie's heart since childhood. When she left Greenlawn and shut him out of her life, it hurt, but he never forgot her. Her return gives him an opportunity to win her heart. He's ready to help her, but will her determination to prove she can handle life's challenges on her own stand in his way?

Get your copy here:

https://scrivenings.link/aheartsjourney

Her Heart's Longing

The Three Sisters—Book Three

In her heart, registered nurse Katie Mann carries the painful memories of her teen pregnancy and the baby boy she gave up for adoption. Only the people closest to her remember that time in Katie's life.

She can't convince the baby's biological father, the charming and fickle Nathan West, that she isn't interested in giving him a second chance at a relationship.

When she meets Jackson Stone, a former college classmate at the senior citizen residence where she works as a nurse, sparks ignite. Jackson, the grandson of Katie's favorite resident at the Senior Home, thinks she's hiding something, but that doesn't stop him from pursuing a relationship with her. Katie can't deny her growing love for Jackson, but she's afraid to tell him the truth about her past.

Will telling Jackson the truth keep Katie from the man she loves and the family she longs to have?

Get your copy here:

https://scrivenings.link/herheartslonging

Pets Amore

A novella collection—including "Snowflakes and Puppy Love" by Beth E. Westcott

Snowflakes and Puppy Love—When Cooper Stiles walks in the door of Archer Books, his stunning blue eyes and friendly smile pull at Brianna Kinney's heart. He's the first man she's attracted to since becoming a widow. The new clerk in Robin Archer's bookstore catches Cooper's eye.

Brianna's love for children and her cute puppy are captivating, but he doesn't have time for dating. His current priority is caring for his nephew and niece while their mother, his dead brother's wife, fulfills a work commitment overseas. And he's not going to get caught up in any more match-making.

Get your copy here:

https://scrivenings.link/petsamore

Stay up-to-date on your favorite books and authors with our free e-newsletters.

ScriveningsPress.com

www.ingramcontent.com/pod-product-compliance
Lightning Source LLC
Chambersburg PA
CBHW070624100726
47907CB00007B/1849